# SPOILER'S PREY

# SPOILER'S PREY

## Robin Blake

**SEVERN
HOUSE**

First world edition published in Great Britain and the USA in 2024
by Severn House, an imprint of Canongate Books Ltd,
14 High Street, Edinburgh EH1 1TE.

severnhouse.com

*British Library Cataloguing-in-Publication Data*
A CIP catalogue record for this title is available from the British Library.

ISBN-13: 978-1-4483-1145-3 (cased)
ISBN-13: 978-1-4483-1146-0 (e-book)

*All Severn House titles are printed on acid-free paper.*

Typeset by Palimpsest Book Production Ltd., Falkirk,
Stirlingshire, Scotland.
Printed and bound in Great Britain by TJ Books,
Padstow, Cornwall.

# Praise for the Cragg & Fidelis mysteries

# About the author

**Robin Blake** is the author of eight previous Cragg & Fidelis mysteries, as well as acclaimed works on the artists Van Dyck and Stubbs. He has written, produced and presented extensively for radio, and is widely published as a critic. He lives in London.

www.robinblake.co.uk

For my granddaughters Esme and Ivy

They hang the man and flog the woman
That steals the goose from off the common,
Yet let the greater villain loose
Who steals the common from the goose,
So goose will e'er a common lack
Unless she dare to steal it back.

Anon. 17th century


Thus came enclosure – ruin was her guide,
But freedom's clapping hands enjoyed the sight;
Tho comfort's cottage soon was thrust aside
And workhouse prisons raised upon the site.
E'en natures dwelling far away from men
The common heath became the spoiler's prey;
The rabbit had not where to make his den
And labour's only cow was drove away.
No matter – wrong was right and right was wrong
And freedom's brawl was sanction to the song.

From 'The Fallen Elm' by John Clare

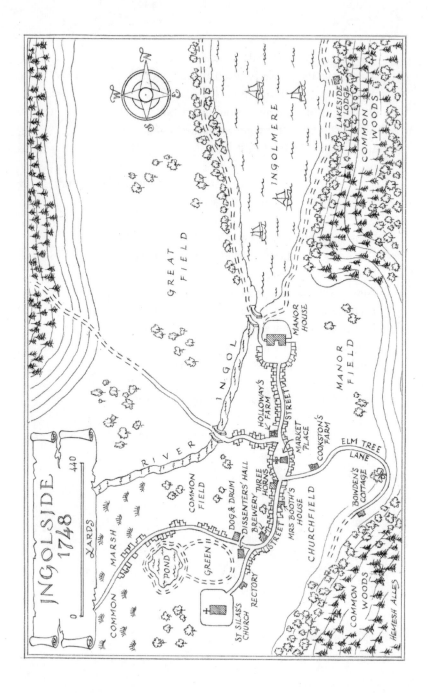

# PROLOGUE

I suppose it was usual for them to come before first light, when they could be sure the farmer was at home. The men, with their guns slung across their backs and carrying lanterns, hammered on the door and shouted for him to present himself. A low light from the ground floor, perhaps just a single lamp, betrayed the life within, but for a minute or more there was no reply.

'Come out! Come out now, or face the consequence.'

One of the men lit a taper from his lantern and applied it to a torch of tallow. It flamed up, lighting their faces as they stood in a semi-circle around it. There was a slight sound from above their heads and they looked up. The face of a child, like a spectre at the window, looked down at them for a moment before it was pulled away. The man with the burning torch stepped a few yards away from the farmhouse threshold. He drew back his arm and tossed the burning brand so that it wheeled upwards into the night and came down high in the thatch.

The little farmhouse stood at the marsh's edge, many furlongs apart from the village. Beside it lay a scrubby field in which a donkey and a goat grazed and, beyond that, a streaky dawn mist across the marsh like strands of cold grey wool. But now, stealthily, a slight orange warmth began to flicker among the mist, like the first kindling of the dawn light.

But dawn itself would not break for another half an hour.

# ONE

No one knew for certain how Cornelius Quexton first came to the faraway place called Ingolside. Quexton was as inexplicable as his strange surname, his comings and goings as mysterious as a comet, or the sparks that flash from a horse's hooves across cobblestones. His legend had many ramifications. There were those who said Quexton was a former preacher and friend of John Wesley until they fell out over the nature of the Trinity, or some other theological quibble. Others had heard he was previously an actor and writer of plays for the London stage, until caught in bed with a duke's daughter and forced to flee the town. Still others told of his time as a soldier of fortune and free rider in the interests of certain Italian princes – or was it the Sultan of Turkey? Perhaps he had been all of these, or none of them. Whatever the case was, most agreed him to be a man of a singular charm and accomplishment, but one also of strong views, most forcefully expressed, about the state of the world, the state of the nation and, now, the state of Ingolside.

What was Ingolside? It was an unremarkable village in the most northern part of the County Palatine that is known as Furness, where people had for centuries lived what would appear to be blameless, uneventful lives. In homes clustering around the foot of the lake of Ingolmere, they were for the most part tenant farmers, small holders or copyholders and cottagers living under successive lords of the manor.

The most recent of these was the Lumsden family, who had come by their lordship in Oliver Cromwell's time. The productive land over which the Lumsdens lorded was in the form of long fields farmed in the old way of strips. The rest – more than half – was outwoods, rough pasture and moor that was spread across the valley of a small river, of the kind known to Lancastrians as a beck or a pull. The greatest part of the pasture and woods in Ingolside were common, as were almost all of the moors and

marshes, and it was on this common land that the smallholders
relied for additional grazing to that of their own three or four
acres. The cottagers meanwhile depended almost entirely on
being able to put a cow and small gaggle of geese to graze on
the common, while trapping eel in the marsh and rabbits in the
woods for meat, while picking up the firewood they needed to
cook it on.

But when I went to Ingolside, in the early summer of 1748,
the village's peaceful existence had been violently disturbed, and
there were those who blamed it on the coming of Mr Quexton.

I made my own journey on receipt of the following letter from
Dr Luke Fidelis, physician and friend of many years.

> *Dear Titus,*
>
> *As I told you before leaving, I came to Ingolside three
> days ago to attend to old Mrs Sarah Lumsden at the Manor
> House. My patient is approaching sixty and possibly mori-
> bund. I have stayed on to keep an eye on her while suffering
> her peevishness as patiently as I can. However, I write not
> to inform you of this, but to tell you that the peace of the
> village has lately been breached by an unpleasant outbreak
> of strife between the Squire, Arthur Lumsden, the larger
> farmers and the cottagers, and this has suddenly come up
> to the boil in a manner worthy of the sensational theatre.
> In short, a man died during a public disturbance.*
>
> *The death is very doubtful. Whether it is criminal or
> accidental is not certain. I have had no chance to examine
> the corpse as no one will give me the authority to do so,
> but the rumour is that he was struck by a bullet. Some say
> he was handling a pistol, which discharged into him, though
> no one admits to seeing this happen. I therefore urge you
> to make haste to come and take the enquiry in hand.*
>
> *Your friend, Luke.*

I have consulted Luke Fidelis's professional opinion many
times in the run of my duties as Coroner for Preston, and later
for the County. His judgment is always solid when applied to a
body, and often astute in considering persons in their motives
and ways of thinking, their weaknesses and strengths. Yet my

friend is susceptible to charm, which is his own – I might say his only – weakness.

'Oh, I know Ingolside,' said Elizabeth, my wife, when I told her I would have to leave immediately on a journey to the place. 'By which I mean, I have been there. It was when I was a girl.'

'You are still a girl to me.'

'When I was properly a girl. Thirteen. An awkward age. We went to visit one of my mother's brothers, Mark Holloway. There was a handsome young man in the place, I remember, by the name of Arthur Lumsden. The Squire's son.'

'Handsome, was he?'

'Oh yes. I fell for him, naturally, but he regarded himself as superior and me as no higher than a peasant wench. I might have been good for a roll in the hay but not for amours or displays of gallantry.'

'A roll in the hay? Did you indulge him?'

Her laugh, lovely as a bell, rang out.

'He offered me a bag of sugared nuts if I would. I told him to show me the nuts first, but he never had any, the liar.'

'So there was no roll in the hay?'

Elizabeth cupped my ear with her hand and whispered into it. 'I swear I never had a roll in the hay until I had one with you, Titus.'

'And I never even offered you sugared nuts.'

'I had grown out of those by then.'

'Yes, I remember. But tell me, your mother's brother, is he still living there?'

'He was, the last I heard.'

'Shall I call on him, then? And if I do shall I be pressed to his bosom?'

'I doubt he would go that far, but he is a decent enough soul. He would welcome you I think. Shall I write and tell him what a splendid, reliable and lovable fellow you are?'

'I will carry your letter myself and present it to him as my credential. What is your uncle's profession?'

'He farms.'

'With much land?'

'A fair deal of land. He has a tenancy from the Lumsden

family, one of the largest of the manor I would guess, though it's more than ten years since I last clapped eyes on him.'

It was a long road and, after four days of continuous rain, a muddy one, not least in the last half-mile where the road crossed a desolate marsh. When I arrived at the Dog and Drum inn, Ingolside, the clock of St Silas church, which stood on the other side of a wide green, would shortly strike nine. Having seen to it that my mare was in the stable enjoying her nosebag of oats, I was being pulled this way and that on a lobby bench by a decrepit boot catcher heaving and hauling on my footwear. My clothes were soaked and my buttocks were stiff and sore. I was hungry. In short, I was not in a kindly humour. This was not improved by the innkeeper, Curly Berry, telling me the fare he proposed to me for supper.

'There's cheese and pickled eggs.'

'You have nothing hot? I need a stew or, at the least, a bowl of soup. I'm cold as well as hungry.'

I attempted to twist my leg to assist the boot's removal.

'A townsman, are you?'

I told him I was from Preston.

'Oh! Another Preston man, is it? A doctor from there stayed the other night. Well, as we do in these country parts, my kitchener's gone to bed by now and the oven fire's been wanzed for the night.'

'You might un-wanze it, might you not?'

'Flame up the fire late as this? Not likely.'

'You should know I am here on the King's business. I—'

Berry held up his hand to shut me up.

'If you were Lord Derby himself I could not go above a pickled egg and a wedge of cheese. I must be thrifty with my firing these days.'

At last both boots were off.

'Oh, very well,' I said. 'You do have a bedroom for me, I take it?'

A few minutes later I stood in my wet-stockinged feet holding a single candle up to inspect the fireless and dismal bedchamber Berry had assigned. The small plate of food lay on the table, brought up by the bootcatcher, whose seventieth birthday was certainly behind him. The egg when I ate it was as vinegary as my mood. And when I rolled into bed I could not be sure which was colder – myself or the damp bed sheets.

For all my tiredness I slept badly and in the morning I was still feeling crabbed.

'Mr Berry told me that Dr Fidelis has stayed here,' I said to Maggie, the black-haired young woman serving my breakfast.

At the mention of my friend's name she blushed (I was used to female blushes in connection with my friend) and said, 'The doctor did stay here but only for a night. A very handsome gentleman, he is.'

'He only stayed one night?'

'That's right, Sir.'

'So where did he go? I'm sure he's still in the neighbourhood. Has he been put up elsewhere in the village?'

She shrugged.

'They say he's taken up with—'

'With whom?'

She looked up to the ceiling and sighed, then looked at me again.

'I couldn't just say, Sir. But he's here in Ingolside all right, 'cause I saw him round and about only yesterday.'

After I had eaten breakfast, which meant more cheese and egg, though with the welcome addition of fresh bread, I sent again for Mr Berry.

'Where is Holloway's Farm?' I asked him. 'Is it far out from the village?'

He laughed as if my ignorance were some joke.

'It's *in* the village, beside Market Place. That's halfway along Street. Solid stone house as you'll see. Prosperous, is Mr Holloway.'

He said the word 'prosperous' as if it meant a booby. That was Curly Berry's way: his words were superficially polite enough. All the offence was in the tone he used to say them.

'I wonder if you know Dr Fidelis from Preston? Your servant told me he stayed here recently, although just the one night. Is there another inn he might have moved to?'

'Not unless he's sleeping in a charcoal bed. The Three Horns had its guts burned out a fortnight since.'

'Well, according to your servant, the doctor is still in Ingolside somewhere.'

'As he's attending Mrs Lumsden, Squire's mother, you'd best go to Lumsden's before you go elsewhere asking after your friend.'

'At the Manor House?'

He laughed again.

'Aye. It's where Lumsden lives'

I was tired of Curly Berry's thin, sarcastic laugh and pinched face. I like wit in a man but Curly Berry was out of the room when that quality was handed around, though he seemed to think otherwise. So I told him good day and went out.

The rain had relented in the night and the air was dry, with a light breeze. I wondered whether to seek out Luke, or pay my respects at the house of Elizabeth's uncle, Mark Holloway. My decision to go first to the latter was not without calculation. Holloway was of my family: with luck he might offer to spare me another night at the Dog and Drum. So I walked down what was clearly Street, being the widest of the village's few inter-connecting lanes. A butcher and a baker had their shops there and I noted a wood turner who (I imagined) would have been able to turn out a candlestick to order. But a good proportion of the premises on Street were simple cottages, many with ragged thatch and hollowed door-stones on which ragged cats lay asleep. And about halfway down, just before crossing the Market Place, I passed a blackened, roofless premises outside of which, propped on the ground against the door post, was a charred inn sign with three horns.

The people of Ingolside stared at me with frank curiosity, taking note of the appearance and clothing of the stranger in order to pass them on later as matter for gossip. I raised my hat here and there, but no one so much as spoke, and one or two conspicuously crossed to the other side rather than confront me. I had rarely been to an unknown place that seemed less welcoming.

I came to the Market Place where stood the house that Berry had spoken of. It was a storey higher than the cottages and workshops nearby and stood on the corner of a side lane, over-looking it through a set of mullioned windows. The front door, which butted directly on to the main thoroughfare, was approached by a flight of four railed steps. I climbed these and drew down the bell pull.

The door was opened by a maid in working clothes who, when I asked for Mr Holloway, showed me into the hall and disappeared into the recesses of the house. A few moments later a woman of about thirty-five came out to greet me.

'You are Mrs Holloway?' I asked.

'Oh no, Sir. Mr Holloway is not married. I am his niece, Amelia Hart. I keep his house for him.'

I brought Elizabeth's letter from my pocket.

'I am Titus Cragg,' I said. 'And I am married to another of Mr Holloway's nieces. She sends this letter to her uncle. She was Elizabeth George.'

Miss Hart took the letter and thrust her face close to it to make out the writing. Her face then broke into a wide smile.

'It is the handwriting of Cousin Elizabeth! Oh my goodness, yes! And you are her husband? Oh, we played together as children so happily. She was the very best of playmates.'

'And she still is.'

Miss Hart looked at me, unsure if this was meant as ribaldry. I hastened to add, 'I mean, she has a great sense of fun. She laughs very often, which is a joy to hear.'

'I remember that so well. Welcome to the house, Mr Cragg. Mr Holloway is afield this morning but I am expecting him for dinner at midday. Will you return and eat with us then?'

I gave her a bow and said I would be honoured. I thought that, if the household dined as early as midday, it clearly ran according to old country customs: a reminder that, no more than two days' ride from the civilization of Preston, one found life being lived in more ancient, rougher ways.

Miss Hart then gave me directions to the Manor House, which stood on a slight mound overlooking the end of Street, where it widened out into an open flagstoned space. Like Holloway's Farm, the Manor House was built of stone with tall chimneys rearing above a roof of slate. Yet it was a far more extensive house than Holloway's. You would not call it stately, but its size and position endowed it with unquestioned mastery over the humbler dwellings that surrounded it.

Instead of going immediately up to the door, I walked around it and down to the shore of the lake which gives Ingolside its name. Ingolmere is a narrow body of water more than a mile long with a steeply sloping, deeply wooded shore on the eastern side and a wide and level tract of agricultural land on the other, stretching away from the lake shore for hundreds of yards as it rises gradually, and then more sharply, to the skyline of high fells above. On this morning the wind gently rippled the water. Half a dozen skiffs bobbed here and there on its surface. The fishing rods that projected upwards from them shifted this way and that, like insect antennae.

Looking along the shore I saw a path, on which at a distance of about three hundred yards two male figures appeared to be dancing. They were of quite disproportionate size – one short and slight, the other bulky and half as high again as his companion. I watched them for a while as they circled and leaped, stepped forward and shuffled back, but could make no sense of the dance. The pair were some sort of Morris men, I supposed.

Approaching the Manor House again I saw an elderly clergyman, who walked in the same direction. He caught up with me and spoke, his words tumbling out in rapid, breathless bursts.

'Good day, Sir. My name is Cuthbert Cumberledge.'

'I am pleased to meet you,' I said.

'I hold the living here in the parish of St Silas,' Cumberledge continued, 'and I am come to the Manor House on pastoral business, that is to say, to visit the sick, by which I mean old Mrs Lumsden who, poor lady, is grievously stricken. Perhaps you, Sir, are on the same mission. Whom have I the honour of addressing?'

'I am Titus Cragg, Mr Cumberledge, the County Coroner. I have come to Ingolside on official business.'

For one moment his jaw dropped and I caught a glimpse of his gappy teeth.

'On business? Oh! Yes, I see. Of course, I see! The unfortunate occurrence we have had, the death of . . . the death of . . . someone whose name I know perfectly well . . . Lavenham! That's it. Well, you were bound to come, I suppose.'

'Yes, I was bound to come. Can you tell me where the corpse lies? I hope it is still above ground.'

'The corpse? Yes indeed. It is above ground. We have not
buried it, not yet. It lies, I believe, in the care of his colleague,
with whom he has occupied lodgings for the past several weeks.'

'What name does his colleague, as you call him, go by?'

'His colleague?'

'Yes. His partner, you might say. They were working together.'

Cumberledge seemed to be having difficulty with these
questions.

'I don't know,' he said at last. 'He's not from round here. A
stranger.'

'You do not know his name?'

'Ah, I have it! Yes! Wilkin Tree. That's his name. And, you
know, his colleague's death is most inconvenient, coming as it
does at this ticklish time.'

'Why ticklish, may I ask?'

'Why with Whitsun coming up and preparations for our Great
Whitsun Ales, you know. As a clergyman I look forward with
dread to that unholy feast. The people give themselves over to
nothing but gross pleasures – and overlying all is this hidden
current, if I might call it that, of unpleasantness over Mr
Lumsden's plans for the future of the manor.'

'Mr Lumsden, Sarah Lumsden's husband, is that?'

'Oh no. I speak of Mr Arthur who is Mrs Lumsden's son.'

We were now at the Manor House door. The Reverend
Cumberledge stood a little behind, granting me precedence in
knocking. To my surprise, it was Luke Fidelis who came to the
door.

# TWO

Old Mrs Lumsden was evidently a demanding patient who required her doctor to wait on her almost continuously.

'I am glad to see you, Titus,' said Luke, standing aside to let us enter. 'I am at the lady's beck by day and her call by night, and it is exhausting. Her spirit still asserts itself even as her body fails.'

He turned to the clergyman.

'Good day, Mr Cumberledge.'

He tilted his head in the direction of the stairs behind him.

'You should go straight up to the sick room. She has asked for you three times already.'

As Cumberledge headed up the stairs, Fidelis took my elbow and walked me into a parlour within.

'The Rector is my only relief,' he said. 'She will make him pray with her a good hour, and then lecture him on doctrine for another.'

'Does she make you pray also?'

'Oh no. With me she likes medical conversation. She enjoys hearing of the variety of diseases I have treated in my career. I describe the course of them and she follows every detail. In conversation she is strong though she wastes away physically.'

'What is her affliction?'

'She's fallen into a marasmus. Her flesh is shriveling and she eats less each day that passes. I assume there is a morbid underlying condition, which will show itself in due course.'

'And will she then die?'

'I will try to prevent it. I may even succeed. She is not yet sixty and may live another twenty years if I or nature can find a way to fatten her.'

'Tell me about the matter that you wrote to me of.'

'It was a day or two before I came. According to what I have heard, a mob of men came down Street, possibly the worse for drink. They marched in close formation through the Market Place and on to this house. Having arrived in front of it they shouted and brandished fists, threatening to break the windows or even do worse.'

'Worse?'

'They seemed intent, or some of them did, on firing the house. Some had flaming torches. Squire Lumsden came out with two servants, each of them carrying a fowling piece, and threatened to shoot.'

'And did they, in fact, shoot?'

'I think they did. Warning shots, supposedly. After a fair deal of scuffling the mob gradually dispersed.'

'How do you know all this?'

'The dead man's colleague, Wilkin Tree, told me what he saw from a window of the Manor House, which looks over the forecourt.'

'But no fire was set?'

'Not according to Tree. After the shots, they dispersed.'

'But you wrote me that a man had been killed.'

'Quite so.'

'Was he shot?'

'I don't know. I have not seen the body. Some say shots were aimed above the mob's heads, as a warning. The agitators drew back under the threat of the guns, so I heard, and the dead man was later found lying in the Market Place. Nothing could be done for the man. He was dead.'

'Who was he?'

'His name was John Lavenham.'

'A villager?'

'No, a stranger. A commissioner or some such, looking into the land holdings hereabout. He was invited to come in some weeks ago by Mr Lumsden along with the colleague I mentioned, Mr Wilkin Tree.'

'For what purpose?'

'For a purpose not popular with everyone in the village, it seems.'

'Well, I suppose this will become clear when I speak to the Squire. Is he at home?'

'He is away on business.'

'I assume he is the local magistrate. I can myself have you examine the body, of course, but I prefer to have the agreement of the bench. In the meantime, I ought to speak to Mr Tree. Where shall we find him?'

'He stays in a house that belongs to the Squire, just beside the lake. It was reserved for the use of both men on their arrival five or six weeks ago. Shall I take you there?'

But before he could, Mr Cumberledge came hurrying down the stairs, considerably out of breath.

'Mr Coroner, Sir, you must attend Mrs Lumsden. She expressly wishes to see you and I am to take you up to her.'

Sarah Lumsden half sat, half lay in bed with duck-down pillows heaped behind her. She wore a cambric nightcap elaborately trimmed with Dutch lace. Her face was bony, and age had made her nose and chin as sharp as each other.

'You have come here in a time of strife, Mr Craig.'

The voice was hoarse and harsh. The words seemed forced out from a constricted throat.

'It is Cragg, Mrs Lumsden,' I said.

'What is?'

'My name. Titus Cragg at your service.'

Mrs Lumsden sniffed.

'I cannot think what service you might do me, Sir. Now Cumberledge here is my vicar and also my spiritual advisor, even though he is inclined to forgetfulness. Young Fidelis is my medical man, bound to me by the fees he charges. And of course in my time I have had numerous subjects to do my bidding: a reeve, a bailiff, dairy women, ploughmen, men and women of all kinds who strive to please me, and who rally at my command. I am a small monarch in this place, Mr Crane. I am Queen Anne brought down to scale. So do not suppose I need your service. You have come instead to try what service I can do for you, is that not so?'

'Well, Madam, I—'

'Mr Cumberledge!'

She gesticulated toward the clergyman.

'I am of a mind to give Mr Crabb refreshment. Go at once to the kitchen. He shall have barley wine and you small beer. I shall take a glass of warm milk with cinnamon stirred in. Go, and look sharp.'

Cumberledge left us scurrying and Mrs Lumsden let out a sigh. For a moment her features creased at a twinge of pain somewhere inside her.

'As I say, you have come when we are all at sixes and sevens. But there is worse to come, you know: our eights and our nines at least.'

She laughed at her joke with a kind of croaking gulp, then wriggled her body so as to sit more upright in bed.

'So you are the Crowner, Mr Clogg?'

'Cragg, Madam. Yes, I am,'

'What have you come to crown? There is only one crowned head in this village and it is mine, as I have been telling you.'

'If I had the right jewels and diadems I would be glad to oblige you, Madam.'

'I am sure you don't mean that, Mr Clark. Leastways I want more than words from a man if I am to trust him. But trust is in short supply nowadays and treachery is to be found everywhere in this little country of mine.'

There followed a long silence. She remained still with eyes shut, breathing laboriously. It was not easy to know what to say, so I sat and waited in silence.

Eventually the Reverend Cumberledge returned followed by a rosy-cheeked girl carrying three pewter mugs on a tray, and now Mrs Lumsden roused herself. She took her drink, sipping noisily. I tried my barley wine. It was distinctly sour.

'Mrs Lumsden,' I said, thinking I should at least try to gather some information from the woman, even if she seemed semi-deranged. 'What do you know of Mr Wilkin Tree and the late John Lavenham?'

'I know nothing of them except that they be agents of the Devil. They came to Ingolside to carve my realm up into parcels, all by the device of my accursed son.'

'They are in the service of Mr Lumsden?'

Suddenly she became fully animated, sitting forward once more and beating the covers with a bony fist.

'Yes, these men are his creatures. Who else would spite me and defy me so? Of course my son brought them to Ingolside.

He hates me. If he could depose me, he would. But he cannot depose me. My reign continues and while it does he is impotent except in plotting and scheming. The villagers are right to cry out against him, and cry honour to me. I am their Queen in all but name. I am their solace and their seawall. I hold back the drowning tide of darkness.'

Exhausted by her outburst of vehemence she slumped back against her pillows and lay as before with eyes shut. I looked at Mr Cumberledge, who gave me a baffled smile as he shrugged.

'I shall go down now,' I mouthed, moving my thumb in the direction of the door. He nodded and I withdrew from the room.

'That woman thinks she's Queen Anne,' I said.

Fidelis and I had skirted the house and were heading for the lake shore.

'She does,' he said. 'In little. There is a certain peculiar truth in it, you know. In the days I have been here – and became part of her little court – I have felt this place to be much as she imagines it herself: a sequestered little commonwealth. With the high fells surrounding it on three sides and the marsh that guards the fourth, it is hard to enter. Once entered you find that every-thing is done by local custom.'

'Where are you lodged? Not at the Dog and Drum, I take it.'

Fidelis laughed.

'One night was enough. Then I found alternative quarters. I have taken a room with the Widow Booth at her house in the street they call Street. You?'

'I arrived at the inn late last evening for supper. Pickled eggs. I arose for breakfast this morning. Pickled eggs. The only escape from pickled eggs is to escape the inn entirely, which I shall do this day, or die in the attempt.'

'And put up where?'

'Perhaps with a farmer here, Mark Holloway. It happens that he's Elizabeth's uncle. I am hoping that he will take pity on me. I am invited there for dinner.'

We had by now reached the shoreline, and began to follow it. Fidelis pointed to a house half-hidden amongst trees on the southern shore.

'That's the house where John Lavenham's body lies. It is ten minutes' walk.'

I hesitated.

'Before I go there I should notify the Parish Constable of my arrival. It is a usual courtesy. Do you know his name?'

'I have not heard it. I don't know who he is.'

'Ah! Then let's go and take a first look at the late Mr Lavenham. An unofficial look only. I'll speak to the parish officer this afternoon.'

The house, which was called Lakeside Lodge, was approached by the stony track that skirted the shore. It was a kind of hunting and fishing lodge, oak framed and of modest size, standing a little above the level of the lake and a little back from it. At the waterside there was a boathouse and a jetty.

I hammered on the door and waited, listening. There came some creaking sounds, and footsteps. A voice called.

'Go away.'

'I am County Coroner.'

'I know no one of that name.'

'It is my title. My name is Titus Cragg and I am here on the King's business, it being my duty to look into the death of John Lavenham whose body I believe lies here. I require you to show him to me.'

There came a rattling as hasps, locks and chains were undone and the door opened a crack. An eye appeared, looking at us, and a fearful voice was heard.

'I don't recognize you, Sir. You must say who you are, whether from this parish or beyond.'

'I am not from here. I come from Preston.'

Luke Fidelis stepped into the line of his sight behind me.

'You know me, Mr Tree, in any event. We were together at Mr Lumsden's house on several occasions, as I hope you remember.'

'Ah, yes, the doctor,' said Tree. 'Do you vouch for this man, then?'

'I do. Mr Cragg is exactly who he says he is.'

The door swung back and we looked on a dressed-down figure of a man. He was thirty-five and of more than medium height, well-built and with very straight sandy hair protruding from under his house cap. He wore a well-cut coat over a shirt closed at the neck with a silken stock and he held in his fingers a long-stemmed tobacco pipe. He looked at us warily then jerked his thumb over his shoulder in the direction of the house's interior.

'You are on the King's business, you say. Then I would like His Majesty to remove Lavenham's body. I don't care to sleep in a house so close to a corpse, not to say its rising stink and the endless noise of flies.'

'I will see what can be done about that.'

'Then come in.'

The odour in the hall was like wet, rotten sacks, very old ones, mixed with a strong hint of sour vegetables and yeast. Looking to my left I could see through a door a room with a table covered by papers, pens, inkstands and drawing instruments.

'He's in the outhouse,' said Tree.

He led us along the passage beside the stair that led into what proved to be a kitchen, where a mountainous woman stood at the sink peeling potatoes. Tree took no notice of her, but led us out by the kitchen door to a small green with a laden washing line stretched across it. Ranged along one side of this green was a low line of brick compartments for the storage of logs, the washing of laundry and similar purposes. The sound of buzzing from one of these told us where we would find the remains of John Lavenham. Tree opened the latch and pulled the door open for Fidelis and me to enter. He himself remained outside.

The interior had a flag floor and whitewashed walls. It contained nothing else beside a folding laundry table in the middle of the space. On this lay the bulk of a person, his unbooted feet protruding out of the far end of the grimy sheet that covered him. Taking a handkerchief from my pocket, I pressed it to my nose.

'Go on, Luke,' I said.

Fidelis pulled away the sheet and dropped it on the floor. A cloud of flies immediately rose, buzzing and darkening the air, but he ignored them. Slowly he began to walk around the table, his eyes noting every particular of the body.

Lavenham seemed to have been a few years younger than Tree. He was dressed in shirt and breeches, neither of which looked either new or clean. His shirt was undone at the neck to expose his throat but his coat was closely buttoned. He was of less than medium height and stocky, with a protruding belly, though whether it had been like that in life was uncertain. I had seen enough bloated corpses to know this one may have been swollen with the gas that all decaying flesh produces. He gave off a smell like a sweetened dunghill, if such a thing is conceivable.

Fidelis bent to scrutinize Lavenham's bald head. He looked carefully at the crown, and then paid as close attention to the ear, the cheek, the nose. He prized open Lavenham's jaw with his fingers and looked into his mouth.

He let the jaw go and with a sigh continued circling around the body. He parted the coat between the buttons and looked inside but did not open the coat completely. At one point he leaned down and sniffed deeply.

'Interesting. It smells of something burned. Like malted cereal.'

'I am surprised you can smell anything above the decay of flesh.'

'It is a question of discrimination, that is all.'

Fidelis sometimes claimed this almost preternatural skill: that he alone, in his eyes, could tell the difference between, let's say, an eyelash and a single hair from a crow's feather, or between a drop of old dried blood and a coffee stain on a black coat.

'But can you discriminate what he died from?'

Fidelis shrugged, giving a disarming smile.

'There is a minor head wound but I cannot be sure what it signifies. His jaw seems oddly aligned. There's also a hole in his waistcoat and shirt, which may continue into his flesh. There is what looks very like blood on his shirt and at the back of his coat. So I need to take a closer look not just under his clothing but under his skin, and to that end I must come back with my instruments.'

'Then let's get out of this noxious room at once. As well as wanting to breathe, I want a talk with Tree.'

We stepped with relief out into the air. Wilkin Tree was standing in the middle of the green, looking out over the lake. I approached.

'Mr Tree, shall you and I walk a little?'

Leaving Fidelis, I gently guided him by the elbow towards the lakeside. We set off to stroll further along the lakeside path.

'You do not speak very kindly of your late colleague,' I said.

'It is nothing but that Lavenham was a very untidy person. I myself do not like disorder.'

'The woman I saw in the kitchen, is she not employed to tidy after you?'

Tree shook his head.

'Lizzy cooks well enough, if you like to eat nothing but stewed meat, potato pie and dumplings. She also washes our clothing, but that is her limit. She does not scrub floors or clean windows and I'd be surprised if she knows the difference between a besom and a feather duster.'

'Were you present when John Lavenham died?'

'I was not. I was inside Mr Lumsden's house and knew nothing about it until word came back he had been found slumped on the steps below the Market Cross.'

'Did you watch the assembly of villagers in front of the Manor House?'

'The riot, you mean. Yes, I did.'

'From what point of vantage?'

'From one of the windows of Mr Lumsden's house.'

'You say it was a riot. Was it really?'

'It was, in Mr Lumsden's language. There was a lot of noise. Then a stone was thrown and broke a window. Squire fetched a paper with the Riot Act printed on it and went outside with two servants, all three of them carrying fowling pieces. He showed them the paper and threatened to shoot at them.'

'Did he read the act out? Did he formally warn them?'

'It is said he did. I did not hear it.'

'And did the Parish Constable attend to keep the peace?'

'There isn't one that I know of.'

'No Constable? Then who knocks people's heads together after a fist fight? Who keeps an eye on the goodness of the ale at the Dog and Drum?'

'Don't ask me. I am a stranger here. I only know as much as I have learned in a few weeks' residence, which isn't much as no one but the Squire and a couple of the farmers will talk to me. I fear for my life, Mr Cragg. I fear that what happened to Lavenham could happen to me.'

'Do you think Lavenham was deliberately killed?'

'What else can I think? He was shot, wasn't he?'

'Is this the Squire's opinion also? He is magistrate here, I suppose. Has he not looked into the matter?'

'You must ask him about that. He has not told me.'

'I have yet to meet Mr Lumsden.'

'He is away on business at present.'

'And meanwhile can you describe *your* business at Ingolside?'

'Counting trees. Pacing boundaries. Estimating distances. That sort of thing.'

'You mean you are a surveyor?'

'Yes. And map maker besides.'

'And Lavenham? Was he a surveyor too?'

'Of a kind. I survey land. He surveyed writings. He had a fondness for old documents in a lawyerly way.'

'In a lawyerly way? Was he an attorney?'

His face acquired a mysterious smile, which I could not quite account for.

'Not exactly.'

'Aside from the matter of his untidiness, were you and John Lavenham on friendly terms, living here together?'

Tree spat into the bracken that lined the edge of the woods. His spittle lodged there, winking in the light.

'We rubbed along. But I did not know him as friends know each other. Lavenham and I had never met before we came here. We did not even travel together, so we met here as strangers. We remained so, to a large extent.'

'You must have talked together, of an evening.'

'Oh yes, we talked together, but he told me little of substance. He told me once of how it might feel standing before the cele-brated Magistrate de Veil in Bow Street. I felt, though he did not say so, that he was talking about himself. Yet this was contradicted by his being a well-spoken, educated sort of fellow. Not one who would fall foul of the law.'

'He was trusted by Squire Lumsden, as you are.'

Tree laughed, though not exactly from good humour.

'Lumsden is very well disposed to us, as he should be since he invited us here. But the cottagers and common people regard me and Lavenham as agents of the Devil. They learned to call us that from the old woman, of course, Mr Lumsden's hag of a mother. They unjustly love her while unjustly hating her son.'

'I have had a talk with her. She feels deeply aggrieved at what I believe are her son's schemes to enclose parts of the manor. She detests it as you might a plot.'

'There is no plot. Is it a plot to desire improvement? And prosperity? Is it conspiracy to make the land give of its best? It is something all will benefit from but they are too stupid to see it.'

I remembered the grumbling and discontent at Preston over the people's loss of common rights in the marsh. But this looked like a project on a much bigger scale. Looking across to the far shore of the lake, I saw a huge, gently sloping cultivated field, which was evidently worked by the ancient system of strips with neither boundary hedges nor fences to divide it up. It stretched away as far as the lower slopes of the fell, while its boundary to the right was lost in the distance. These fields, I knew, existed under the lordship of Arthur Lumsden but were not exactly his property. They would be worked by the people of the village as much on their own behalf as his. It was an ancient, commonly agreed system of rights and obligations.

'I see. So you confirm that Mr Lumsden does intend to take personal control of the farming here, through a scheme of enclosures?' I said.

'Through that and other improvements.'

He waved an arm towards the land between the lake and the fells.

'He wants to see all the great plough lands that lie over there, and the two lesser fields at Church End, all divided into parcels and all hedged around. They will thus be managed by him and the larger tenant farmers on a better, more rational system because they will be under clearly defined ownership and not the muddle of competing rights and claims that there is now.'

'And what of the woodland behind us here?'

'It will be felled and cleared for sheep, and he will make more pasture by draining the marsh. There's much money in sheep.'

'And you and Lavenham came here to provide the information he needs for the Act of Parliament that will make all this legal?'

'Yes, and it is work I glory in, Sir. There is nothing that will serve this nation better than to sweep away forever the wasteful and irrational practice of dividing the fields into unfenced strips.'

'I see. Sweep away, you say. There might be cause in that for a riot, not just in Squire Lumsden's but in anyone's language. And for bad feeling against anyone such as you and Lavenham who are allied to the Squire's project. You say you fear for your life. Have you received threats?'

'If hostile looks are threats.'

'I would be grateful if you would inform me should anything more tangible in that line come your way.'

Tree picked up a stick and hurled it furiously into the lake.

'What can you do to help me? You're a lawyer.'

'If I can name whoever harmed John Lavenham, that would help you, Mr Tree. Shall we go back?'

# THREE

A s we retraced the way back towards the house I told Tree about the process of inquest, and that the body of John Lavenham could not be removed immediately for burial, but would be taken away just before the inquest began. Then Fidelis and I returned to the village. I told him along the way what I understood about Lumsden's scheme for enclosure.

'I have heard rather much of this myself,' he said. 'In their cups the people here speak of it. Squire Lumsden is in partnership in the scheme with a few of the richer farmers, on the understanding that he will have the greater part of the enclosed land, and they will share and share the rest alike between them. Production will be thereby wondrously increased.'

'It isn't surprising that it is opposed, Luke. People have farmed this way since very ancient times.'

'You can't stand in the way of improvement, Titus. This country requires sweeping changes if it is to be prosperous.'

'Sweeping again! You and Wilkin Tree are of a mind on this question, I see.'

'It is only a question of applying reason, a simple matter.'

'It does not seem simple to me.'

We had passed in front of the Manor House and on to the Market Place, where Fidelis led me directly to the stone cross at its centre, raised on a three-step plinth. He started to walk around it, looking down carefully at the steps.

'Lavenham was found lying on these steps,' he said. 'But I wonder where exactly. Ah! It may have been here, I think. Look.'

He had stopped and gone down on one knee to inspect the steps that ranged along the side facing the Manor House.

'Look at these marks on the stone,' he said.

I looked and saw the faint remains of some brown staining. They were not more than smudges.

'It doesn't look much. Do you think it is blood?'

'It is possibly but not certainly blood. And, if blood, it is possibly but not certainly human. But despite all this uncertainty, if this is where Lavenham lay, the coincidence suggests it was his blood.'

'The bleeding doesn't seem to have been very great.'

'There has been rain, however.'

At this moment, I noticed the parson coming towards us from the direction of the Manor House.

'Ah, Mr Cumberledge,' I called, beckoning him over to join us. 'Did you by any chance witness the discovery of Mr John Lavenham's body at the end of the supposed riot that took place here?'

'Did I, Mr Cragg?'

'I am asking you, Mr Cumberledge. Think back.'

'Well, yes, I did. The riot was over and I was on my way back to the Rectory. I was following two of Mr Lumsden's servants who had been sent after the mob of demonstrators as they went their ways. I saw them on this very spot looking down at his corpse.'

'Will you point out where he lay?'

Cumberledge pointed to the exact spot where the brown marks discoloured the stone of the steps.

Fidelis now left me to hurry back to his patient – Sarah Lumsden must be paying him a pretty fee, I thought – and Mr Cumberledge likewise took his leave. I crossed to the corner of Market Place, rapped on Holloway's door and was admitted by Miss Hart. She brought me into the dining room where I found Mark Holloway himself at table awaiting his dinner. I apologized if I had made the meal late, but his smiling, weather-beaten farmer's face showed he was not put out.

'Think nothing of it, Mr Cragg. Take a seat. Before we continue, there is something I must say. On no account spend another might under the dubious – and I think we may fairly suspect infested – roof of Mr Curly Berry. The man is a slovenly wretch and keeps his house accordingly. You must instead stay here, with us. My niece will put a room at your disposal and we will allow you a key to the front door.'

Does the reader suppose I refused this invitation? Of course, I said yes.

'Splendid,' said Mark Holloway. 'It will be a pleasure to host the husband of little Elizabeth George. It is strange to think of her as a grown woman and a mother. I remember her only as the liveliest and prettiest child. My sister writes to me from time to time with news from Preston. I think you and my niece have a son, yes?'

And so the talk continued, with Holloway questioning me about the growth of Hector and the health of Elizabeth's parents, Mr and Mrs George. I in turn got acquainted with Holloway's own domestic circumstances. He was a widower with no living children and Amelia, child of another sister, had been keeping his house for ten years. She herself had never married. There seemed a natural and quite innocent affection between them.

A meat pie was brought and divided up between us. As we ate, the talk turned to my business at Ingolside. I told of that morning's visit to Lakeside Lodge.

'I met Lavenham, of course,' said Holloway. 'The villagers in their ignorance regard him and Wilkin Tree as agents of evil.'

'Yes, I've heard that already.'

'What those oafs do not understand is that in the long run they will all prosper by a scheme of enclosures.'

'From what you say, may I infer that you are one of the larger farmers who have gone into partnership with the Squire in the scheme?'

Holloway nodded as he chewed a mouthful of pie.

'I am, and I have put money into it,' he said, when the obstruction had been swallowed. 'And I expect a good return. But as I say the whole village will benefit. Even the poor cottagers.'

'How so, if I may ask?'

'They will work for wages rather than scrape a living by themselves.'

'I remember something similar at Preston when there was a question of the riverside marsh being drained and built over,' I said. 'Those who had the right in common to trap waterfowl there, and to graze their beasts, did not welcome it.'

'A couple of pigs on the common! Killing a few inedible scrawny wading birds. Such are paltry rights. We will take the draining of our own marshes in hand and the sooner the better.'

I held up my hands.

'I am not here to entangle myself in questions of agricultural economy. I only want to know how John Lavenham died. His body was found within a hundred yards of this house. I wonder if you saw what happened.'

'I was not at home,' Holloway said. 'The month of May sees many summer cattle and horse fairs in this county. I was attending the fair at Trimbleby on the Saturday and did not return until the next day. But Amelia was here, were you not, my dear?'

'I was, Uncle.'

'Did you see anything of the evening's events, Miss Hart?' I asked. 'From the window perhaps.'

'I knew little of the disturbance of the peace outside the Manor House, but after the crowd had gone their ways I happened to glance out at the Market Place, which my window overlooks. I saw what I thought was a man, a drunken fellow I imagined, sitting facing towards me and propped against the Market Cross. The area had become very quiet for a Saturday night.'

'Was there anything particular about the man as far as you could see? Did you know him?'

'I did not recognize him. His hat was pulled down low. But he had a paper of some kind on his coat.'

'What writing was on it?'

'It was growing dark, Mr Cragg, and from such a distance quite impossible to see.'

'Have you not heard any talk about that, though? What might have been written on this paper, do you think?'

'Nothing has been said about it, Sir. I only know what I saw, two men coming into Market from Street and going towards the man. When one of them touched him he slumped sideways, lying quite still. The two men knelt and I suppose tried to help him. I couldn't see what they were doing. One of the two men ran back towards the Manor House. Then Mr Cumberledge came up and looked at the body. I recognized him all right.'

'So what are people saying about this?'

'No one will admit to knowing anything,' said Holloway.

'There is gossip that he was shot,' Miss Hart said.

'At all events,' her uncle continued, 'it is a grievous assault on the Squire's plans, if it turns out that Lavenham was assassinated.'

'I hope this will all come forth when the matter is inquested,'
I said. 'More than anything, what puzzles me is why Lavenham
was out and about where a hostile mob had assembled, when he
himself, and his work, were the object of the hostility.'

'It is odd, perhaps, and suspicious certainly,' said Holloway.
'How well did you know the man?'

'A little, as I say. He was sensible enough, I thought. A more
pleasant sort of character than his colleague Tree, in my opinion.'

'You do not like Wilkin Tree?'

'Oh, you know, I do not dislike him. He has a sharp tongue,
though, and a southern manner. In general he has little to say
for himself.'

'So you had more liking for John Lavenham.'

'Yes. He would go to the alehouse. He would talk to anybody.
Tree is not inclined to society. The only friend he's made here,
so far as I've heard, is the Lumsdens' gamekeeper. He's been
out with him on his rounds at night a few times, so it's said.
Otherwise when he's not working Tree shuts himself up and
reads books.'

This caught my attention.

'Is he a reader? That surprises me. He made no indication of
it when I saw him today.'

'They say there's always a book and a pair of reading spectacles in his pocket.'

'I too am very fond of the literary arts. Do you have a library
yourself, Mr Holloway?'

He looked at me astonished, as if I had asked if he kept a
camel.

'What use are books to me, Cragg? Tales, verses? Practical
matters are my concern. You must look to my niece if you want
to speak of books. She has ruined her eyesight, so fond is she
of reading.'

I did look to her.

'I read with the aid of eyeglasses, Mr Cragg,' she said.

'And what reading do you prefer, Miss Hart?'

Amelia glanced up from her plate, then looked down again,
avoiding my gaze.

'Well, the Scriptures, of course, and verses and hymns such
as those of Dr Watts.'

'The non-conformist divine?'

'I am not of the Wesleyan persuasion, Mr Cragg, but I greatly admire those hymns, which are divine poems to me.'

'And aside from spiritual reading, what else?'

'I like moral tales told by means of imaginary letters, as Mrs Eliza Haywood's *Letters from a Lady of Quality to a Chevalier.* Mrs Rowe's *Friendship in Death* is very good too, and of course I have read Mr Richardson's *Pamela* and the first two parts of his new story *Clarissa.* I am so impatient to read the next instalment, which has been such a long time in coming.'

The buoyancy I often feel in discussing books with a fellow reader subsided a little. These romances are certainly worthy and often formidable, but as my bookseller Sweeting would say, worthiness and wit are rarely found within the same covers.

'You do not have much longer to wait,' I said. 'Our bookseller Sweeting tells me he is in daily expectation of receiving copies of parts three and four of *Clarissa.* Elizabeth will be in his shop as soon as they arrive, I am in no doubt. Richardson is a favourite author of hers.'

'Oh! That is indeed exciting. Our nearest bookshop is in Keswick. I must write and order the book. And what are you reading, Mr Cragg? What book have you with you in your valise?'

'I have the letters of Alexander Pope with me, Miss Hart. They are highly enjoyable to anyone interested in the literary life of the past thirty years.'

I did not tell her that I also had with me the recently published memoirs of the notorious Graf Pontius von Schpifflerghun, mercenary fighter in the armies of the Tsar of Russia, the Sultan of Turkey and the Empress of Austria, and possibly more than one of these monarchs at the same time. I had been finding the book as abominable as it is exciting and amusing. Absurd episodes abound, not least being the account of his own near stillbirth on the first page. But, given that the stillbirth was avoided by the insertion of a live farmyard cock's beak into the baby's fundament, followed by the pumping of air through the cock by way of its own back passage, it is not a tale one would pass on to a lady partial to the works of Mrs Haywood and Mrs Rowe, or the poems of Isaac Watts.

We therefore spent the rest of our meal discussing more general matters. I was questioned about the world beyond Ingolside, and of any news that might not yet have reached Ingolside's ears. I described what I had read of the fire in London that had started in a wigmaker's shop, and laid waste to a hundred houses. Holloway received this news with a hotch of his shoulders.

'We matched that here, when the Three Horns burned out. It was that bad, our vicar in his sermon called it a conflagration and, though I don't go to the Dissenters' Meeting House, the preacher there, so I was told, likened it to the fire that rained down on Sodom and Gomorrah.'

'I've seen what's left of the place,' I said. 'I hope the loss of life was less grievous than in those biblical cities.'

'A goat, a rooster and a few hens killed in the back yard. Goody Greenhalgh who kept the inn got her leg burned. A few of her customers were coughing for a week after.'

'How did the fire start?'

'There's suspicions but nobody's sure.'

'You mean it was started deliberately?'

'I do not say that, Mr Cragg. I do not say that.'

As I walked back up Street to collect my mare and my luggage from the Dog and Drum, I stopped for a closer look at the remains of what had been its rival inn. The Three Horns had been thoroughly destroyed. Where the inn sign had hung was only the twisted metal of its bracket dangling above the boarded-up door. The roof was gone entirely and the glass too, giving the place a gaunt, hollow and sinister appearance. I peered through a scorched aperture that had once been a window. The room was blackened and choked with debris, the floor of the room above having collapsed to leave a heap of charred beams on the ground. Birds building nests flitted here and there above, which made me smile. Nature is so quick to assert itself where humans leave a ruin.

Going on my way, as I neared the Dog and Drum my attention was drawn to a plain building of yellow brick, which stood at the very top of Street, in a position that faced directly down it. The simple portico at the entrance, and the tall windows lined up along the side walls, suggested it was a dissenting chapel – which is what it turned out to be, though in use this day for a meeting without prayers or hymns. Half a dozen men had gathered under the entrance, smoking their pipes and listening through the open door. I recognized Curly Berry among them and approached him.

'What's happening here, Mr Berry?'

'A meeting of the village. It's finishing up now.'

'What was it for?'

'Supposed to be about preparations for Whit Fair but they won't fix their attention on that. They only want to air their grievances.'

'Grievances for what?'

'What you like.'

He gave me a cynical smile.

'They've grievances about everything here. It is a village of grumblers.'

I thought this was a good opportunity to make myself known to these grumblers. So I went inside.

It was a plain interior, with three high windows running down each side and a small raised platform at the end of the room, on which stood a wide rostrum, rather like a stage, which presumably served as a pulpit. Whoever had conducted this meeting had by now vacated the platform and it was unoccupied. Pushing through the crowd, I mounted and turned to face the room, raising my hands and calling for quiet.

The hubbub diminished a little as every face turned towards me. A voice shouted from the crowd.

'You what, Mister?'

'I am the Coroner to the County,' I said more loudly. 'My name is Cragg and I have the job of looking into any death that is doubtful. In this case, it is Mr John Lavenham's death.'

The people did not stop murmuring, though I could not tell if it was from discontent or simple commentary. I went on, raising my voice even more.

'I must tell you it's my intention to hold a public inquest in a few days' time to determine why Mr Lavenham died. Some of you will be asked to act as jurors, to decide on the evidence.'

There was a noticeable increase in comment. I raised my voice by a few more intervals.

'But take note, if you please: the hearing is an open one, with nothing concealed or underhand. All may attend and hear the proceedings but anyone with evidence will be required to come forward and speak up. The prime object is not to point a finger of blame towards anyone in this village. I have nothing to do here but get at the truth.'

'Truth's not open-handed, Mr Coroner,' shouted someone. 'It's not a bargaining token neither. It isn't for sale.'

'Of course it is not for sale, Sir. But it should be open-handed, you know. In justice this man's death must be accounted for by fair means.'

'Why should we care about the death of this or that stranger?' shouted a woman at the rear of the crowd. 'This Lavenham wasn't one of ours.'

Many jeers were heard in support of this. I thought of Sir Thomas More's speech in Shakespeare's play *Henry VIII* when he addresses the London street mob rioting against incomers. There was a time when I could recite the whole of that speech word for word. Now I merely borrowed from it to make a shorter speech of my own.

'Of no account? Let me put aside the matter that this is the King's business and ask you something else: would *you* like to go into a strange country and find people spurning you like a dog, and saying you were of no account? And find when one threatens to cut your throat, and even does so, he will be allowed to go free because your life is of no account?'

I grew hot and, while speaking with double loudness, was trying not to shout.

'Common humanity says you should give strangers justice equal to that which you hope for yourself.'

A hoarse voice boomed repeatedly above all the noise, a sound like a shepherd's horn call. I identified this heckler as a large figure in the middle of the room, with huge side whiskers, a broken nose and heavily weathered face. The woman at the back of the hall shouted over this man's roars.

'Equal justice? There is none of that from the London direction.'

Another man echoed her.

'That's right. Lackeys they are, licking the spit off the chins of the rich.'

I pointed to the author of this last remark.

'Do you mean Mr Tree and the late Mr Lavenham, Sir?'

'Aye. Who else?'

'Then I would like a word with you. Will you approach?'

It was not this man but all the people together who now advanced towards me. In a moment I was surrounded and under siege. They were shouting things and jabbing the air with their fists and for a moment I was afraid I might be pulled down and given a kicking, if not worse.

Then I was aware of another man standing beside me on the platform and holding his hands in the air.

'Listen,' he called. 'Listen, won't you? Mr Cragg is only from Preston. He isn't London. He isn't a danger to you. Stand back. Stand back and let him be.'

Whoever the man was, it was clear he commanded their respect. He and the rest of the crowd edged back. Their oaths and threats receded to the level of low growls, then whispers and finally nothing but thoughts.

The man turned to me and I took note of his appearance. He wore his reddish hair tied in a tail and without a wig. His face was shaven clean and his clothing was that of a small tradesman. He was of less than medium height and I put his age at thirty-five.

I thanked him for his intervention.

'I think you saved me from harm. Broken ribs at the least.'

'Don't blame them, Mr Cragg. Their patience is extremely tested in these days. But you are safe enough alongside me. My name is Quexton, Cornelius Quexton. Will you join me in a mug of ale at my lodging across the road?'

'I will, Sir.'

He led the way and only then did it come to me that he was one of the two men – the smaller one – that I had seen that morning dancing on the shore of the lake.

# FOUR

Quexton's lodging was a narrow cottage facing the Green, just two minutes' walk from the Meeting House. Its parlour was not unpleasant, though a little dark, having only a single small window. Its furniture of plain elm was typical of cottages and its floor was stone-flagged. There was little to be seen of Quexton's personal tastes except for some books lined up along an exposed beam beside the fire nook.

Quexton went into a room at the back and while awaiting him I ran my eye along the row of books. The collection may have been small but it was certainly varied. He had Chambers' *Cyclopaedia*, some plays of Shakespeare, *The Faerie Queene*, a treatise *On the Law of Nature* and another about Rational Agriculture. Then to my great surprise I saw *The Memoirs of Pontius Von Schpifflerghun*, the very same little volume as I had myself brought to Ingolside.

We sat down at the table on which Quexton placed a jug of ale and pewter mugs. He poured for us both, we clinked pewter on pewter and drank.

'Is it locally made?' I asked.

'The brewer is Oswald Gillow. He knows his business.'

As we talked I began more and more to like Quexton, and he in turn had pleasant words for me.

'I approve of what you said to the meeting,' he told me. 'I too am an incomer here. When I first came last year, I felt no one at all would give me a welcome. Since then I have come and gone, keeping my lodging here and slowly getting to know them, and letting them know me. As you were saying to the people earlier, one who can fancy himself wearing the boots of another thinks more charitably of him.'

'My words were not exactly mine. I am afraid they were filched in paraphrase from a speech in Shakespeare's play about King Henry the Eighth.'

'Ah! Shakespeare.'

He nodded towards his miniature library.

'I have a large number of books in stores here and there. I cannot carry them all from place to place. But I do always make sure I have some of his works to hand. He had a way of hitting the mark smack in the middle.'

'I am delighted you are a reader of Shakespeare.'

'Of all his kings, which do you like the best?'

I said there were not many likeable kings in Shakespeare's work.

'I nominate Henry the Fifth. He was the only one who *did* try on the people's boots for size. You will remember he went incognito amongst the ranks on the eve of Agincourt. Most of the other monarchs are either tyrants or arrogant fools.'

'Shakespeare wrote that greatness is abused when it disjoins remorse from power.'

'Which powerful men are apt do. Tender feelings are not usual in the great. Remorse is alien to them. The Squire in this village would do well to learn the lesson.'

'Lear learns remorse at the end, does he not? Granted that is only when it is too late to save his poor daughter Cordelia.'

'Too late? Does she not marry and start a happy family?'

'Only in the version generally known now. I myself prefer the story as Shakespeare wrote it.'

'I have not read that. Everyone dies in it, I suppose.'

'That is what tragedy is.'

'Ha! I suspect as a Coroner you secretly love a tragedy.'

'I can admire a tragic play, where the invented characters die. But not the tragic death of people in the world. That would be to extract pleasure from misery.'

His face wore an ironic smile.

'It might fairly give you some pleasure, though, as it provides you with employment.'

He was teasing me.

'Ah yes,' I said. 'I suppose I can enjoy death rather as a gravedigger does. Remember what Horatio says to Hamlet about that? That death has for the gravedigger "a property of easiness", which is why he can sing while he digs. Like him I must accept death. I must look it in the face and become easy with it.'

'Easy? I think it must often be difficult in the extreme to

explain a death that occurs without witnesses. That is what I take
to be your legal task.'

'Supposedly the jury explains. I merely gather evidence to lay
before them. Through that process, it is hoped the truth will be
found and I do prefer to know the truth myself before the inquest
itself convenes. I do not always know it, I will admit. Sometimes
the evidence is buried too deep.'

'I see your difficulty with evidence. The one most directly
concerned cannot testify, being dead. So you must rely on the
*ipse dixit* of others among the living.'

'You use a legal term, Mr Quexton. Are you an attorney?'

'I have studied the law.'

'At the Inns of Court?'

He did not reply. I went on: 'I count my time at the Inns of
Court as a very happy time.'

'Happy, perhaps, but lacking point. Students are blockheads
for the most part.'

'So you don't practise the law now?'

He dismissed the question with a wave of his hand.

'To know a little of the law is useful for one who does what
I do.'

'Which is, more precisely?'

He wafted his hand again, unwilling to be precise.

'Oh, I have done many things. Now I concern myself with
justice.'

'We are one of a kind then. I too am on the side of justice.'

'I speak of common justice, Mr Cragg, public justice. That is
distinct from the kind you read about in your law books. It is
why I tour around and make observations. I sometimes speak in
public.'

'Then you are a little like a travelling dissenter.'

'If it's John Wesley you refer to, I know the man and I sympa-
thize, even agree with his views. I have even attended prayer
meetings here, at the Dissenters' Hall. But I am quite different
from the Wesley brothers. They are bent on founding a sect, whereas
I am a lone wolf. Nor do I presume to interpret God's system, but
am concerned only with arrangements made by people.'

'And in this case, those of the people of Ingolside?'

'Yes. Petty, vindictive and complaining though they are, I am learning to understand them. And understanding leads to liking, I find.'

'The man who died here was called John Lavenham. He came to Ingolside to look into some old documents. Do you know anything of what happened to him?'

'I travelled on business into Yorkshire. So I know very little – less than you.'

'Which is not much. By the way, did I not see you this morning at the lakeside? You and a man of great size. Were you rehearsing Morris dancing for the Whit Fair, I wonder?'

Quexton tilted back his head and roared with laughter.

'Dancing by the lake? Dancing! That's a good one. Wait till I tell Charlie that. Dancing, now!'

I rose to my feet, picked up my mug, drained it and put it down on the bookshelf. But before bidding him goodbye I picked out Von Schpfflerghun's *Memoirs*.

'It is a remarkable coincidence that I myself am looking through these memoirs. I have brought the book with me. It is hard to believe most of what he writes, is it not?'

'I knew the man, Mr Cragg. He is a habitual liar. Four-fifths of his anecdotes are inventions.'

'You *knew* Von Schplifflerghun?'

'Met him during my travels, when I was younger and moved much around the Continent. In fact, I served with him briefly in Bohemia, until I tired of playing the military adventurer. I have found a more just way of life now.'

'So he did not in fact seduce as many women as he claims?'

'Seduce? He was incapable of it. The only bed games he could manage were forcible. When it comes to Von Schplifflerghun, the split between remorse and power was absolute.'

It was time I left. I extended my hand.

'It has been a pleasure talking to you, Mr Quexton, and I bid you good day. We'll speak together again, I am sure.'

As I returned to the street it came to me that we had indeed had a beguiling conversation, but I'd learned very little of practical value either about Cornelius Quexton or the matter in hand – that of how Lavenham was killed, and why. Quexton was well read. He had been a soldier of some irregular kind. He had had some legal training but never finished it. He leant towards religious dissent but without any noteworthy commitment. The man was likeable, certainly, but elusive. I did not even know where he was born, who his parents were and how he lived, or made a living, whether he was married and had children. In short, I knew none of the usual things that arise when one meets someone for the first time. I had met Quexton, yet I was acquainted with very few of the fundamental facts of his life.

In the afternoon I called at Luke Fidelis's lodging. I had delivered my belongings and horse to Holloway's Farm and walked back up Street until I found the house of the Widow Booth, which stood to the south of the Market Place, on the opposite side of Street from the burned inn. It was the last in a row of decent cottages that abutted a craftsman's shop, tidily thatched and with clean windows. A queue of three people stood outside, who became agitated when I directly approached the door.

'Wait your turn,' growled one as I was about to knock. 'You get here last, mind you go in last.'

I turned to this man, an old one leaning on his stick, who shook as with an extreme case of palsy.

'What do you wait for, Sir?'

'The physicker.'

'You mean Dr Fidelis? Is he seeing patients here?'

'So we've been told.'

'Well, I am not a patient,' I said, rapping on the door. 'I am here on other business.'

I don't know exactly what I expected in Fidelis's landlady. I found when Mrs Booth opened her door to me that she dressed cleanly, but very simply, was not over thirty and, with all that, was extremely handsome.

I said who I was and asked if her lodger was at home. She gave me a wide smile.

'Come inside, Mr Cragg. Dr Fidelis is in the back parlour with Mrs Shanks who has a bad case of the dropsy.'

'There are more outside in a queue, waiting to see him.'

'The word has got around that he will give medical advice at no charge. He is a marvel. Mrs Lumsden had him on almost continuous duty all day and yet he will not rest even when he comes back to his lodging.'

I saw the admiration in her eyes. I smiled, having seen this aspect in Fidelis's lady friends many times before.

'Come in here and have some refreshment while we wait for him to finish up.'

She took me into the parlour whose window faced the street. A tray with a plain teapot and cups lay on the table before the fire. She poured for us both.

'Is there no doctor here in Ingolside?' I asked.

'Not since old Dr Rigg died ten years back. He had been so incompetent, and his earnings so meagre, that his wife found it impossible to sell the practice. We have to make do with our wise woman, else we must travel to Dr Hornby at Kendal. This is not a prosperous parish, Mr Cragg.'

I could see that Helen Booth herself was not prosperous. Lodging Dr Fidelis for the time being was a windfall in money terms, whatever else it brought her in bodily pleasure. And, by the way, I could guess at that else: from the look in her eye, I reckoned he had probably already found his way into her bed.

We talked together as we drank our tea, or rather she got me to talk, so full of curiosity was she about my work, the cases I had seen, the occasional adventures they had landed me in; and then about myself, my circumstances back in Preston, and the make-up of my family. She on the other hand would hardly speak of herself at all.

Fidelis then came in, thirsty enough to drink two cups in quick succession. Our hostess poured him a third and left us, saying she must cook their supper.

'She told me since Mr Booth died five years ago she cannot afford meat, not even once a week,' Fidelis said. 'So I've brought home a hare for the pot.'

'Home, is it now, Luke?' I said. 'Will you be removing here from Preston, then?'

Fidelis looked at me gravely.

'We may have differing ideas about the meaning of home, Titus.'

I let this mysterious remark pass.

'And she is as long as five years a lone widow,' I said. 'I am surprised. She is rather a beauty.'

'She is, Titus. But Booth cannot have been any hand at business, as he left her hardly a brass farthing. Her only income is a pittance she gets for going into the Manor House twice a week as an assistant maid, brushing cobwebs and scrubbing floors. Her fine appearance is not enough to attract a new husband. They think more of hard cash than soft love hereabouts.'

'What was the husband's business? I had no chance to ask during our conversation just now.'

'Well, what do you think it was, Titus? Look around you. Make an educated guess.'

Fidelis frequently laid down these challenges and I generally failed at them. However, I tried, glancing at the simple cottage furniture, the sparse ornaments, the boiled curtains, the ragged rug on the stone floor. These spoke of the woman's poverty but told me nothing else. I also noted a few prints hanging on the wall and on a shelf a row of books, many being other than mere almanacks. I shrugged.

'It is a literate household, it seems. Let's see. Was he the schoolmaster?'

'No, no, Titus! The clue is not in her books, but her boots. She wears a dull old dress, woollen stockings, no jewellery, but she is finely shod. The boots are not new but very well made, and made to last. And what business do we see standing right next door to this house?'

I went to the window, opened it and peered out. A sign swung above the next door, with a picture of a cobbler's last. I withdrew my head.

'He was the village shoemaker.'

'Well observed, Titus, though you needed a prompt.'

I laughed.

'You are ever the more discerning observer.'

'There is a science in observation, as Mr Aristotle might have put it, and I am merely a practitioner of the science.'

'I rather think it's your stock in trade, Luke. Cobblers work with their hands on leather, lawyers with their eyes on statutes and long precedent. But doctors need their hands and their eyes. They must be quick in front of their client, or they may miss an under-lying morbidity. Your eye has been valuable to me many times.'

'I blush.'

'And, by the way, it is kind of you to see the sick people of this place, purely *pro bono publico*.'

'I do not claim any virtue in that; it is purely professional self-interest. I like to get acquainted with the diseases of a place when I visit for the first time. It's for my own instruction, and in order to know the place better.'

'And what have you learned about Ingolside?'

'It is home to many agues, owing to the proximity of the marsh. And there has recently been a fire in a public building.'

'Yes. The Three Horns. The ruin is just across the road.'

'An inn, as it happens, but it might have been a church, or a meeting hall. I have today seen three men, not related to each other, each with a cough they can't get rid of, and their sputum in each case blackened. I recall the same effects when the Skeleton Inn burned at Preston – you remember it?'

I certainly did, and the bout of trouble the event had brought me.

'These men each told me they were at Three Horns when it caught fire. The flames spread with deadly speed and they – intoxicated I suppose – were slow to respond. They were carried out in the end, semi-conscious, and all are lucky not to be suffocated and dead.'

'Speaking of the dead, what of Lavenham's corpse? When will you examine him? It had better be soon as he stinks like a midden.'

'I'll do it tomorrow in the morning if you authorize me. I'll look at the superficial wounds and the deeper chest wound. I shall also look for internal disease. Have you discovered the constable?'

'It seems there is none. But listen, Luke. I have heard from a witness that there was possibly a written letter or sign found with the body. I would like to see that. Do you know when the Squire returns? I am hoping he has it. It will be hard, anyway, to get on with my work without speaking to him, as he is the magistrate and also as far as I can tell the employer of Lavenham and Tree.'

'At the Manor House they told me that he is expected tomorrow. He has been to the town of Penrith, I have heard, on business with Lord Lonsdale.'

'Lonsdale?'

'Mrs Lumsden in her more lucid moments spends considerable time cursing Lord Lonsdale and the whole Lowther family. You know that she holds herself to be the last guardian of feudal agriculture in this parish?'

'She told me so herself.'

'The Lowthers are the biggest landowners in these north-western shires and have engrossed their estates in the last generation and done so with – according to Mrs Lumsden – particular ruthlessness. Her son has his own like ideas. He may have gone there to get his lordship's advice.'

'On how best to batter down any objectors to his schemes.'

'Yes, and he needs it, for he's got a fight on his hands.'

'It is reasonable that the death of Lavenham may have something to do with that fight. He came here with Tree specifically on the business of the enclosures.'

Fidelis drank a mouthful of tea.

'I feel your inquest will face many contrary questions as a ship faces contrary winds.'

'And as any competent ship's captain will tell you, the most important thing in such cases is to have your ropes neatly coiled. Shall I meet you at Lakeside Lodge at eight o'clock?'

# FIVE

Fidelis being habitually the worst morning riser since the seven sleepers of Ephesus, I was there before him. I had had a comfortable night at Holloway's Farm, after an evening in which we played at Gleek after supper, being the only three-handed card game we all knew. After that Holloway and myself listened to Miss Hart singing and playing on the spinet. I was privately steeling myself beforehand, but afterwards felt ashamed because she had a true voice, which stayed perfectly in tune throughout her recital.

After a full night's sleep I came to Lakeside Lodge at eight o' clock, to find Wilkin Tree had already gone out. Waiting for Fidelis, I passed the time in the kitchen talking to the servant, Lizzy Duckham. She was a rich source of information, once I had her on the subject of Ingolside and its people. I asked how the land was held. Were there those that owned their strips of land, or held it as copyholders from the Squire.

'Them that work land here are all copyholders: Squire lays claim to the land, but we have our strips of it to work by ancient right. The Duckham strip's been twenty generations in the family. The Lumsdens have been here for three. Squire's been buying out some of us lately, and trying to bully more into selling. He wants to get the whole lot into his own hands but I reckon he's now got as much as he'll ever get by buying. My man won't sell his rights for certain, and nor will most. So Squire's changed his attack. The talk is he's going to try to break us by force of parliament. He reckons to make it law that him and his friends get all the fields and have us working them for wages day by day. Duckham says they're no better than robbers doing that.'

'And the common?'

'He reckons he'll take that an' all. The forest alongside the lake where he'll be felling the trees for sheep pasture, and the marsh, that he says he'll drain of its water and fashion new fields.'

'Some would say that he will benefit all by increasing the agricultural acreage.'

'He'll benefit himself and his friends. No one else will. The cottagers that have no copyhold depend for everything on the common. They grow a little in their yards but they can't get by without their gathering and their grazing a few beasts in the woods and on the marsh.'

'It's no wonder Mr Tree and Mr Lavenham are not liked.'

'Oh, they are only Squire's tools and it's Squire we've the grudge against. Truth is, Lavenham was liked, in his way. He was a one to tickle a smile out of you, or even bring you to laughing. Always ready with a joke, he was. Handsome an' all. There's quite a few that think it's a crying pity that he's dead, instead of this other one.'

'Mr Tree, you mean?'

'Just by opening his mouth he sets people at odds with him. I'm not saying I don't get along with him, me, being as I work here. But if he came from my sow's litter, he'd be the weanling I'd send to the butcher first, if you get my meaning.'

'What are people saying about the cause of Mr Lavenham's death?'

She looked at me shrewdly.

'They're close about it, Mr Cragg. Maybe some can account for it, but I can't.'

'I have heard there was a paper on the body, a letter perhaps. Have you heard this?'

'No, I've never heard of such a thing. People are asking if Lavenham was killed on purpose, but there's nobody answering why or how, and no talk of any letter that would give a reason.'

At this moment Luke arrived with his bag of tools and went straight in to where the corpse lay.

It took two hours for Luke Fidelis to complete his examination of the corpse, which was now so overripe that my friend, who was usually impervious, emerged looking not a little nauseated.

'There was a bruise at the base of the skull, but I don't think it was serious enough to have killed him. His jawbone was bruised, which could have happened by falling over. He had an external wound to his neck and a hole in his chest, but no other apparent wounds. I am sure the dried matter on his shirt is blood. The hole is from a gunshot.'

'A gunshot?' I repeated.

'Yes. Here, I found the ball inside him.'

He opened his hand and showed me the thick lead pellet.

'I believe it was fired at close quarters,' he said.

'And how is that?'

'Because there appeared to be residue of burned powder around the wound.'

'That would kill him instantly, wouldn't you say? But did he shoot himself dead, that's my question.'

'Dead men cannot commit suicide, Titus.'

'By which you mean?'

'He was already dead when that shot was fired into him.'

'In truth, Luke? So the gunshot didn't kill Lavenham.'

'No. The flow of blood was insufficient. I have several times seen the blood flow from bullet wounds in the chest, and it is truly copious. Looking at his blood-stained clothes the amount of blood was insignificant by comparison. Besides, no one has mentioned a great flow of blood from the body, and our own eyes could only see light traces of it on the steps of the cross. I am not even sure that it was his blood, either on the footing of the cross or the stains on his clothing.'

'Surely the stain on the shirt was his own blood.'

'If he was shot after death, his heart would not be beating. In that case there would be little if any bleeding.'

'What else did you find?'

'I opened him up further and looked for signs of sickness. The heart, liver, stomach, kidneys, spleen were all in order. It wasn't until I inspected his lungs that I found anything of note.'

'Which was?'

'They were blackened and clogged.'

'What with?'

'Ashes. He had been in a fire, Titus, and had breathed noxious ash-filled smoke, just like the village patients I have been seeing.'

'His lungs were injured, then?'

'To some extent. At all events, we may be sure he was drinking in the Three Horns Inn when fire broke out, and inhaled a good deal of the smoke.'

'Did that make him sicken?'

'I don't know, but I have an experiment in mind which may help us.'

'And did he suffer burns?'

'His hair was intact. The neck wound might be a burn. There's no scorching on his clothing.'

'What about his head wound? Was it accidental?'

'It might easily have been. The flames were near, the air was full of smoke, spars and stones were falling from the roof and Lavenham was in a drunken stupor.'

'So we do not know if he crawled out or someone carried him out of the building. What is your opinion, Luke? Could he have survived the inhalation?'

'Yes. Others did.'

'Why was he then shot? And when? And how did he end by sitting dead in the Market Place three days later?'

Fidelis shrugged.

'Someone knows, but I do not. We need a human witness.'

'One cannot be far to find. This is a village. Almost everyone knows almost everything.'

'Do you know how the cynic Diogenes defined the difference between a city and a village, Titus?'

'I know you will tell me.'

'He said that in a city the law defeats gossip by rising above it. In a village gossip defeats law by subverting it.'

I sighed.

'That is clever of Diogenes but I suppose it only helps us prove what we already know about this place. It doesn't help us establish how Lavenham died.'

'Or why.'

'I can almost never settle on why until I know who and how. In short, as you say, we need to find a witness to his death.'

On our way back to Ingolside I was still feeling the lack of witnesses like an itch. The nearest I had was Miss Hart with her faulty eyesight and her idea that there had been a note with the body.

'I wish I knew what happened to Lavenham in the fire. There must be people who saw him at the inn when fire broke out.'

'And some that know what happened to him after.'

'Why does no one come forward to tell the truth?'

'These country people are like a clock that will charge you for the telling the time.'

'Have you heard of Goody Greenhalgh?'

'I have treated a woman by that name for the after-effects of burns.'

'She is, or was, the landlady of the Three Horns, I believe. I must speak to her about this. Do you know where she lives, Luke?'

'When I saw Mrs Greenhalgh she was at her brother's house which overlooks St Silas churchyard. He took her in after the Three Horns was destroyed.'

'I will go there now.'

'You will be wasting your time. On my advice she has now left Ingolside. She is at her sister's at Trimbleby.'

'That's some miles away.'

'Yes, I believe it is.'

'Which is not convenient, Luke. She's a probable witness. And she went away by your advice, you say?'

'She was in pain from her burns. They were quite serious on her legs and arms where the skin looked in danger of suppuration. I told her I might prevent that with honey dressings and frequent immersions in sea brine, which she said was convenient as her sister lived near the sea and kept bees. I told her to go there at once.'

'Honey and seawater? It sounds like the makings of some old witch's brew.'

'Sea bathing is recommended by Hippocrates, specifically for cases of burned skin. But I have seen more recent reports that when a ship burns, the scorched sailor who jumps into the sea prospers more than the one who takes to the longboat.'

'Unless he drowns.'

'That is beside the point. I consider it worth a try. And I have many times seen the good done by honey when smeared on a skin wound.'

'So Mistress Greenhalgh has gone to her sister's at Trimbleby. Oh well. It is there I must go if I am to talk with her.'

We had covered four hundred yards along the path leading

back to the head of the lake when we saw a man hurrying towards us. He was red-faced, on the portly side and dressed in a gentleman's riding clothes.

'It is Squire Lumsden,' said Fidelis, 'returned from his business in Penrith.'

A minute later we came face to face and I looked with curiosity and not a little dubiety at the fellow who had once tried to have a roll in the hay with my wife. Traces of the handsome boy she had described still remained, though after twenty-five years it was overlaid by the beginning of corpulence and a reddened and roughened face. I gave the Squire a bow.

He said, 'Who are you, Sir?'

'I am Titus Cragg, the County Coroner. I have come expressly to look into the unfortunate Mr Lavenham's death.'

Lumsden stared at me up and down.

'Who the devil sent for you? It was not by my authority and that affronts me. I am the magistrate here. I am the law. You cannot simply come here and look into things, as you put it, without commission from me.'

'I do not need an invitation. Lavenham's death is enough invitation.'

'Well you will not be able to proceed because we are going to bury Lavenham. I have been away on business since the unfortunate event, and have also been awaiting a letter, and was therefore unable to order the burial immediately.'

'What letter, if I may ask?'

'I had written to London to enquire after any relatives, which I saw as my duty before putting him in the ground.'

'Have you received a reply?'

'I haven't and it's no good waiting any longer. He must be buried.'

'I am afraid he cannot, not yet,' I said. 'I am here to inquest him.'

'Is that quite necessary? I have ruled that the death was an accident caused by himself, when the fellow was cleaning a gun.'

He turned to Fidelis.

'As for you, Doctor, what is your interest in this?'

'Mr Cragg asked me to open the corpse and I have just finished the procedure.'

'With what result?'

'He did not die from cleaning his gun.'

For a moment Arthur Lumsden couldn't hide his disappointment. Then his spirit returned.

'If I say he died in that way, then that is so. I hope you have not abused your position, Sir. You came on to my land merely to give medicine to my mother in her sickness, did you not? Not to dissect corpses and give opinions about them. It is none of your business.'

'It is my business, however,' I said. 'And I hold the King's commission in all such matters. I am also entitled to seek whatever assistance I need from whomever I like. It was I that asked Dr Fidelis to make a medical examination of the deceased.'

He took a pugnacious step towards me and, seizing my lapel in his hand, pushed his face to within three inches of mine.

'I don't like lawyers coming here unless it is my own lawyer on my own business.'

'But do you not want to know who killed Mr Lavenham? He was here on your business, I think.'

Lumsden let go of my coat and bared his teeth in a forced smile.

'I know who did it.'

'Then you must give me the name.'

'I don't know the name. I don't know the *particular* hand that did it. But I am sure of who is morally responsible, and be in no doubt I will exact punishment in my own way.'

He swung away, striding on towards Lakeside Lodge. Fidelis and I continued on our way and, before we parted at the Market Place, where I was expected at Holloway's for dinner, Luke took something from his pocket.

'There is one more thing that I found on Lavenham's body. It was attached to his coat and I think I can guess its significance.'

He put into my hand a pin, and a scrap of paper, no more than an inch across, with two pinholes in it. It was a fragment of a paper's edge from which the rest of the sheet had been torn.

'Where was this pinned on the coat?'

'Below the left shoulder, over the clavicle.'

'The collarbone?'

'Exactly.'

I looked carefully at the scrap of paper. I could see it had the lines of stave with some musical notation and under them the words *so amazing so.*'

'Is it a broadside ballad, Luke? For singing?'

'It might be. But why would a ballad be attached to his coat, and torn away?'

'That will emerge. It confirms what Miss Hart who lives with my host Farmer Holloway told me. She has a view from her window of the market place and saw the body when it was sitting slumped at the foot of the Market Cross. She thought there was a paper attached to the coat, of which this fragment is all that remains. If only we could identify the text.'

'Better still,' said Fidelis, 'identify who tore it away.'

# SIX

Goody Greenhalgh's sister Margaret had left Ingolside twenty years earlier to wed a fish merchant in Trimbleby, one Hogg, who on the evidence of his home was prosperous enough. Next morning, after an easy southerly ride of two hours towards the coast, I had no difficulty identifying the Hoggs' house in the centre of the little fishing town. It had a porticoed front door and the five tall sash windows of its principle rooms proudly facing the main street, while its back (kitchen, scullery and yard) looked out over a saltmarsh and beyond that the distant sea.

But I did not call there immediately, going first to the post office where I handed in the letter to Elizabeth that I had written during the previous evening. Enclosed with it was a note to my clerk, Furzey, telling him to join me in Ingolside, and in the meantime to see if he could discover why John Lavenham might have appeared in London before Magistrate Veil of Bow Street. I then went back to the residence of Mr and Mrs Hogg.

On knocking, I was told by a maid at the house that Mrs Hogg had gone with Mrs Greenhalgh to bathe. I asked for directions to the place, at which the maid looked uncertain, as if suspecting me of having a disgraceful motive for going to find the bathing ladies.

'I assure you, I am on the King's business,' I said.

She gave me the directions. I would find the sisters at a small inlet from the great Bay of Morecambe, at a place called Sea Cliff, only about a mile from the town.

It required some finding. On the road down to the sea I passed a smithy, a limekiln and, down a side track, a modest salt mill. Arriving at the shore I found the tide was almost at its height. Several wooden platforms stood on legs thirty yards from the high-water line, linked to the land by walkways. Two merchant ships lay alongside these offshore wharves while carts came and went on the rickety piers, bringing barrels of cargo from them, and provisions to them.

At the shore I turned off along a track and, leaving the piers far behind, came at last to a small hump, from the top of which I had a view across the vast expanse of Morecambe Bay. I guessed that at low tide I would be faced with a prospect of flat black mud and sand, with the deep water away in the far distance. But now at high tide I saw a vast expanse of water stretching for miles to the opposite shore. On it fishermen's boats bobbed, shallow-draught skiffs shaped like walnut shells, as I could see from the half dozen examples that lay bottom up in front of me on the foreshore. I went down to speak to one of their owners, who was mending a fine-mesh net.

'What do you fish for?'

'Shrimp. Blackfish. And anything in between. We're not particular.'

'You enjoy the life?'

He looked at me as if I'd asked him to solve a mathematical equation. He pushed up his oilcloth cap and scratched his forehead.

'I'll say this. I'd rather it to driving a plough.'

'But it may be dangerous, I suppose. After all, a man cannot drown while sowing a field.'

The fisherman looked with squinting eyes across the bay.

'Me, I look at it this way. What happens is at my own charge. Working a boat I can sell what I catch, or feed it to my family. There's no lord of a manor to say where I'm to fish and then take half the catch off me.'

'Well, I hope the fish are plentiful.'

'Plentiful enough.'

'I wonder if you know of two ladies who come to bathe hereabouts in the seawater?'

'Oh aye. That's Hogg's wife and her sister. I've seen them. Mad pair of old hussies.'

'I believe they come to a spot somewhere nearby. Can you direct me?'

With his hands busy he indicated with a jerk of his head.

'Go back up the cliff and look down other side. You'll see them if they're in the water. Mad pair, like I say.'

Re-climbing the hillock, evidently seen as a 'cliff' in the middle of this flat littoral, I looked down on a sleeve of water that spread

around it, filled up for the time being by the tide. Shrill cries
resounded from it and, looking in their direction, I saw two ladies
shrieking with laughter as they sported and splashed together in
the muddy brine.

Dismounting, I led the horse down the slope to a narrow beach.
I tethered him to a bush and sat on a dead tree stump to await
the women coming out.

It was only as they were doing so that they noticed me, and
at once tried with hands and arms to cover as best they could
their bodies, which appeared plump and pink through their soaked
shifts. I swept off my hat and hid my face behind it to spare the
blushes of the two matronly sea nymphs rising from the deep.

'Well might you hide your face in shame, Sir, whoever you
are,' called out one. 'And where in heaven's name is Aysgarth?'

'I have no idea, Madam,' I said, from behind my hat. 'Who
is he?'

'Aysgarth, I say, with the cart and blankets, who is due to meet
us here and take us back to Trimbleby before we catch our
deaths.'

'It seems he has missed the appointment. If I may ask, which
of you is Mrs Greenhalgh, and which Mrs Hogg?'

The ladies were alike in many points: their height, their
complexion, their roundness and their nicely shaped noses and
chins. There was one notable difference, one sister having
hazelnut eyes, and the other's eyes as blue as a cornflower.

'I am Mrs Hogg,' said the brown-eyed one. 'And here is Mrs
Greenhalgh, my sister. But who are you, if we may know?'

I told her my name, and my office, and explained my mission
to enquire into the circumstances of the death of John Lavenham
at Ingolside, adding, 'You ladies are very welcome to ride home
on the back of my horse, if Aysgarth's cart cannot be found.'

They conferred together in whispers.

'We accept your offer, Mr Cragg,' said Mrs Greenhalgh. 'But
first you must walk away for a moment so that my sister and I
may dress. Keep your back turned, mind.'

I strolled away from them along the shore of the inlet. I listened
to the whistles of curlew and plover wheeling and soaring above
me as they waited for the tide to retreat and the mud to be
uncovered once more.

'Coo-ee!'

I turned and the ladies, decent once more, were waving at me. Going back, and able to look properly at them, I saw the livid burns on the skin of Mrs Greenhalgh, visible on her right hand and along her bare arm.

Not long afterwards I was leading the horse with the ladies up, sitting side by side. Their hair was draggling but they were both equally exhilarated after their sea dip.

'You seem to have much enjoyed dipping in the sea,' I said.

'We have,' said Mrs Greenhalgh. 'It's as good as a draught of aquavit, is it not, sister?'

'It is,' said Mrs Hogg. 'I don't know why folk don't do it all the time. It's a power of a tonic.'

'And do you find the treatment beneficial to your condition, Mrs Greenhalgh? I mean your burns. I am a friend of Dr Fidelis and it was he that told me where to find you.'

The mention of Luke Fidelis increased Mrs Greenhalgh's animation.

'Eh, that doctor. He's a marvel for his ideas. Yes, I'm healing up nicely. I'm lucky I did not lose my hair to the flames. Dr Fidelis warned me I'll be scarred but promised I'll heal just the same.'

'I'm wondering how it happened,' I said. 'How did the fire start?'

'They reckon the chimney caught, and we were that roaring busy that nobody inside paid heed. Then the thatch went up on top, and folk were running in and shouting about a fire on our roof. A lot of my customers went out then to have a look but I wasn't afraid, not yet. I thought it would be slow to take hold and maybe get put out by men with ladders and buckets. So I was going around giving a shake to them that were too drunk to take notice and warning them to look sharp. Then, before we knew it, the roof was coming down on our heads.'

'Did you notice Mr Lavenham among the drunkards?'

'I did and he was too far gone to make a move – or get out of his chair, come to that. But all at once the timbers were crashing down and I fainted, I reckon, because the next I knew I was being carried by a pair of strong arms out of there.'

'You had a lucky escape,' said Mrs Hogg sagely.

'My dress was burning but when I was brought outside, a kind person chucked a bucket of water over me.'

'Who took you out of the building?'

'A few men went in with brooms to beat at the flames. Some had theirselves soaked wet with buckets of water and put wet sacks over their heads to lug those left inside to safety. One was Ben Bennett the thatcher. I reckon it was him.'

'And what happened to Lavenham?'

'I reckon Mr Lavenham was last to be got out, I don't know by who.'

'But he was alive?'

'How should I know? I never saw it. I thought I was dying myself.'

'Your burns must have hurt sorely.'

'Not as much as it did watching my livelihood go up in flames.'

'Do you know the names of any of the other men who went to the rescue? I mean the ones with wet sacks over them.'

'As well as Mr Bennett, like I said, there was maybe Quexton, because his friend that goes around with him, Charlie Johnson, was helping. I'm sure of that.'

'Who is that third gentleman you mention? Charlie Johnson.'

Mrs Greenhalgh laughed.

'"Gentleman" you call him! You wouldn't if you saw Charlie. He's got a nose like a misshapen potato and a jaw like a church doorstep. And he's a deal over six foot tall.'

'So, who is he?'

'He's the bruiser who's due to fight the Ripon Rockbreaker at Ingolside at the Whitsun Ales.'

I remembered the huge fellow who had attended Quexton's meeting at the Dog and Drum, with his barker's voice. I also recalled the two men, ill matched in size, that I'd thought were dancing beside Ingolmere. One of them had certainly been Quexton, while the other was built large enough to be the one with an appointment to meet the Ripon Rockbreaker in a few days' time.

We arrived in due course at Mrs Hogg's home where, having unshipped the ladies from my horse, I was invited to sit with them in the Hoggs' flower-crammed, bee-haunted garden.

'Was Mr Lavenham a frequent customer at the Three Horns?' I asked.

'Very frequent. Most evenings he was in.'

'So he preferred your hospitality to that of Curly Berry?'

'Who wouldn't? And besides it was politics.'

'In what way was it politics?'

'Not Whig-and-Tory politics but Ingolside politics. There are two parties, see? There's old Mrs Lumsden's party, and there's the party of her son. Mrs Lumsden owns the Dog and Drum, which has been there longer than anyone can remember. The Three Horns is a new inn, founded by the Squire himself ten years ago. He owns the house.'

'And drinkers in Ingolside split between supporters of the son at the Horns and those of the mother at the Dog and Drum?'

'Exactly. They take opposite sides in everything you might want to name.'

'But are there not matters of principle between the two parties, which would take priority?'

'Yes, if the future of the lands is what you call a matter of principle.'

'Which lands?'

'The lands of the manor, Mr Cragg. The plough land and the common. That is what they argue most about.'

'Did Lavenham take part in those arguments?'

'He was learned in his way, was John Lavenham. Spoke well, knew a lot of educated words.'

'But did he speak of the work he was doing for Mr Lumsden?'

'Now here's something strange. He was almost silent on the subject. All anyone ever learned from him was that he was studying farming in the Manor. He liked to question people about leaseholds, copyholds, gleaning, water rights, commons grazing and cattle owners' rights which he called Levancy and Couchancy. He taught me those words himself one night when there were not many customers in the house.'

'They are words commonly seen on documents concerned with land holding.'

'But for a man that was studying farming, I don't think he really knew much about it. John Lavenham never talked like Squire does. Clearing woods, draining marshland, putting up fences and digging ditches, Squire loves all that.'

Mrs Greenhalgh, as innkeepers often are, was an astute

observer of human society and garrulous with it. She showed no restraint in telling me more.

'What Mr Lumsden's really mad for is all kinds of improvement in breeding and growing. New breeds of animals, specially pigs and sheep. Machines for hoeing and drilling. New ways of manuring, which he calls fertilizing. He even tried digging seaweed and dried fishes' guts into the soil. He's got as many new notions for making farming better as your doctor friend has for making people better.'

'I'm afraid Dr Fidelis doesn't think he can make Mrs Lumsden better. She lies in bed at home gravely sick. Time seems to be against her and there'll be no one to carry on the argument for her.'

'Why, that is the reason she has sent for Quexton.'

'Mr Cornelius Quexton?'

'Yes. To carry on the battle if she herself is unable to.'

'I see. So both sides of the divide have called up help from outside.'

'That's right. First the Squire bringing in Mr Tree and Mr Lavenham, and then his mother sending for Quexton to balance the argument.'

'What was your opinion of John Lavenham's character?'

'He was a good customer. He bought a lot of ale, and rum punches too.'

'He had plenty of money?'

'I don't know about plenty. He had enough, and he used it with charity.'

'With charity? You mean those in need?'

She laughed heartily.

'Yes, the poor thirsty fellows in need. Lavenham would buy a drink for anyone in the house. Men liked him and he had a way with women too. He could make a body laugh, which gave you confidence in him, though I don't know why it should. Wit doesn't guarantee trust but somehow it makes you trust a man easier.'

'I suppose that may be true, Mrs Greenhalgh. One likes a person with wit, but only so long as it isn't aimed at oneself, of course.'

# SEVEN

Riding back into Ingolside, I looked across the marsh that lay around the western flank of the manor. Here and there I saw upright poles for the wildfowlers' baggy nets, and squat hump-shaped hides for the use of shooters looking out for duck and snipe.

I came to the remains of a farmhouse that stood a hundred yards back from the road. The roof had been burned away and though the walls still stood they had been scorched and blackened by fire. Boards were nailed across the windows and the front door. A vegetable garden and a small paddock had been abandoned, a wilderness in miniature. The yard, barn and outhouses were left to the weeds and to ruin.

Having ridden past this melancholy sight I spied over on the marsh a lone figure bobbing in and out of sight as he ran towards me, following a mazy path across the saturated ground. As he got nearer I saw it was the giant whose name I had just learned was Charlie Johnson. I reached the place where the path met the road and there I dismounted to await Johnson's arrival.

'You are Mr Johnson, if I'm not mistaken,' I said when he had done so.

He acknowledged the fact with a grunt. At close quarters he was much as Mrs Greenhalgh had so lively described. Breathing heavily through his mouth, he glowed red both in the face and neck, being wrapped for his training run in several layers of thick woollen clothing. I told him who I was, which he seemed to know already, just saying 'Aye, aye' and nodding his head.

'I think you can help me out.'

'Help you bury the man?'

'No, not to bury him. My job is to find out why he needs burying.'

'I'll help you with that. He's dead.'

Was the man a wit? Or merely stupid? I persisted.

'He is indeed. The question is how he died. I've been told

that, on the night the Three Horns inn caught fire, you went through the flames to get some people out.'

'Me and some others. We wet some sacking to put over us.'

'That is what I've heard. And I've also been told Mr Lavenham was one of those you brought out. Is that true?'

'I carried more than one into the air, then went back and found another before I was done. Fire stopped us then.'

'Was Lavenham moving? Was he talking?'

Johnson had a large handkerchief tucked into his belt. He pulled it out, shook it and applied it to the sweat standing on his brow.

'I've not said I did bring the man out. I said I might've.'

'He was a tall man with fair hair.'

'I know the man you mean.'

'Then you would've known him if you carried him out of the burning building.'

'Fire was all round. Flames. Smoke. We didn't take the time to think.'

'Very well. So the men you carried out, whoever they may have been, were they alive? Did they speak?'

'One was fighting me, blaspheming, trying to get out of my grip.'

'Do you know his name?'

'I do not.'

'What about the other man you saved?'

'He lay quiet as I carried him.'

'Could this have been Lavenham?'

He shrugged. 'Like I said, we had to look so sharp I can't be sure.'

There was a suspicious look in his eye. I had meant to warn him I might call him as a witness, but now I thought better of it. 'Maybe' evidence is of little use at an inquest. Instead I said, 'You know Mr Quexton who, I believe, is your trainer. Was he present at the fire?'

'No, he was away.'

'I was told that he might have been there. That he might have helped to save lives, as you did.'

'No, he was in Yorkshire seeing the Rockbreaker's people, about our fight. The rules we will abide by, and the matter of the purse.'

'Ah! I've heard it will be a big test in prospect and I see you are training hard for it. Will you beat the Rockbreaker? He is a formidable opponent, I suppose.'

Johnson looked me directly in the eyes.

'*I* am a formidable opponent, Mr Coroner.'

The subject of the forthcoming Whitsun boxing match came up again that evening at the Holloways' supper table. The servant was bringing in grilled meats and pouring the ale as I told Mr Holloway and Miss Hart of my earlier meeting with the prizefighter.

'Did you speak to Johnson intentionally?' the farmer asked me. 'Are you a lover of prizefighting?'

'No, not particularly. I spoke to Johnson as a possible witness in John Lavenham's death. But all the same I am curious about the fight. It will be a famous event I think.'

'Richard Elcock has put up a hundred guinea purse and backed it with heavy bets on the Rockbreaker. Mr Elcock is a very wealthy man. He recently came into Yorkshire, having bought Newby Hall at Ripon, and he makes an effort to cultivate his popularity with the local people. He knows they love a fight for large sums.'

'Why is the fight not held at Newby then?'

'It was to be, but Mr Elcock's plans are not popular with all. The local Dissenters at Ripon, who are rather numerous, opposed it. So Mr Lumsden, who is Mr Elcock's friend, offered to stage it at Ingolside Whitsun Fair instead.'

'Will Johnson be a match for this Rockbreaker?'

Holloway was chewing his meat as he thought.

'Johnson comes from the south. No one has seen him perform in these parts, but I hear Lord Lonsdale has taken Elcock's bets and is backing Johnson so he, any road, must believe that Johnson is the stronger man.'

'People will come many miles to see such a contest. Will you attend?'

'I will, if only to see Johnson destroyed.'

'You have bet on the Rockbreaker?'

Holloway shook his head.

'I've better uses for my money.'

'Yet you prefer the chances of the man from Yorkshire.'

'I don't pretend to know who will win the fight, and I would have nothing against Johnson if he didn't associate with that Quexton fellow, who pretends to be his trainer. In my opinion that is only cover for damned mischief and troublemaking. The man is a—'

At this moment Miss Hart, who had attended closely to her food throughout the conversation, interrupted.

'Oh, Uncle. Speak no more of Mr Quexton as it may bring on one of your ingruences.'

Holloway sighed.

'You are right, my dear. That man is not a worthy cause of apoplexy. Let's speak of more agreeable things.'

But, as often happens when the flow of a conversation is diverted from unpleasantness, no more pleasant topic immediately suggested itself and we sat for a time cutting and chewing our meat in silence. I thought about Cornelius Quexton in the character of the prizefighter's trainer. It was certainly not a pretence, as Holloway suggested. On my first day in Ingolside I had seen the two men at what I thought was dancing whereas, of course (as I now saw), they had been sparring, working on Johnson's sharpness and the weight of his punches. Besides, I knew from Johnson that Quexton had travelled to see the Rockbreaker's connections to settle the terms of the contest. Nevertheless, the question I asked myself was: how and why did an educated man come to occupy himself in the prizefighting business? And how did he combine that with what he called his advocacy of public justice?

Mr Holloway now asked me a question about my preparations for the inquest. Many people would be glad, he told me, to have it out of the way in the coming week, before the Whitsun Fair.

'I hope it will be. I have been considering where to hold it and I favour the Dissenters' Meeting House. Who should I apply to? Is there a clergyman in position there?

'There is no clergyman. They have lay preachers, God help them.'

'Then who administers the place?'

'That is Benjamin Bennett. He heads the small board which maintains it.'

'Bennett? I have heard the name somewhere. Where does Mr Bennett live?'

'Pilling's Cottage. It stands opposite the Green.'

'I will go there first thing in the morning.'

After finishing our meal, we went into the parlour. Holloway and I then listened while Miss Hart again played on the spinet for almost an hour, throughout which Holloway sat with his face split by a sugary smile, while I fought to keep my eyelids apart.

But in the course of the recital it made me wonder if the player might by some chance recognize the scrap of music that Luke had discovered pinned to Lavenham's coat. When she had at last finished playing I fetched it and showed it to her, without saying where it came from. She adjusted her spectacles and peered at it.

'There's not enough of the music to tell anything about it,' she said.

'Ah well, I thought it was unlikely.'

'But I can help you with the words, you know: *so amazing so*. They can only be from the first line of Dr Watts' "Love so amazing". It is a wonderful hymn and very moving.'

'You mean to say, this is a fragment from a hymn sheet?'

'Yes, Sir. That is what it must be.'

She handed the scrap back to me, suppressing a yawn.

'It is late, Mr Cragg. I will say goodnight.'

I thanked her and, having begged pens and paper, I went up to my room and sat down at the writing table.

*My dearest wife,* I wrote, *the talk in this place, when it is not about prize fighting, is all on enclosure and agricultural improvement. The Squire is in no doubt that only he knows how the land should be managed. Your uncle supports him, and so do the other more prosperous farmers. The poorer people are in great doubt and the Squire and his mother are at loggerheads on the matter. She says the land has been farmed and used in a certain manner for a thousand years and more, and it is madness to change, for once the old ways are lost, they can never be found again. I am certain this quarrel is at the root of the death I am here to inquest. The Ingolside Whitsun Ales is to be held with plenty of revelry. There will be a famous pugilistic contest between a fellow from the South and a Yorkshireman known as the Rockbreaker. I doubt I shall stay to see the outcome, as the inquest will be over by then.*

# EIGHT

Pilling's Cottage stood at the top of Street, opposite the Green and close to the house in which Quexton lived, although Bennett's was the larger cottage. Beside it a path led to his yard in which stooks of reed were stacked under canopies, and scaffolding planks and poles, with ladders in a variety of lengths, were stored in open-sided sheds. It was a thatcher's yard, which brought to mind just where I had heard the name Bennett before. *'Ben Bennett the thatcher, I reckon.'* They were Charlie Johnson's words when I had asked him who had helped carry out the laggards from the burning inn.

In response to my knock on the door of Pilling's Cottage, Mrs Bennett came out. A woman of perhaps forty, she seemed of strong and serious character, befitting her status as the wife of the village's most prominent dissenter.

'You want Bennett?' she said. 'You'll find him over at the Hall. You've come to preach, am I right? I can see you're an educated man.'

I have been mistaken for many things in my life but never, before this moment, for a preacher.

'No, not to preach,' I said hastily. 'It is to ask for the use of the hall that I want to see him.'

'Just so long as it's respectable business you want it for. There's folk think that just because my brother's a brewer, Bennett'll open the place for ale-bibbing and dancing and all sorts of going on. He won't mind. D'you know the way to it? It's nothing but three minutes' walk.'

'I know it. I've been there.'

When I reached the hall its door was unlocked and, going inside, I saw first of all a boy of maybe sixteen sweeping the floor with a besom. Hearing the door bang he looked up, giving me a steady blank stare but saying nothing.

'Is Mr Bennett here?' I asked.

I followed the boy's gaze upwards and saw a tall, strong-looking man on a ladder applying putty to a pane of glass in one of the high side windows. At the foot of the ladder lay an enormous mastiff dog who shuffled to his feet when I came in and, opening his cavernous mouth, rimmed by gigantic teeth, issued a succession of gruff warning barks. The boy dropped his brush and went to the dog, placing his hand on its head. His touch instantly calmed the animal, though he did not cease to turn his creased and worried-looking mask watchfully towards me.

'Don't mind Limer,' Bennett called down. 'He may be the biggest dog in the county but he's a softling at heart and loves children. He'll never do what's dangerous without the say-so of his master. That's our Daniel here. Isn't that right, Danny my boy?'

The boy was stone-faced, as if he'd never heard the question.

'And what is your name, Sir, if I may ask?' said Bennett.

I gave my name and said I was sorry to interrupt his work.

'Never fret, Mr Cragg. It's almost done. A follower of the Established church, as I think, chucked a malicious stone yesterday. So I have had to replace the pane.'

Evidently a good-humoured man, he chuckled.

'I shall not lay it at the charge of the Reverend Cumberledge. We are on good enough terms, all in all.'

Limer lowered his haunches, and then the rest of him, while watching me steadily. Danny went back to his work.

'You are the Minister here?' I said, keeping a wary eye on the dog.

'We have no Ministers, Mr Cragg. We have no hierarchy. Them that wants to preach may preach, as the Lord directs.'

He made some finishing touches with his putty trowel then replaced it in the canvas bag slung from his neck and began to climb back down to earth. Arriving at the floor, he turned to face me so that I could now fully take in his appearance. This was a man in his fifties, muscular and long-boned and with a jutting, hawk-like nose through which his breath faintly whistled. In a wide gesture he indicated the room in which we stood.

'The day will come,' he said, 'when there will be halls like this across the land, in every town and village. Mark my word. I may not live to see it but the fire of Mr Wesley and Mr

Whitefield's preaching has caught hold too well and will never be extinguished. So, what can I do for you, Mr Cragg? As it happens I already do know the reason for your appearance in our township – to do with Mr John Lavenham, isn't it?'

'Yes, Mr Bennett, it is a question of where I can hold the inquest into his death, which I must do in the next few days. My thoughts have turned to this hall as a most suitable place. I need a room of more than the usual size, as may be found at an inn, and that is where I am generally accommodated. But at Ingolside, one inn has burned down, and the other is not in my opinion adequate to the purpose, whereas this is a very well-proportioned building and, although a religious one, it is sometimes, I believe, used for more secular meetings.'

'There will be neither eating nor strong drinking at this inquest? There will be no dancing or profane singing or lewdness?'

'I will make sure of it.'

'And it will not take place on the Lord's Day?'

'It will not.'

'Then I see no reason why you should not have it. A small payment *ex gratia* will be appreciated.'

'The usual sum of six shillings and eightpence can be paid.'

'That is acceptable.'

'And do you have a separate room, a small one will do, where the body can lie during the proceedings?'

'Aye, we have one.'

'That is excellent. And may I ask if you yourself know anything of how Mr Lavenham died? He was in a crowd of people who walked from a meeting here, through Market Place, to the Manor House. When that crowd dispersed, Lavenham was found lying dead under the Market Cross.'

'That meeting was not of a religious nature. It was summoned by friends of Cornelius Quexton, I believe. And the payment for the hall came from them too.'

'Friends of Quexton, you say? You are sure?'

'Yes. He told me he intended to tell the people how they could protest against the reforms proposed by the Squire. Quexton travels all over the country, you know, speaking about enclosure and trying to prevent the loss of common land.'

'Does he indeed? And what success does he have?'

'He stopped Lord Duffleton from felling woods in Dorset, so I've heard, and was also able to stay the hand of the Marquess of Rockingham, who wanted to dig coals out of a common in Nottingham.'

'You are sympathetic to Quexton's ideas yourself?'

'They interest me as news, but I am neutral. These disagreements about land use are a matter between those farmers who are well-to-do and those who are poor. I do not have a loaf of my own in that oven. I am only a craftsman, neither rich nor poor.'

'Well, I am much obliged to you for making the Hall available to me. But there is another matter arising. I have been told that it was you who helped bring out some men from the burning Three Horns inn.'

'That's right, I did. What's that to do with Mr Lavenham's dying?'

'He was inside the inn when the fire started. Were you also drinking in there?'

Bennett's good humour left him in an instant. He shook his finger at me.

'Shame on you for that suggestion, Sir.'

The dog's ears pricked and he got into a sitting position. He wrinkled his nose and began to growl in a way that sounded like a low snore.

'I'll have you know,' Bennett went on, 'I would no more go through an alehouse door than through the gates of Pandemonium. I am a God-fearing man, me.'

'Of course. I apologize if my question offended you. Yet I have heard you did enter it on that evening in spite of your scruples, did you not?'

'The place was burning. There were lives to be saved. Godless, unworthy lives, it goes without argument. Yet Scripture says "if any man's work shall be burned he shall suffer loss, but he shall be saved".'

'And was one of those lives John Lavenham's? Was he carried by you out of the burning building?'

Bennett shook his head.

'No, Mr Cragg, he was not.'

'You can be sure? Even though the room was full of smoke.

Flames all around. Would you have taken note of who exactly it was you carried to safety?'

'I knew the man. I had seen him about the village. But I did not carry him out.'

By Luke Fidelis's standards the hour was still early, so it was reasonable to suppose he'd only recently have risen from his bed. I therefore walked to Mrs Booth's and found my supposition correct: Fidelis was at breakfast. Pouring myself a cup of tea, I settled into a chair at the table opposite my friend.

'Have you uncovered the facts behind Lavenham's death yet, Titus?' he asked.

'Far from it. I am fishing in muddy waters, Luke. I cannot see the fish let alone the bottom.'

He laughed.

'People here are wary.'

'There is something in particular I am puzzled by,' I said. 'It is about Cornelius Quexton. I know that he trains the prizefighter Johnson and will be his second for the match against the Ripon Rockbreaker. But my supposition would be that the trainers of fighters must generally be retired fighters themselves, while Quexton is nothing like an old boxing-booth bruiser.'

Luke Fidelis drank from his cup, and then began to saw contemplatively with his knife into a thick rasher of bacon, reducing it to a number of small segments.

'I don't see that it signifies, Titus. Any man can train another man up, if he has studied how to do it.'

'But to what end? Quexton is evidently an educated man. Cannot he apply himself to some more useful profession? Can he even make a living out of this?'

'He will take a cut of the purse if his man wins, and the purse is prodigious.'

'Very well. But, leaving aside the distinct possibility that Johnson may lose, I am not sure that training the boxer is his main preoccupation. I have learned that Quexton goes around the country as an apostle against what he calls improper improvement of the land. He speaks against enclosures as a kind of self-appointed tribune of the people.'

'A stirrer? An agitator?'

'So it seems. Anyway, as I was asking Mr Bennett for permission to use the Dissenters' Hall for the Lavenham inquest, he told me the meeting was called and paid for by men close to Quexton. They marched from there to the Manor House, after which Lavenham's body was found.'

'You would think Quexton would have spoken at that meeting. And if he did, perhaps he incited the audience.'

'Yet there's nothing that says he was part of the mob that marched to the Manor House. The story is he was out of the county on business. I don't comprehend that. Why was he not present at what we must assume was his own meeting? Surely he would have spoken, otherwise what was the point of it?'

'Well somebody stirred up the people so much that they marched in a mob to the Manor House. From what you say of him, that is the sort of thing Quexton did in his work.'

'Then why have we not heard of his part in this disturbance?'

'Because the people here are tight in the mouth. What they go by is, "Say nowt, pay nowt, keep it close or make it worse."'

'Does Squire Lumsden know something, then? He told us he was certain of who was behind the death. He meant Quexton, didn't he?'

'I wouldn't take the Squire's word on a matter like this. He doesn't like Quexton.'

'I, on the other hand, rather do. I find him genial and intelligent.'

'So are many villains. Witness Macheath in *The Beggar's Opera*.'

'Yes, I know. And Iago is a delightful fellow to drink with at the tavern. I just cannot sum Quexton up. He has a pleasant manner but is very close. It's hard to take the measure of a man who will not admit to having a past or talk seriously about his future. What do you make of him?'

'I have not even met him, Titus. But now that I know he is training one of the Whitsun prizefighters, I will attempt to make his acquaintance at once. I may place a wager on Johnson.'

During the first part of our conversation about Quexton, we could hear Mrs Booth in the background rattling crockery and coppers. Now this noise had stopped. Wondering why, I looked around and saw the woman standing in the doorway.

'Have you been visiting with Ben Bennett, Mr Cragg?' she asked.

'I have. We agreed in the use of the Dissenters' Hall for the inquest.'

'A good man, is that, about as good as any in the parish.'

'He had his son Danny with him. A very silent boy.'

'Not his son but his nephew, that he took in as charity. Not right in the head, is Danny, though nobody knows any harm in him.'

She spun around and returned without another word to her scullery.

My father, who preceded me in the post of Coroner at Preston, used to state it as a prime rule that, when enquiring into an unexplained death, one must begin by compiling a detailed memorandum of the dead person, in terms of character, property, means of living and domestic circumstances. In the present case I was conscious that I had until now neglected my father's principle. So, putting aside for the moment my curiosity about Cornelius Quexton, I made up my mind to devote the rest of this Monday to finding out everything I could about John Lavenham.

Thinking it reasonable to begin by learning more about how he came to Ingolside, I went first, with Fidelis, to the Manor House and asked for an interview with Squire Lumsden. I was shown into the manorial business room, in which there were two desks, at one of which sat a bald fellow in the black habit of a dissenter bent over a ledger. I introduced myself and asked his name.

'I am Martin Mansfield. I am Mr Lumsden's bailiff and see to the estate business.'

'I hope to speak to Mr Lumsden.'

'The Squire is up in the woods. There has been a wolf reported and he has gone to see what trace he can find.'

'A wolf? Surely the animal is now extinct everywhere in England.'

Mansfield sighed, like a man addressing a question that wearies him.

'That is the general belief, Mr Cragg. But there are many matters on which the general belief cannot be relied upon. Wolves

are one of those matters. You may hear its howl one moonlit
night, and then you will be persuaded.'

'I will listen out. Now, if the Squire is not here, perhaps you
may help me.'

'In what matter?'

'In the matter of John Lavenham. As you may know, I've come
here to look into his death and hold an inquest. It appears he
came from London, with Mr Tree and at the Squire's bidding,
to assist with the improvement of the land.'

'Wilkin Tree is a clever devil with that measuring equipment
of his, and a good mapmaker by all accounts. That's what we
need because, without an accurate map of the land, you are hard
pressed to make any rational division of it.'

'I can understand that. But for what reason was John Lavenham
engaged? He was not a surveyor. I heard he had at one time
studied law.'

'Perhaps he did. I do know he came here to study some old
documents in Squire's possession and to see just how Ingolside's
land lies. Squire must assert his title to any ground he means to
reform and entitlement is recorded in old rolls.'

'Where are these rolls?'

'Normally they're locked up in the manorial chest that is kept
in this house – charters and leases and such.'

I myself had had, in the past, occasion to consult such documents in my own legal practice and knew it was sometimes far
from easy to make out their exact meaning. I had had to rely
more than once on the keen, experienced eye of my clerk, Robert
Furzey. John Lavenham must have had a similarly sharp eye for
our ancestors' legal terminology, as well as their handwriting,
with its own peculiar contractions and abbreviations.

'It is exacting work,' I said. 'Where did he do it? Did he
scrutinize the documents at Lakeside Lodge?'

'At first. Later we gave Lavenham a room to work in here at
the Manor House.'

'I would appreciate a chance to have a look there. There may
be indications as to how and why he was killed.'

'I can help you as to the why myself.'

'You can? You have some evidence about that?'

'Only an indication.'

He opened one of the drawers in his desk and drew out a single paper on which a message had been written.

'This was delivered to this house one night, meant for Mr Lumsden.'

He passed the paper to me. The hand was crude but the import could not have been clearer.

*Tha black weezing fat guted Rougue of a Sqire guzling down meat and wine while tha mashinates to bring Poor men to sterve May you chawk your last and that soon with a goodly helpin hand and you may tell yore lackees the same to witch all the Poor of this parish say Amen.*

'Was this found with Lavenham's body?'

Mansfield was startled by my question.

'Why do you ask that? No. No, it wasn't. Like I said it was pushed under the door.'

'Who wrote it?'

'It is anonymous, I believe that's the word. Unsigned.'

'I can see it is. I mean do you have any ideas about who it came from? Anyone making other threats against the Squire.'

'There is always snide talk against a strong landlord, and some of it rough. Squire is not mealy-mouthed himself when he speaks out. There's many in the parish have had hard words from him and didn't like it, not least when he sits in judgment on the bench.'

'The person or persons responsible for this letter do not much care for the Squire, that is plain. The question that interests me is whether they have also had a hand in Lavenham's death and for that reason I would like to take the letter and examine it more closely.'

He nodded his head.

'If you like. But it may not be the work of a killer. A threat is only a threat. Is doesn't mean action must follow.'

'That is true. But in any case, this is evidence as to how some people here are thinking. A squire who does not enjoy the people's broad approval will never feel quite comfortable. Aren't you afraid yourself, with that reference to the Squire's "lackeys"?'

'I know how to protect myself, and my family.'

'Those who went out with guns to face the mob on the night Lavenham was found dead – were you one of them?'

'Aye, I was.'

'There were two, I believe, as well as Mr Lumsden. Who was the other?'

'Charles Bowden, that's gamekeeper on the estate. He is a trusted man.'

'And which of you fired his piece?'

'I did not. Charlie and Mr Lumsden both did.'

'You are sure?'

'There were two shots close together without time to reload. So they must both have fired.'

'Where is the room Lavenham used? I should like to see inside.'

'It is the room right next door, but that door is kept locked and Mr Lumsden keeps the key himself. You must apply to him.'

With Arthur Lumsden absent, I wondered if his mother could help. I thanked Mansfield and returned to the hall where I found the rosy-cheeked maidservant arranging a vase of flowers. She told me her name was Betsy.

'I would like a word with Mrs Sarah Lumsden, Betsy,' I said. 'Will you find out if she is alone and will see me?'

Betsy agreed to go up immediately.

# NINE

As I climbed the stair of the Manor House towards old Mrs Lumsden's sick room, a door above me clunked shut and Curly Berry appeared at the stairhead. He waited for me to reach him, then said, with carefully modulated sarcasm, 'You're comfortable where you are lodged, I hope, Mr Cragg?'

I said that I was, seeing as they were my relations and therefore exceedingly hospitable. I added a question of my own.

'You have been with Mrs Lumsden?'

'Yes, if it's anything to you. I give my monthly report on takings at the inn.'

'Do you tally the eggs you have pickled? It is a speciality of your house, is it not?'

Berry arched his eyebrows in surprise at my question.

'Eggs? Yes, that's right. Eggs is economical food, compared to meat.'

I nodded at what he carried, a drawstring purse bulging with coin.

'I was thinking you should be bringing your takings to Mrs Lumsden, but instead you are collecting money from her.'

'Business is slow, Mr Cragg. Mrs Lumsden is kind enough to give assistance. Now, if you don't mind . . .'

He edged past me and trotted down the stairs.

'Clegg, is it?' Mrs Lumsden said as I entered, looking me up and down as if for the first time. 'What the devil do you want?'

I dragged a chair to the bedside and sat down.

'It is Cragg, Mrs Lumsden. Titus Cragg.'

Sarah Lumsden was exactly as before, sitting up against a bank of pillows, wearing a lace night cap and a blanket around her shoulders.

'I am hoping,' I went on, 'to continue our conversation that we began on Friday.'

She drew breath and let it out in a heavy sigh.

'If you wish. Remind me. What did we talk on?'

'It was the matter of the death of John Lavenham, whose body was found lying on the steps of the Market Cross on the evening of the riot. Do you remember the riot?'

'I do not call it a riot. That is Arthur's nonsense. Yes, I saw the event from the window. I am not so sick that I cannot walk to the window, or remember plain facts. But it was no riot. It was men and women coming together to cry out against someone who would deprive them of their customs and their commons. By whom I mean my son.'

'I am gathering intelligence where I can on the nature of Lavenham's work in that connection. He was invited here by Mr Lumsden to examine the manorial documents, I think.'

'When not raving about his future flock of sheep, my son is besotted by parchment. Where he finds a deed that seems to give him the right to make an eviction, engross a field or trample on a custom, he gives shouts of joy. I have heard him. Shouts of joy and triumph, he gives.'

She wrinkled her nose.

'To me those scrolls are nothing. Musty old parchments. Terrible smell coming off them. God knows how old.'

'Yet do they not record the people's ancient rights, and those of the lord? They are the law, after all, however venerable, and of the essence in most questions of land use.'

She waved her hand in front of her face as if brushing away a cobweb.

'The people know the truth without the need for ink and parchment. It is handed down by mouth, grandparents to parents, parents to children, generation to generation. It is printed on their minds. If you want to know what a man has the right to hold, you only need ask him.'

'But memory can play false, after all.'

'So can documents. I know which of the two I trust more.'

'I wonder if John Lavenham had discovered certain parchments in the manorial chest that contradict the popular custom.'

'I don't know what he discovered, Mr Crack, or claimed to have discovered. Arthur has long since stopped speaking to me about these matters. But mark my words, Sir, John Lavenham was doing evil work, as I think I told you the other day. You talked a moment ago about essence, Mr Crick . . . or is it Crock?'

'It's Cragg.'

'Well, no matter. What I am saying is that custom is the real essence of life among the people, and anyone who denies it is doing the Devil's work. Now, if you please, be gone. I am tired.'

'I am sorry if I have tired you, but before I go I would like your leave to examine the room in this house that was set aside for John Lavenham to do his work in.'

'Room? I know of no such room.'

'Mr Mansfield has told me of it. Perhaps the Manor Chest is kept there. I would dearly like to see that.'

'I do not have jurisdiction, if that is the correct word, over the Manor Chest. My husband never looked into it. Indeed, he often talked of making a bonfire of it. But as I have already told you my son is besotted by those mouldy old rolls. So as far as I care, you may examine away, Mr Clegg. You may examine away. It's not for me to stop you.'

'I am stopped by a locked door. Can you have it opened for me?'

She looked at me, her eyes watery and dull.

'No, Mr Clack. As I say, I do not have the right and nor do I have the key. You must ask my son.'

As it happened, my chance to do this came almost immediately for, descending the stairs, I met Arthur Lumsden coming in by the front door. He wore a buff jerkin and cap, and carried a long-barreled hunting gun. He was followed by a spaniel, its tongue lolling, whose name I gathered was Herbert. The Squire was in unexpectedly good humour.

'Still swimming in circles like a deaf and dumb otter, Cragg?' he said.

A large ewer and a bowl lay on a table. Lumsden splashed water from the jug into the bowl and laid it on the floor. The dog lapped noisily.

'If I am like that it is because the case of John Lavenham is complicated. May I tax you with a request? I must raise a jury of at least a dozen men ready to serve. I would in most cases have the help of the Parish Constable.'

'There is none.'

'So I understand, and it is unusual. I wonder how does the parish manage in general without a Constable?'

'We had Constables in my father's day and before. Always a Digby. But thankfully the last of them never had a son and there was no one else would serve in his place. The Constable was always a Digby. Had to be a Digby. So: no Digby, no Constable.'

'Did that not concern you? As Magistrate.'

'It didn't. A family of lazy mattress worms, the Digbys. They were a wasted expense.'

'Then if you have no Digby to help me, perhaps I may have leave to recruit the jury myself? I have the power to do so when there is no parish assistance.'

'Yes, carry on and do it, if it will hurry up this confounded inquest.'

'If I may trouble you with a small question in connection with the case.'

'Go ahead.'

'Between the fire at the Three Horns and the arrival of the mob in front of your house, three days elapsed. I wonder if you saw John Lavenham about the place during those three days.'

'No, I did not. I suppose he was buried in his work.'

'He is reputed to have been an affable fellow, much given to drinking in the inns. It seems he was present in the Three Horns when it caught fire, but I cannot establish what happened to him after that.'

'Shot, wasn't he, by accident? That's what everyone's been telling me.'

'He was shot but it was very doubtfully an accident. Do you know anything of a paper or some such that may have been found with his body?'

He looked at me sharply, suggesting that my mention of a paper was disturbing to him.

'No. I know no such thing.'

'It was your servants who found the body and, as you are the magistrate here, I take it they reported to you on the matter.'

'So they did. But there was nothing about a paper.'

'How you did you come to hire John Lavenham? Were his services recommended?'

'There is no mystery about that. His name was mentioned to me by one of Lord Lonsdale's people, who also gave me the name of the mapper, Tree. Lavenham was suggested as one who could read old documents. I know no more about him than that.'

'You have not heard that he had in his time attended Bow Street Court as the defendant in a criminal case?'

'I have not. But if such a thing happened, I would expect he was a defendant in error and it was trumped up. He seemed an honest man to me. I am an excellent judge of character.'

'I am told that a room was set aside in this house for Lavenham to work in.'

'That is correct.'

'May I see the room?'

'I think not.'

'Can you give me a reason why I may not?'

'The reason is that I prefer not.'

After a flat refusal like that, I knew I could do nothing to force the issue. I would need a magistrate's warrant and Lumsden himself was the magistrate. In his days as Coroner, my father sometimes talked about how, moving around the county from jurisdiction to jurisdiction, he required above all the stamina and the tongue of a diplomat. Diplomatically, therefore, in the interest of smoothing our dealings, I changed the subject.

'I have had a pleasant talk with Martin Mansfield,' I said. 'He tells me you have been out hunting a wolf today. I said I was surprised there is any of the species left anywhere in the realm.'

Lumsden offered me a knowing smile.

'Many people think that. But the wolf is not extinct in England. He may be scattered, but he is still dangerously numerous.'

'And that number is reduced by one from today, I hope.'

'I must disappoint you. Our object was only to look for traces. You cannot hope to hunt and bring down the wolf as you do the deer or fox. A wolf is cunning, lying low by day and coming out when light is fading. To kill him you have to locate his lair and trap him. If he is not trapped or at least cornered and shot he will outrun any pack of dogs, any horseman. He will escape as far as the next county, or the county beyond that. So any campaign against him must be carefully planned.'

'I hope he will not in the meantime come here and terrify the people.'

He looked hard at me for a few moments, then said, 'Come with me.'

Seizing Herbert's collar, he led the way through a corridor that ran to the back of the house. I followed him past the kitchen, scullery, pantries and servants' hall, and out into a back yard. This was flanked by barns and storerooms as well as a stable block and kennels. He shut the spaniel up, deposited his gun in the neighbouring gun room and then led me out through an arched passage to open ground. Here was a small stone hut and an adjoining pen from the middle of which a short-legged animal, with curled horns, and a coat even shaggier than the dog's, watched us approach with (I thought) a certain disdain.

'Ah! A fine ram,' I said.

The Squire made a show of astonishment.

'So the townsman knows a sheep from a goat!'

'That surprises you?'

'You are a lawyer, an indoors man. Your horse is a chair. What would you know of agricultural things?'

'I assure you that a lawyer's horse is his horse, Mr Lumsden. Or in my case, his mare. I go about continually on her. And besides, my grandfather was a farmer and I have rich memories of getting mud on my shoes.'

'Then perhaps, muddily shod as you are, you will grasp why I am not concerned here about the people of the village. They will look after themselves, but sheep are another matter. They have no defence against a predatory wolf. This fine creature here is my sheep Adam, the foundation sire of my flock – that is, the sum of his concubines and their progeny. He cost me dear and I will not put his life at risk.'

'His progeny will yield you plenty of wool by the look of him.'

Squire Lumsden raised his head, stretched his neck and drew in a long breath through his nose.

'Wool gathering is not the shepherd's prime concern, not these days,' he said. 'The profit is in meat and I assure you that the lambs this animal sires will be more meat-heavy than any that has ever come before. Plentiful sheep meat for every man, that is the promise of this ram and all his kind. But not, most assuredly not,

for every wolf. Therefore the wolf must die. More, he must be—'
He clenched both his fists and banged them together. 'Exterminated,
once and for all, so that modern men of vision may provide sheep
meat across all the tables of the nation. We talk of beef as the
mainstay of the British diet, do we not? Yet beef is beyond the
means of most of the people, most of the time. We are offering
a meat every bit as satisfying, but at a price all but the poorest
can afford.'

In a certain way, Lumsden was now talking to himself. A
glassiness had come into his eye, signaling that my presence had
been temporarily forgotten. Whenever I see that glint of obsession,
I know rational discourse has gone for a walk and the best thing
to do is the same, in the hope reason will reassert itself later.

'I shall leave you with your sheepish Adam,' I said. 'The
inquest into the late John Lavenham will be convened at ten in
the morning on Thursday. I would be grateful if you would attend
and be ready to give evidence, if required.'

'Very well, if I must.'

'Then there will be no need for a formal summons from me.
I bid you good day, Sir.'

The problem now arose of just how, without detailed knowledge
of the population and, faced by the hostility of many, I would
find suitable men for the inquest jury. Returning to Holloway's
house for dinner, I mentioned my difficulty, and at once Miss
Hart spoke up.

'Oh, Mr Cragg, I would be very pleased to assist you, if you
will accept my help. What type of man do you require?'

'They must be householders. Perhaps following a trade, or a
craft. In any event they cannot be men such as labourers or servants, or landless cottagers.'

'I think we shall be able to satisfy you. After dinner I will
take you from door to door up and down Street and together
we'll gather them in.'

And so we did, proceeding first around the marketplace, and
then up Street until we reached the Green, calling in on all the
eligible men on either side.

At first the villagers were wary, and some even surly. Many
had heard my speech at the Dissenters' Hall and had shared the

suspicion of me that I'd heard voiced there. But Miss Hart's
presence at my side was enough to sway them in my favour, so
that I was able to penetrate their defences well enough.

I asked each man two questions. Firstly, had they seen
Lavenham alive after the fire? And secondly, would they serve
as jurors at Lavenham's inquest? As we went on, I found a new
side to Miss Hart. Out of her uncle's company she shed her
demure manner and spoke animatedly about her life and, in
particular, her charity work. She told me she helped to maintain
a small orphan's house, and joined with some other women to
provide relief to the poorest Ingolsiders.

'We try to help villagers left alone and decrepit after their
husbands or wives have died. And others come in from the
countryside, unable to support themselves. They scrounge scraps
of food unwanted by the stallholders at the end of market day.
Some are too old and friendless to gather wood for their fires.'

'They are not entirely without friends, then, if you provide
help.'

'There is not very much we can do positively to save them,
but we take them soup and bread, and logs if we can.'

'It is commendable work,' I said. 'Elizabeth does similarly in
Preston. How many do you have on your list of needy people?'

'Up to two dozen. But between us, Mr Cragg, if the Squire,
my uncle and their friends have their way, the burden of hunger
might be ten times what it is now.'

'Oh? What do you mean, Miss Hart?'

'I had better not say more. Look, see that man there?'

She pointed to a respectably dressed farmer walking towards
us.

'Who is it?'

'That's Andrew Duckham, a tenant of Lumsden but of middling
prosperity, not like some of those we've been speaking of.'

'I believe I've met his wife. Why do you point him out?'

'We need one more man for the jury and I think he'd agree
to it. He's a man of good judgement.'

Duckham was willing and his name was added to the list of
jurors.

Reaching at last the village green and standing opposite the
Dog and Drum, we took stock of our list. We'd found no one

who had seen the late Lavenham alive or dead between the fire and the riot. But we had filled all the seats of my jury. As well as Mr Duckham, the butcher, the baker, and the candlestick maker, whose premises on Street I had previously noticed, had all agreed to serve. So did the blacksmith, the saddler, the cutler, the clog maker, the wheelwright, the brewer, the potter and the poultryman. It would be a compendium of all the business of Street lined up on a single jurors' bench.

'Eh, Coroner,' a voice called. I looked up to see Curly Berry coming out of his inn and hurrying towards us. He was still wearing his tapster's apron.

'I hear tell you're wanting men to serve on the inquest jury. I've sat juryman myself, not here but before I came here I did. So you'd best put me on the bench with the others.'

'Mr Berry, we have all the men we need now.'

'Yes, but you must put me on the jury along with them. It'll be expected that I'm on it, as I have all the experience.'

I tried to fend him off but, undeterred, and in a froth over the prospect of being a juror, Berry pressed on and on until I was battered down.

'Very well,' I conceded, as being the only way to shut the man up. 'I'll take you as first reserve.'

'That is handsome, Mr Cragg.'

Curly Berry's self-esteem had been bolstered up, which was why he for the first time adopted a more respectful tone towards me.

'I can also bring you some business on the day,' I went on. 'We will need to victual the jury: will the Dog and Drum provide some fare for them? I will pay a tariff of one shilling and sixpence a head.'

Berry rubbed his chin for a moment, though I knew he would say yes. And he did.

'Aye, I can do that, Mr Cragg. I'll be glad of the business. Will we also be feeding yourself and your clerk?'

'I think not, thank you. But for the jurymen, I shall be disappointed if you do not furnish the table with your own favourite delicacy.'

'My favourite, Mr Cragg? And what would you mean by that?'

'I mean pickled eggs, Mr Berry.'

# TEN

I now had my jurymen, as well as excellent premises. By tomorrow Furzey would have arrived, with time in which to complete the papers in the case, issue any further summonses and have the hall ready before Thursday, the day I had decided to hold the inquest.

Yet there was still much to do. The list of witnesses was by no means complete. It already included Arthur Lumsden, Luke Fidelis, Wilkin Tree, Martin Mansfield and Mrs Greenhalgh (to whom I had by now sent word confirming that she would be needed). No villager had yet come forward with further information on John Lavenham, though I was sure there was more to learn about him. In my experience it is not unknown for the truth of a case to emerge only when witnesses are examined under oath. But that did not stop me trying to know beforehand what the jury's likely verdict would be.

I thought again of the room assigned to Lavenham at the Manor House. A visit in there of even five minutes might bring revelations, but Martin Mansfield had insisted I would need the Squire's permission as only he had the key. Could that be true? What of the servants who tidied it and cleaned? I wondered if I could corrupt the rosy-cheeked girl, Betsy, to let me in there. No, she would surely be too frightened of discovery and dismissal. On the other hand, she might do it on Sarah Lumsden's order.

There was a more direct route into the room, though. I again felt an old crock for not seeing it immediately: Lavenham himself must have had a key. What had happened to that? Why should it not be lying somewhere in his lodgings?

Another conversation with Tree, and a summons for him to appear as a witness, was needed anyway. So, calling at Holloway's on my way to pick up a printed summons form, I set off for Lakeside Lodge.

\*     \*     \*

It was late afternoon when I got there. Wilkin Tree opened the door much as before, unlocking and peering out at me with the caution of a fearful man.

'You may come in, but I don't want to see that doctor.'

'I am alone, Mr Tree. Have you taken against Dr Fidelis?'

Tree's face contorted and his body visibly shuddered.

'I cannot abide the idea of keeping company with a man who has cut open a corpse, and dabbled amongst the organs with his fingers.'

'Then you are quite safe with me.'

He led me into the room to the left of the hall, where his drawing board and writing table were. I noticed how orderly the room was: everything here had its appointed place and there was nothing extraneous. On the board was the beginnings of a map, which might have been of the great field that lay on the western side of the lake, with names indicating how the cultivated strips were apportioned.

'In view of what happened to Mr Lavenham, your caution about who comes into this house is understandable,' I said. 'You told me the other day that you feared for your life. Have you received any threats since then?'

Tree opened his desk drawer and took out a sheaf of papers. Removing the pin that secured them, he leafed through until he found one in particular, which he handed to me. It bore a message, no less shocking for being so very crudely written and so very short.

*If yo want to live leeve.*

The handwriting had much the same crudity as the letter Mansfield had shown me earlier.

'How did you get this?'

'It was pushed under the door during the night. I found it when I came down this morning.'

'And no one was seen delivering it, or skulking around at the time?'

'There is no one else nearby to see. I suppose it was night and I was alone. I was also asleep.'

'Do you recognize the hand?'

'No. It is hardly a hand at all. An uneducated person wrote that.'

'It may have been, although one who forms letters well can also do it badly, such as by writing with his unaccustomed hand – for instance his left, if he is right handed.'

'Oh, yes, that is a possibility.'

'Has anyone in Ingolside threatened you to your face?'

'Not in so many words, but as I said before I feel unwelcome, I do. That's why I keep away from people. I don't see many coming out here, which contents me. That bruiser Johnson runs by every day at breakfast-time. I see him go past my window. He is friend to Cornelius Quexton who is no friend to me, so I stay out of his sight.'

'When you say Quexton is no friend to you, do you mean he is actively hostile? Has he spoken to you?'

'No. I haven't exchanged a word with the man. But I have heard tell of his views, and I can make a good guess at what he thinks of me and the work I do for Squire Lumsden.'

'Because he is against enclosures?'

'He is against any change in the use of the land. He loves woods and hates sheep. He has the stupid idea that the land belongs to the common people and should remain unchanged, when everybody knows it belongs to the King, the lords and the gentry, and if they want to change it they have that power. I am here to make maps of the manor specially for Mr Lumsden, not for the benefit of the people.'

'Perhaps after getting notes like that one you feel even more unsafe, living out here in isolation.'

'It was in the village that Lavenham died, not here.'

'You did say you were afraid when I spoke to you last.'

'A manner of speech. I've more cause to be worried about this wolf Lizzy Duckham's been gabbing on about, that's living in the woods up above, than I am of people coming out here to do me in.'

'That is not what you implied the other day.'

'I had not then heard about this wolf.'

'The wolf didn't bring you that threatening note to your door, Mr Tree.'

'Whether it is wolf or man, I am ready for all comers.' He nodded towards a hunting gun propped in the corner of the room. 'I keep it always primed and ready.'

'Do you know if John Lavenham received any threats similar to the note you received?'

'None that he told me of.'

'Would he have told you?'

'He might not. As I said to you before, we were far from being birds of a feather.'

'May I look in his bedroom here? There might be something.'

'I have no objection. I was not his keeper and nor am I the keeper of his possessions.'

Lavenham's sleeping quarters had a pleasant outlook over the lake and towards the great, cultivated field that stretched away from the far shore. The distant fells beyond rose up majestically to the sky, in hazy colours of green, blue and purple. If I had been in his place I would have enjoyed living there, but I would have kept the room a good deal tidier. It was in a state of considerable chaos, with shoes, clothing and balled-up handkerchiefs thrown into the corners, and more clothing falling out of the wardrobe and drawers where it had been stuffed incontinently. The wig stand was empty but two wigs lay on the floor. The writing table was strewn with books and letters lying open, an array of pens – reed pens as well as quills – and also ink, sand, sealing wax and other writing materials. The mantelpiece was a litter of small change, pipes – some broken, others unused – a tobacco pouch, tinderbox, tapers, and candle ends. There was a box of hair powder, and three snuff boxes containing different grades of snuff.

I gathered up all the papers lying on the table and made a bundle of them with others from inside the table's shallow drawer. These I would take away with me. I then began a search for the key of his room at the Manor House. It was not on the writing table, on the table by the bed, in the table's drawer, or on the floor around the bed. I lifted the worn Turkey rug, looked inside the slippers, emptied the candle box. I made a thorough search under the bed. Nothing came to light.

Before leaving I handed the formal summons to Wilkin Tree.

'A second piece of paper delivered to you, Mr Tree. I hope you will not act on the other one before you answer this one. And in the meantime, I will take that note in evidence, if you please.'

\*     \*     \*

'If that's all you want, I can let you into Lavenham's room at the Manor,' said Mrs Booth.

On my return from Lakeside Lodge I had found a note from Luke Fidelis inviting me for a bite of supper at Mrs Booth's. Now, sitting at the table with herself and Fidelis, I had just finished telling them of my unsuccessful search at Lakeside Lodge for the key to Lavenham's work room. As soon as she spoke I remembered that she worked as a sweeper and cleaner at the Manor House.

'Do you sweep and tidy that particular room yourself?' I asked.

'I sweep. I was told not to tidy. It is like it might be after a tempest in there. Chaos.'

'It is the same in Lavenham's bedchamber. He was not a systematic person. What have you noticed there? What form does Lavenham's work take?'

'I see many scrolls of parchment. There is a large table on which they are sometimes spread.'

'What writing is on them? Can you read it?'

'No, that is beyond me. The handwriting is cramped and very old fashioned. The words may as well be ciphers. My eyes cannot make sense of them.'

'Do you work at the Manor tomorrow?'

'I do.'

'Then how shall we manage it? It must be when Lumsden is out.'

'He will be. He goes with Martin Mansfield to the livestock market at Keswick tomorrow. He never misses it. Come with me to the Manor House at ten in the morning and I will let you in.'

That night, at Holloway's, I retired to my room and went through the papers I had retrieved from Lavenham's lodging. Although Lavenham had a room to work in at the Manor House, he evidently also continued to work on at Lakeside Lodge. What I now had in front of me seemed for the most part to be his own copies of leases or in some cases sworn agreements concerned with land holdings. Most were of ancient date, written in the style Mrs Booth had described: much abbreviated and in arcane legal language. Then my attention was drawn to a notebook in which he had jotted information about numerous villagers in plain style. Knowing that Lavenham had come to Ingolside to examine the documentary contents of the Manor Chest, I had expected that he might make notes to accompany the transcripts. But the notebook did not contain the sort of information to be found in ancient rolls: these were details of the present time – the names and ages of the tenants, with other personal and family details, as well as a note on the land holding they farmed.

*Fenby – aet 34 – two strips of thirty yards he says by ancient copyhold. 2 sons.*

*Langhorn – aet 41 – cottager with one strip approx sixty-five yards — illiterate ignorant. Holding kind unknown. Daughters.*

*Moorhouse – two 70 yard strips allegedly ancient copyhold. N.B. tenant is aged & likely to die soon. Married son.*

*Bradshaw – aet 25 – four short strips Church Field – type of holding unknown. Unmarried.*

Shutting the notebook, I leafed through the remaining bundle and came across another piece of paper that gave an utterly different and unexpected angle on Lavenham's life. It was a letter, addressed to him from a Covent Garden address in London, from a lady who signed herself Françoise.

*Cher John, I receive your letter this morning. All I can say is sooner you return the better. What you do so far away playing the inky scribe and poring over ancient parchments when I need you here I am at a loss for to say. Business is so slack. The days have been wet and the gentlemen prefer to stay at home or in the coffee house by the fireside than come around to Françoise's. I try sending my young Gaston around the town but it is no good. Such a clumsy awkward* marmot. *He entirely has none of your disposition to drum up business. But I also fear our offer in the house is getting stale and we must find new blood you and I. So this is only*

*to say come back to town. The Bow Street affair is forgot*
*already and I think there now you have* rien à craindre. *I*
*embrace you.*
            *Your Françoise.*

Lavenham, it seemed, was not exactly the upright citizen that
Arthur Lumsden had taken him for.

# ELEVEN

I n the morning I called again at Helen Booth's house, finding
her in her working clothes, with her hair bound up in a head-
cloth. Fidelis came down with his medical bag and the three
of us walked down Street and across the market place to the
Manor House. Fidelis and I stood at the front door while she
went around to enter by the servants' entrance at the side.
Moments later she opened the front door and let us into the hall.
Fidelis, whose role in this subterfuge was to occupy the time and
attention of old Mrs Lumsden, went straight up to the patient's
room.

'Wait there,' Helen told me and hurried away.

She came back a minute later wearing an apron and carrying
a broom and a dusting cloth.

'You have the key?' I said.

'No, Mr Cragg,' she said. 'I have not. I don't understand this.
I went to take it from the hook board in the servant's hall but it
is not there. We had better go and see if the room is open.'

I went with her to the door of Lavenham's work room and
stood aside while Helen Booth tried it. It was an old oaken door,
its panels framed by thick ribs, and with a heavy ring handle.
She took hold of the ring, turned it and pushed. The door would
not budge. Asking her to make way, I put my eye to the keyhole
but saw nothing I could recognize. But then something crossed
my narrow field of vision: just a flitting shadow, the slightest
movement.

I stepped back, tugging Helen with me by the arm.

'It is locked from the inside,' I whispered. 'Someone is in
there. But who?'

Helen shook her head and spread out her hands. I nodded at
the next door, which was immediately alongside.

'Do you also sweep in that room?' I whispered.

'I do.'

'Then let's wait there and catch them as they come out.'

This was the Manor House's business room, where I had previously spoken with Bailiff Mansfield. It was unlocked. We slipped inside and I stood, holding the door open by the width of my finger while listening for the sound of the next door's opening while Mrs Booth went about her business, dusting and sweeping according to the usual routine. Five minutes passed before I heard the clunk of the lock and the creak of hinges. I darted out into the passage.

Betsy the rosy-cheeked maid was coming out of Lavenham's room. She clapped her hand to her mouth and her eyes widened in shock at being discovered.

'Good morning, Betsy,' I said. 'I wonder who else is in there.'

In a sudden movement she darted into the passage and swung the door shut, pressing her back against it.

'There's nobody, Sir. Nobody at all.'

She flashed a defiant look at me. I said, 'Betsy, step aside if you please. I must have a look. Remember I am on the King's business.'

She hesitated, then, after a brief moment, and with a grimace, she stepped away from the door and, running down the passage, disappeared into the rear part of the house. I grasped the ring handle and pushed open the door of John Lavenham's workroom once again.

The room was lit by a single window and sparsely furnished. In the middle stood a large table on which were strewn all sorts of writing materials and document scrolls and, behind it, a chair. Sitting in that chair, very much at ease, sat Cornelius Quexton. A parchment scroll was lying partly unrolled in front of him.

'Cragg! Come in!' he cried, in a welcoming tone, just as if the room was his to use as he liked.

I walked into the room, looking around. There was no one else there.

'What is your business here, Quexton?' I said. 'I first thought it was Betsy, but now I see you have been here with her.'

He shrugged his shoulders.

'Betsy is a delightful young woman. She is my friend and my helper, that is all.'

'Your helper in what business?'

He tapped the scroll he was examining.

'I am reading one of the old documents that John Lavenham was working on.'

He nodded towards the great oaken chest scored and stained by years of use that stood next to the wall.

'The Manor Chest is crammed with more of them – old leases, charters, that sort of thing.'

The chest's lid was open and the interior was filled to the brim with more parchment. I moved towards it, noting the strong smell of decay and, closing the lid, sat down on it.

'Much of it is of antique interest,' Quexton went on. 'Are you an antiquarian yourself, Cragg? Did you intend to have a rummage on your own account?'

'I am here officially. I am looking for material evidence in my enquiries.'

My words seemed empty, pompous.

'But without the leave of Mr Arthur Lumsden, I am guessing,' said Quexton. 'I am in the same position. Conveniently for us both, then, he has gone to Keswick today with his bailiff to admire the sheep.'

He smiled with a suggestion of mischief about his eyes.

'What is your interest in these scrolls?' I said. 'Do you read them on your own behalf or hold a commission from another? Old Mrs Lumsden perhaps?'

'She approves my activity, and indeed it was she who asked her maid to unlock the door for me. But no, I am not employed by her. She pays me no fee. I am my own master in all things, which I am proud of.'

'Master in doing what? Surely not merely the training of prizefighters. You yourself said to me you were concerned with justice.'

'Mr Cragg, I may train prizefighters, but as I did indeed tell you the other day, I have weightier interests outside pugilism.'

'Weightier than your prizefighter?'

It was a feeble enough joke. I was hoping to continue the teasing tone of the conversation but Quexton did not smile.

'There is weight and there is weight. The poor of this parish are heavily oppressed by their Squire. He constantly exceeds his authority – indeed, I believe he abuses it – when he overrides the customary regulation of the manor's land, which he does constantly. He tries to take all under his personal control, which is a tyranny by any definition. Therefore, I am looking for documents that would prove his tyranny over Ingolside.'

'You are not native to the place. What is it to you?'

'I take an interest in the matter, here and in other places, out of philanthropy.'

'But if the law is on Mr Lumsden's side—'

'It's not!'

'That has not been tested.'

'Then it should be.'

'If you mean in court, be warned. As an attorney I can assure you that going to law is a very long process.'

Quexton banged the table with the flat of his hand, as if swatting a fly.

'Good, Cragg! As long as possible I say. As long as it takes to wear the fellow down so that he desists and returns this place to its previous tranquility.'

'Tranquility is a worthy aim, of course. But as well as being lengthy, legal cases are expensive. That is why in court the poor never prevail over the rich.'

'We will agree on that. The object must therefore be to obstruct the movement to a trial. Among the means of doing so is to make known the contents of the old rolls, which specify the people's rights and which Arthur Lumsden keeps close in order that no one but himself should read them.'

'John Lavenham was reading them.'

'In the desperate search for anciently sanctioned legal ways of enclosing and engrossing the manor. I hold that none such will be found. Enclosure is a modern procedure.'

'And what do the rolls show instead?'

'They are not kept in any systematic way and are very hard to search. But I have found indications that the mandate of the Squire over this land is anciently restricted. Stinted, in the legal language. There is evidence in that chest which he cannot afford to have made public.'

'Have you seen anything that throws light on John Lavenham's presence here?'

'He was copying the rolls. I find pens and ink, paper and parchment in this room.'

I rose and went to the door. I opened it and stood waiting for him. Any chance I might myself have had of a discreet look around the room was gone.

'I suggest the room be left now to its cleaning,' I said.

Quexton hesitated.

'By *both* of us,' I added.

He sighed and rose from the chair.

'Very well. To its cleaning.'

Outside the door, Quexton wished me good day and left me sharply, striding away towards the hall of the Manor House to let himself out. I turned the other way, heading for the servants' hall, which I found filled with the pungent smell of vinegar. Betsy and another housemaid were cleaning silver and pewter. I asked for Mrs Booth but by now she was working in another part of the house.

'Betsy,' I said, 'is there somewhere you and I can go for a quiet word?'

She dropped her polishing cloth and silently led me into a small adjoining parlour.

'It's the housekeeper's room, Sir,' she said, closing the door.

'Who is the housekeeper?'

'It used to be Mrs Barlow. She was dismissed, or she left, any road.'

'And she has not been replaced?'

'Mrs Lumsden and Mr Arthur cannot agree on who will be next housekeeper, so there isn't one.'

Evidently, if they could not agree on a housekeeper, there was little hope the mother and son could agree upon any matter.

'Well,' I said, 'if there is no housekeeper, we will not be disturbed having a talk in here. But who pays out your wages and settles the tradesmen's bills?'

'Mr Mansfield does it for now.'

'And I am surprised to see you having cleaning to do. Are you not Mrs Sarah Lumsden's maid, with duties confined to looking after her needs?'

'We are short of people so I have to double as housemaid.'

'I see. Then what, Betsy, did you observe on the night of the so-called riot? The night when John Lavenham was found dead at the foot of the stone cross?'

She shook her head.

'Nothing, Sir, I was in my room which looks out the other way.'

'Have you heard any talk about the matter around the village?'

'No, Sir. Not a word.'

'I understand two of the male servants stood with Mr Lumsden when he read the Riot Act, Mr Mansfield and the gamekeeper.'

'Charlie Bowden.'

'Yes, Bowden. Where can I find Mr Bowden? I would like to pay him a visit.'

'He lives in Two Chimneys Cottage. You go all the way down on Elm Tree Lane, off Market Place. The house has two chimneys, you see?'

'I do and I thank you. Will you please go up to Mrs Lumsden's room and ask the doctor to come down and join me outside the house?'

I left the house and sat on the steps while I waited for Fidelis. He came out after ten minutes.

'I have been cupping her. It is a rather laborious treatment but she feels some benefit.'

'You have been drawing her blood? You usually say bloodletting does no good but only harm.'

'You refer to wet-cupping, which I never use. This is dry-cupping. We simply apply the glass cups to the skin and warm them with a flame. The heat causes the loose skin under the cup to be sucked outwards. It swells like a bubble into the cup.'

'In what possible way is that medicinary?'

'Patients find it a pleasant effect, and it is certainly a striking one. That is sometimes all the medicine one needs.'

I have never understood the esoterics of medical treatment. I changed the subject.

'I am expecting Furzey to arrive later today. I wonder if there might be a room for him to stay at Mrs Booth's.'

'I think so. I am the only guest for the time being. You must ask her later, when you come for your dinner, which I hope you will do.'

'Willingly.'

'For now, I have been sent for to see a sick man on Elm Tree Lane.'

'Not one by the name of Bowden?'

'No. It is Moorhouse. Who is Bowden?'

'Lumsden's gamekeeper. I want to speak to him. He was one of the two servants with Lumsden when he confronted the mob. He also lives in Elm Tree Lane.'

'Then I'll walk with you.'

Halfway down Elm Tree Lane, which ran eastwards from the Market Pace, we came to a small neatly kept farmhouse behind a low stone wall, the home of Fidelis's patient. His name was familiar from somewhere but I couldn't think for the moment where I had come across it. Leaving him to his business, I walked on and at a bend passed the great tree after which Elm Tree Lane was named. Another fifty yards on I came to the two-chimneyed cottage in which Charles Bowden lived.

The woman who came to the door with an infant in tow said she was Mrs Bowden. I told her my name and asked for her husband.

'You are in luck, Mr Cragg,' she said. 'Charlie's just popped back home to collect some traps for setting in High Wood, then he'll be straight off out again.'

'Who's this?' growled a voice behind her.

A muscular, thickset man, less than forty years of age with a full red beard loomed up. I repeated my name.

'And who are you to me?'

'I am the Coroner, come to inquest the late death of John Lavenham.'

'Oh, aye?'

'You were there when he was found?'

'That's right. It was me first spotted him.'

With a sharp cock of his head to his wife and child he pushed past her and came out. He was carrying two large iron devices with jagged teeth, which I assumed must be the traps his wife had mentioned.

'I'll not talk of it in front of the bairn,' he said. 'A corpse and a disturbance – it wouldn't be good for her. Come with me into the lane.'

'As you prefer,' I said.

He strode ahead of me into the rutted track. As far as I could see, Two Chimneys Cottage was the last dwelling before the lane entered the woods that clad the steep land that rose above the eastern shore of Ingolmere.

'Those are formidable traps, Mr Bowden,' I said.

'For the wolf. I'll get him, no danger. He's up in them woods biding his time but I'll get him.'

'I hope you will,' I said. 'A wolf is always an unwelcome visitor, I suppose.'

'Specially a lone one. He's rare, mind you. I only ever saw two before this one. But you never can tell with a lone wolf, a male. It's what any keeper'll tell you.'

'I wonder if you would mind telling me something else, though. Just how was it that you first saw Lavenham dead?'

'We'd gone out in front of the house when the mob of people came up. That's Squire, myself and Martin, see? And Mr Arthur read the Riot Act off a printed paper to the crowd. They had been shouting and jeering, and making threats against his property, and even his person. But they went away then and a little while later Squire told Mansfield and me to follow behind and make sure they'd dispersed. We got to the Market Place which was quiet by this time with nobody out. That was when we saw the man, half sitting he was and half lying on the steps under the stone cross. I'd just shaken him to awaken him, like, when he just rolled down the steps to the ground. I felt his face and it was stone cold. He had no more life in him than that gate post.'

'Was there a paper on him? Or a message of some kind?'

'I don't recall one.'

'Very well, Mr Bowden, I shall count you as the first finder. That means you will be required to give your evidence at the inquest. You will be the first witness.'

'Oh yes? When will that be?'

He seemed quite unafraid of the prospect.

'It will be this Thursday morning at the Dissenters' Hall. I should tell you that I have it in mind to ask about something more than how you found Lavenham and ascertained his death. Martin Mansfield told me that all three of you, Mr Lumsden, you and Mansfield himself, carried guns when you went out.'

'Yes, we did. For our own protection.'

'Mansfield says that two shots were fired.'

Bowden frowned. He paused, thinking.

'Was it two?' he said. 'I know Squire aimed a shot over the people's heads, as I was standing on his left side. Martin was on his other. Happen he shot too. I cannot be sure. It was only to frighten anyway. Get them to disperse.'

'You yourself didn't shoot?'

'I did not.'

'That's strange, Mr Bowden. Martin Mansfield says he never fired his own piece, but asserts you did.'

'He is wrong, Sir. The two shots – and I am fairly sure there were two – were fired by Mr Lumsden and Martin.'

# TWELVE

Coming away from the gamekeeper's house, I had just heard the first blatant contradiction in the investigation. Bowden and Mansfield had directly gainsaid each other about who had fired their gun during the riot.

In the lane I found Fidelis sitting hatless and wigless in the shade of the elm tree waiting for me. I sat down beside him and gratefully put aside my own hat and wig. The day was warm and close.

'So what did you learn from the gamekeeper?' he asked.

I gave him an account of my conversation with Charles Bowden.

'It means one of them, either Martin Mansfield or Gamekeeper Bowden, is lying,' I said. 'But why? The shots were fired above the heads of the crowd, were they not? It was innocuous. No one was shot.'

'If someone had been, there would be every reason to make it known and none to hide it.'

'You could not hide it in any case. Not in a place like this. To say the least the case would have been brought to you for treatment. There has been nothing of the like, I take it.'

'Nothing.'

We set off to walk back. Passing Moorhouse's Farm, I asked how Fidelis's patient was faring.

'Old Henry Moorhouse is in a bad way,' he said. 'Likely to die soon, though I couldn't say how long it will be.'

*Likely to die soon.* That was where I had seen the name of Moorhouse. Exactly the same phrase was used in connection with it as I had seen underlined in Lavenham's notebook, where details of the farm's holdings were listed. So why exactly had Lavenham interested himself in old Moorhouse's state of health?

'His son is in a fury over it,' Fidelis went on. 'He stormed at me to cure his father. It was an extraordinary outburst. He was beside himself, as if his father's death could not be tolerated and there would never be a sun or a moon after if he died. And his wife, she went down sobbing on her knees to beg me to cure the old man. She's rather younger than him – twenty, I would say, while he is over forty.'

'A second wife?'

'Perhaps. I could see no sign of any children. Anyway, she was quite as distressed as he was angry. She even seized my hand and kissed it, as if that would give me additional power to save her father-in-law.'

'And can you?'

Fidelis shook his head.

'He is much too far gone. I estimate he might last two days. If he is still alive in three it will be a miracle.'

'Not many are truly prepared when their parent dies. We all know with certainty that those we love will one day be taken from us. But then, when it happens, we are taken unawares.'

'Grief is just as blind as love, but it is more afraid. Part of grief is fear for the future: that, I am sure, is Thomas Moorhouse's case. The question of funeral expense, for one thing, may have no answer. The Moorhouse family are not rich farmers like your Uncle Holloway. The house is bare of comforts and their clothing is old and well worn.'

'Do not these country people form clubs, just as the poor do in Preston? Box clubs. They put in a few pennies every month and years later the club buys them a coffin.'

'But you have to be able to lay hands, each and every week, on those few pennies.'

'They have a farm, Luke. They have the means, surely.'

'No. They eat all that they produce and copper pennies don't sprout from the plough.'

Mrs Booth's house, when we walked in, was filled with the smell of roasting meat, got as before by Fidelis himself. It was a well-cooked meal, which we washed down with a good ale from the brewery of Oswald Gillow, who had been one of those in the Street agreeing to sit on the inquest jury. In the course of the meal I told her about Furzey and asked her if she could accommodate him.

'Of course I'll put your Mr Furzey up,' she said. 'I presume he is agreeable and respectable.'

'Robert Furzey is usually respectable,' I said. 'Whether he is also agreeable, I shall leave it to you to decide.'

After the meal we sat out with our pipes in Mrs Booth's garden. The afternoon was warm and our chairs had high backs against which we could rest our heads. The air was filled with the sound of bees working in the flowerbeds. After a while we both fell gently asleep.

It was consequently only as the afternoon was waning that I returned to Holloway's house and let myself in by the front door. Two women's voices could be heard coming from the parlour and, putting my head into the room, I found the tea service was arranged on the low table. Robert Furzey was sitting beside the window, balancing a cup and saucer awkwardly on one of his knees while, to the left of the fire, Miss Hart sat in the attitude of a hostess. Opposite her, laughing delightedly at something Miss Hart had just said, was the woman that I knew better than any other, and loved even more.

'My God, Elizabeth!' I said, astounded. 'How did you get here?'

'Mr Furzey was so clever,' Elizabeth said. 'He found us a charming little ship at Preston called *Jennifer*, a merchant vessel that flew us direct up the coast to Trimbleby. We had such fair winds that *Jennifer* took only six hours to get here. And so, after just two more hours on a pair of livery horses, here we both are, all in a single day. Isn't it wonderful?'

I glanced at Furzey, who nodded and greeted me with a low, 'How do?'

'Yes,' I said, 'it is wonderful that a storm did not blow up. The sea is not the most regular or most safe way to go from place to place. It is hazardous, to say the least.'

Elizabeth stood and faced me, looking distressed.

'Oh, dear Titus! That sounds as if you are not pleased to see me.'

Instantly my gruffness dissolved. There is nothing to be said in favour of spoiling a happy reunion, and least of all one with her. Whenever we were reunited after a few days apart, I was always filled with amazement at her beauty, and my good fortune in being her husband.

'Forgive me,' I said. 'I should have said that it is wonderful that you were not shipwrecked but even more wonderful to see you.' I kissed her. 'But why, in any case, did you come?'

'To renew my acquaintance with my old playmate Amelia, whom I haven't set eyes on for twenty years. That's right, isn't it, my dear? We were fifteen when we were last together?'

'We were,' said Miss Hart. 'They were happy times.'

The talk turned to what Elizabeth and Amelia Hart would do the next day. A walk through the village and a visit to the church was proposed. There was a marble monument to a predecessor of the Lumsdens who had gone to the Crusades, the splendour of which was not to be missed. There was also Mrs Cumberledge, who was an intimate of Amelia and would, we were assured, welcome a visit at the vicarage.

That night Elizabeth was in bed before me, reading.

'What's the book?'

'John Gay's *Fables*. You know them. Like Aesop in verse, but more satirical. Amelia has lent it to me. It is so amusing and full of clever ideas about life and society.'

She put the book aside as I got in beside her.

'Tell me your progress in this business you came here for.'

'I have so many unanswered questions. For example, I cannot see that Lavenham – who came to Ingolside to assist Arthur Lumsden's improvements to the estate and manor – would have voluntarily, at great danger to himself, gone out among men who objected to those improvements and were on the edge of riot. They even threatened to burn the Manor House. His body, you know, was found in the middle of the Market Place immediately after the near riot had dissipated. And here's another question. His lungs were congested with soot as from the smoke of a fire, which Luke says might have been fatal. Now, others had similarly sooty lungs who escaped from the burned-out inn. But that fire was three days before the people came out and publicly protested against Squire's projects. If Lavenham died from suffocation at the fire, what happened to his body in the interval?'

'Did someone reserve his corpse, for some reason or other?'

'What possible reason could there be? The notion is repulsive.'

'There's a fable in my book which might be rather to the point. It is called "The Greek Philosophers and the Ass". Do you know that one?'

'Please remind me.'

'They go around from town to town with a poor old donkey, which they horridly beat and beat to make him carry all their things. And then one morning they find the donkey dead from exhaustion, so what do they do? They make a drum out of his skin, which they carry around beating to advertise their lectures.'

'My dearest wife, I am not sure I can see—'

'Yes you can, Titus. The donkey is dead so he's no use to them as a beast of burden. So they put him to a new use, still beating and beating him.'

I was tired, which prevented me, perhaps, from seeing the merits of the case. I only said, with a yawn, 'I still cannot follow what you mean, my love?'

'That they were doing the same thing with poor Mr Lavenham's body. They saved it for a new purpose, like the ass's skin. They used it to make a point.'

I yawned again.

'Well, I would much prefer him to have been alive when the mob threatened the Manor House. This idea that he was already dead makes our whole task more complicated.'

'Oh well,' she said, 'perhaps there is a simple explanation after all, and you will find it in the morning.'

First thing after breakfast I collected Furzey from Mrs Booth's house and walked up with him to look over the inquest room. On the way he gave me an account of the progress of some of the legal business we had in hand at Preston. Then, as we were approaching the hall, I said, 'Have you any intelligence on John Lavenham, by the way? You remember I wrote that I'd heard he had appeared at Bow Street Court, but not the nature of the charge or the outcome.'

'Yes, and I have smoked him out all right.'

He paused. It was something he often did: keeping back a morsel of information just to tease, because he knew I was itching to know it.

'Well? What have you found out?'

Before he could answer, my name was called from across the street. It was Ben Bennett, who had spotted us as he came out of his cottage door. He hurried across the road and I made introductions, adding that Furzey as my clerk would be making the Dissenter's Hall ready for the inquest on Thursday.

'Then let me show you around,' said Bennett.

He led the way and once inside we agreed the room could be used without any great alteration. In particular the rows of forms facing the dais would provide more than enough room for the public.

'I will require a good solid table for me and the Coroner which will be placed facing the people,' said Furzey. 'Also a dignified chair for Mr Cragg, a chair for myself and one for the witnesses, to be also of a dignified character, and a bench long enough to sit twelve jurors and the spare man, making thirteen in all.'

Bennett assured us there was a suitable oaken table and chairs in the building and proposed that the foremost public bench or pew, which was long enough, would be shifted on to the dais and placed at a right angle to the table for the use of the jury. The witness chair would be at the other end of the table so that witnesses and jurors would face each other. I was just telling him this would be satisfactory when I heard Elizabeth's voice saying my name from the hall's entrance. I turned and saw her standing there with Miss Hart, both women in their outdoor bonnets. It had been arranged that we would go together from here to visit the church. I went down the room to greet my wife and her cousin while Furzey, a natural Whig with more than a dash of Dissent in him, began a friendly conversation with Bennett about the disagreement between John Wesley and George Whitefield on the great question of Predestination.

'I am Anti-Predestination, myself,' said Bennett. 'I find it would render impossible the operation of divine grace.'

'I'm right with you, Sir,' said Furzey. 'Predestination cannot be correct. Of course the Lord knows what we do, but it is we who decide to do it.'

'Does Whitefield think we are made as machines? We are created with our will free, whether to do good or evil.'

Leaving them to their theology, I walked with the ladies to the church of St Silas.

It was a crumbling old church, with some of the stonework in the arches along the nave gone out of alignment like snag teeth. Miss Hart showed us the tomb of Sir Hereward, the old warrior, tucked into a niche at eye level in the north transept, with his escutcheon carved into the side of the stone box inside which he lay. On top of the lid was a marble effigy of the man, portraying him asleep in death – a lean figure the size of life, wearing chain mail, with helmet on head and broadsword by his side. His face looked severe, with prominent cheekbones and compressed lips, like a man who rather resented one looking over him. With his leanness, his armour and his knightly appearance he bore a faint resemblance to Don Quixote.

'Oh, just look at the dog and the cat,' Elizabeth exclaimed in delight.

A carved smooth-coated cat and a recumbent rough-eared dog were curled up amiably under Sir Hereward's mailed feet. The dog was not unlike our own spaniel, Suez.

'What sort of cat is it?' asked Miss Hart. 'He surely meant a good deal to the knight, that he should be sculpted for his tomb along with his faithful dog.'

'Well, he looks an everyday cat,' said Elizabeth. 'But it is strange. It is not usual for a cat to be shown as a faithful true companion, though a dog often is.'

'I often wonder if the dog went on crusade with his master,' Miss Hart said. 'It would be just the thing to buffet the eye of the Saracens who, I have read, greatly despise dogs.'

'He is rather like our dog at home, Suez,' said Elizabeth, 'who is certainly game enough to go to war. I cannot imagine the cat was a crusader, though I suppose it is not impossible.'

'Shall we go over to the vicarage now and see if Mrs Cumberledge is at home?' said Miss Hart. 'She is a dear friend of mine, and will be very pleased to meet you both.'

# THIRTEEN

Mrs Cumberledge was not in the least put out by our unexpected arrival. She invited us inside and sat us in her parlour, a light and airy room, though furnished in the style of more than a generation past. She rang for an old body of a servant from whom she ordered refreshments and in due course tea, milk, bread and butter were brought in.

'I have been prettifying the garden.'

'You are a gardener, Mrs Cumberledge?' I said.

'Oh yes. I have old Seb Buttley to do all the work, of course, but strictly according to my own design. What we are doing now is for a particular occasion. We invite an assembly every year for the Whitsun Ales, gathering outdoors if the weather permits, but with a tent in case it doesn't.'

'Mr Cumberledge believes the Whit celebrations to be ungodly,' I said, 'which I do not understand as they're designated "Church Ales".'

'They are so called because once the country parish priests brewed ale and sold it at Whitsun for church funds. It was a Papist custom, Mr Cragg, which has survived into the present time because unfortunately sinfulness has not yet been eradicated. Today's Church of England is not, I am glad to say, a brewer so our own Whitsun gathering is a strictly temperance occasion, a tea party where all people to whom sobriety is sacred are welcome. Even Mr Bennett who leads the Dissenters Society will attend. He is militantly sober.'

'So you gather in very defiance of the alehouse, it seems,' said Elizabeth.

'That is well put, Mrs Cragg. I hope you and your husband can be with us. We shall not invite all other strangers in our midst. That doctor in particular is a man of very irregular and even scandalous habits, as well as being a Papist, I am told.'

Elizabeth, although herself a Roman Catholic, made no remark and I followed her example. There was nothing to be gained by taking issue with a vicar's wife on any question of religion. Besides, Luke Fidelis's life really did appear irregular, and he was undeniably a Papist.

'May we hope to see your husband today, Mrs Cumberledge? Is he at home?' Elizabeth asked.

'He is visiting the sick this morning.'

'Mrs Sarah Lumsden?'

'Not this time. It is old Moorhouse, who will very soon be breathing his last.'

'The Moorhouses are afraid for their future, I believe, once the old man dies,' I said. 'Are they not very poor?'

'Yes, they are poor, and not alone in being so in these parts. The parish has seen of late an unpleasant tide of envy from those that are poor towards the prosperity of their betters. But what we say is, why else has the Almighty provided wealth if not to distinguish those more worthy from those less so?'

She sniffed and looked around to see if we agreed. Miss Hart nodded her head.

'How true.'

'As for the Moorhouses,' Mrs Cumberledge went on, 'according to Charles Bowden they are much to the fore in the vice of poaching. They constantly take rabbits from Mr Lumsden's warren in the woods. And yet Mr Cumberledge does his Christian duty all the same, and visits them.'

'Do the rabbits then belong to the Squire alone?' asked Elizabeth in an innocent tone. 'I thought the woods might be common.'

'Well they are common, yes, but the rabbits that live in them are the Squire's. His grandfather established the warren in the nineties and therefore they are Mr Lumsden's game and it is wicked for any other to take them.'

At this moment the rector himself walked in. He took off his hat ceremoniously and bowed to the company.

'I think you have been to see old Moorhouse, my dear,' said his wife.

'Have I? Moorhouse?'

'Yes, Cuthbert, old Henry Moorhouse. He is sick.'

'Ah yes! Why didn't you say that's who you're talking about? Henry Moorhouse. He is very weak, and is hardly able to draw breath. His death is near.'

'My friend Dr Fidelis has seen him in a medical capacity,' I said. 'I am afraid he is of much the same opinion.'

'Doctor, you say?' said the rector. 'No, I have heard nothing creditable of that young doctor. I've seen him round about, in and out of Sarah Lumsden's bedroom. He is full of new-fangled ideas but, if you ask me, they have a way of turning out disastrous.'

'He attends Mrs Lumsden at her own invitation, I understand.'

'But does old Moorhouse invite him? I doubt it as he cannot talk, and certainly cannot pay his fee. He can listen, however, so I gave him twenty minutes from my sermon on cheerfulness, which he heard without interruption, though with every indication of bewilderment. He is beyond hope, I fear.'

'His son is afraid of what will happen to him when his parent dies.'

'Tommy Moorhouse? I rather suspect that young man. He is ill-tempered and I am sure leans towards Dissent. He will come to church in the morning and sneak to the Wesleyan meeting in the afternoon. Not a very agreeable fellow.'

'John Wesley's influence is such a wicked nuisance, we find,' said his wife, turning to Elizabeth. 'People become quite contrary after they have been exposed to that unfortunate man's sermons.'

'Dissenters should be re-named disrespectors, in my opinion,' said the Rector. 'Their conceit is beyond bounds. Do you know? I sometimes find they speak to me as if I were privy to some secret, some hidden truth which I naughtily conceal from them. Ha! The very idea! They derive it from Wesley himself, I suppose.'

'Well, nothing could be further from the truth,' said Mrs Cumberledge. 'If there is any man of probity on the parish, any man that has no naughtiness, it is you, my dear.'

'I hope so,' he said. 'I leave secrets and lies to the Roman Catholics. I leave dogma to them also. King, country and the Thirty-nine Articles, that is my theology plain and simple, and I don't mind who knows it or who discusses it. It is out in the open.'

'Yet Ben Bennett seems an agreeable sort of fellow,' I said. 'I would be surprised if he speaks to you disrespectfully?'

'Ben Bennett? Ah, yes! Ben Bennett. He goes out of his way to ingratiate. Between you and me that is all there is to it.'

When it was time for us to leave, I suggested to Elizabeth that she might go with me to visit the Moorhouses. Lavenham's notebook was still preoccupying my thoughts and I was wondering, if the dead man had had dealings at Moorhouse's Farm, whether this might cast some light on what happened to him. We therefore walked Miss Hart home so that I could collect the notebook, and from there returned up Street and along Elm Tree Lane.

The house was small, neat and well cared for. It showed just five windows, one each beside the door and three above, and each with window pots overflowing with blooms. The short path to the front door intersected two squares of green. In one of these a goat was tethered to a pole so that she could crop the grass but not get amongst the well-tended flower borders. Behind the house was a cobbled yard surrounded by outbuildings.

Thomas Moorhouse was a wiry and restless fellow, with a hard, unforgiving edge to his voice and a permanent frown etched into his forehead. He let us inside and sat us in chairs near the fireplace, though no fire burned in it. I told him that my business concerned Lavenham's death, and that I was speaking to anyone in the Manor that had been visited by him while he was staying in Ingolside.

'Aye,' he said. 'He came here.'

'Just the one visit, was it?'

Moorhouse turned his head and called out roughly, 'Alice!'

A woman younger than him by a good fifteen years came into the parlour. She was slim with a Madonna's smile, but there was a depth and an element of wariness in her hazel eyes as she looked first at me and then Elizabeth.

'The wife,' Moorhouse said. 'We've been married five year.'

'How do you do?' I said.

'They want to know about that Londoner that was here,' Moorhouse said to her. 'John Lavenham, that one that died later. It was just that one time he came, am I right?'

'Yes, just the once,' Alice Moorhouse said.

He pointed to a narrow bench by the wall.

'You can sit there.'

Alice sat and listened to the rest of the conversation, her eyes darting between the three of us, though without contributing any further remarks. Moorhouse returned to the subject I had raised.

'So, this John Lavenham. Like I say, we've had the man here. He was asking after my dad's health, and had a lot of questions about my farm. He had a book with him which he wrote everything down in.'

I brought the notebook out and showed it.

'Would it be this book?'

'Aye, that one, or another very like. He wanted to know my acreage and where it lay, and what kind of crop drilling we do and what else we grow. Wrote it all down, he did, like I said. I've an idea what use he would put it all to, but he never told me himself.'

Turning the pages, I showed him the entry under his name.

'Is this what he wrote?'

Moorhouse looked over the section I indicated.

'Aye, looks like.'

'And is it accurate? Is it what you told him?'

'That's our farm, rightly put down.'

'And was Lavenham with anyone else when he visited?'

'No, he was alone. I didn't like the man. London. Knew better on every subject. And never did me the courtesy of saying what he was at.'

'And did Mr Mansfield call after that?'

'He did, after a day or two. I don't like him either, nobody does. He pretends to have folks' best interests in his mind, which is rubbish for a start as the man's a snake underneath all. It wasn't long before he was telling me, with my old dad soon to be dead, how I would be paying the heriot, and asking if I could afford it.'

'Perhaps you found that a little premature.'

'Aye, call it that if you like. Or bloody cheek, whichever way you want.'

Little enough was heard in Preston of this tax called heriot, but I knew it was a part of every country landowner's income, money due from a tenant when either the tenancy or the lordship changed hands upon the death of one or other of the incumbents.

'So, I says to him,' Moorhouse went on, 'well it's a pound six shilling and eightpence, is heriot. I can sell a pig. And he says you'll do more than that, as Mr Lumsden's set heriot at eight pound now. How much? I said. Not likely. Heriot was always the same amount round here, see: a pound six and eight. Mr Lumsden hasn't the right, I said, to ask eight pound.'

'That's a six-times increase,' said Elizabeth. 'Surely that's excessive, Titus.'

'I would have to look at the old rolls to be sure,' I said. 'But often the amount is not written down but fixed by custom.'

'That is what I told Mr Mansfield and this London prick,' said Moorhouse. 'Heriot is fixed. It cannot be changed. And anyway, I said, the tenancy will be mine by right passed on from father to son. I will not be cast out like an old shoe.'

'What did Mansfield say to that?'

'He had hanging from his shoulder a leather bag and he came out with a roll from it.'

'Parchment?'

'It was, and from the Manor Chest, he said. He said it had the particulars for this farm. He unrolled it and put a part of it under my nose and pointed to it. "It says here," says he, "that the tenancy is not to be passed from father to son unless by the lord's agreement."'

'So he's saying Arthur Lumsden has the right to evict.'

'Mansfield told me he can do just as he likes. I say, unless somebody stops him, though nobody will.'

'And did you look at the document? Did you read it?'

Moorhouse was growing heated now. A flush came to his cheeks.

'The roll? I did look at it but I couldn't read a bloody word. Either there was something wrong with my eyesight, or something wrong with the words, but I could make no sense of them.'

'So you trusted that the roll gave the Squire the right to increase heriot?'

'What else could I do? I couldn't challenge him. An old roll is an old roll. It was written before anyone can remember.'

'And Mansfield, he's saying you would be let stay once you pay the heriot?'

'Oh yes, very good of him. But as I cannot, and he knows I cannot, Lumsden gets his way.'

'Truly, you cannot pay it?'

'Heck as like. Eight pound, man? It would ruin us. We might sell all the beasts and we'd still be running nowhere near. And there's others before have suffered the same under Lumsden's tyranny. More than one lost their farms because of his high hand. Just when they were grieving their old dads being gone, they got turned out of their farms. One was burned out, and all because they couldn't pay the man's demand for heriot.'

By now his face was charged with anger, red as a raspberry and trembling, as he stared into the empty, fireless grate.

'Would the farm that was burned out lie over by the marsh, on the southern road?'

'Brabner's Farm, aye. A wreck of a place now. Ted Brabner never had enough to make ends meet.'

'What happened to him?'

'Gone to who knows where. America, happen.'

'Mr Moorhouse,' I said. 'What you have told me is important. I am here to inquest the death of John Lavenham and I may require you to give evidence.'

'Me? Give witness?' he said. 'I saw nowt. I wasn't there on the night they found him dead.'

'You may be able to help us by specifying what kind of information Lavenham was collecting here at Ingolside.'

'Specifying? I don't know about that. I know nothing.'

Elizabeth now intervened.

'May I visit your poor father upstairs?' she asked him. 'I understand he lies sick in this house and you are worried he may not live long.'

Moorhouse nodded curtly at his wife who took Elizabeth by the arm, led her to the stair and the two of them disappeared into the upper floor. Meanwhile Moorhouse and I talked on. He was not a garrulous man but he had strong opinions, in rather the way Mrs Cumberledge had indicated, and articulated them with considerable bitterness.

'I don't hold with Bishops in their palaces. I'll allow a palace to the King, as that seems the best place for him. But Bishops have too much property and money which is not godly. When the new Archbishop was put on his throne at York – last year, wasn't it? – there was enough feasting, drunkenness and debauching in that city to rival Sodom itself.'

'Do you therefore count yourself among the Dissenters?'

'I do not. I have been to meetings. I heard Wesley when he passed by. But I count myself a loyal Englishman, me.'

I was reminded of Mr Cumberledge's theology. It seemed in spite of the vicar's disparagement of Moorhouse, there was not so much between them as he thought.

'It may go hard with you, Mr Moorhouse, should you lose the farm. You will need friends.'

'I've got friends, but they do not stand very high on the ladder of life, if you understand me. I cannot afford to abide by all the rules of the game, as given us by our so-called betters. I shall have to do what is necessary when the time comes, whatever that is.'

'Do nothing rash, man.'

'Rash? To a squire or a vicar a thing may be rash. A man looking destitution in the eye does what he has to do.'

When Elizabeth came down, her face was grave and at the same time kindly, as I have seen in her many times when receiving other people's distress.

'I am concerned for Alice Moorhouse, Titus,' she said after we had taken our leave and were walking away down the lane. 'She is nobody's fool; indeed I would say she is rather intelligent.'

'He is too. He even has wit. But he is very angry with it.'

'His wife knows that her future is now very uncertain, and she is mortally afraid of her husband. I would not be surprised if he beats her badly, but maybe it is more than that. She said Thomas has a passionate nature but I do not think it is the loving kind of passion.'

I thought of Moorhouse's words to me when we spoke of the possibility of his eviction and I had warned him against doing anything rash.

'Does she fear him, or fear what he might do?'

'Both. I do not think the two of them confide. Or rather he does not confide in her. It is just a sense I had of her fear of his actions, which I admit is not evidence.'

'It may be.'

'Is smelling a rat proof of a dead rat?'

'When *you* smell one, it is. You have preternatural good sense.'

Elizabeth laughed.

'Now it's you being foolish. Sense and good sense are not the same thing.'

'In you they are. However, whatever it is Mistress Moorhouse fears in her husband, I suppose she feels powerless to stop him.'

'Of course she is powerless, Titus. She is a woman in this world.'

'You are a woman, as I thank God, and yet not in the least powerless.'

'I am, though. You are a lawyer, Titus. Nobody knows better than you what the law says about men and women, and where the power lies.'

'Ah, yes, I grant you there is legal power. But that is not the only kind. There is, for instance, the power of love.'

'Well, I hope Moorhouse loves his wife, but I doubt it.'

# FOURTEEN

Elizabeth and I parted at the Market Square, which she crossed diagonally to return to Holloway's Farm, while I turned left and walked up Street. A few minutes later I had passed the Dog and Drum and was soon knocking on the door of Cornelius Quexton's cottage.

It was the giant Johnson who opened the door.

'Is Mr Quexton here?'

Without a word, the prizefighter ushered me inside, where Quexton was sitting at the table writing.

'Mr Cragg!' he said, sounding pleased to see me. 'Is this a social visit?'

'Not exactly. I wanted to tax your memory, if I may.'

He gestured at the chair on the opposite side of the table.

'Sit down and tax away.'

I settled myself and looked up at Johnson who occupied a disproportionate amount of space in the small, low room.

'You may speak in front of Johnson. He has my full confidence.'

Johnson sat down on the bottom step of the stairs that led up to the bedrooms and settled himself to listen.

'It is a matter of the documents,' I said. 'The ones that you were looking at in John Lavenham's room, when I last saw you.'

'What of them?'

'I wonder if you recall any that concerned the farm holding of Mr Moorhouse of Elm Tree Lane? I have just been to see the younger Moorhouse and he told me that Martin Mansfield had shown him a parchment on which the terms of Moorhouse's lease were recorded. Did you see this parchment?'

He considered for a moment.

'No, there was no such parchment.'

'Ah! I just hoped there was, because I am wondering about its validity at law. Oh well. It was a shot in the dark on my part.'

'When I say there was no such parchment, I mean none

specifically relating to Moorhouse, or none that I saw. But there were other such parchments relating to other farm holdings.'

'What about Brabner's Farm, then? I don't suppose there was anything on that?'

Quexton pushed back his chair and stood up.

'I think, if it's Brabner's Farm you're interested in, then you're in luck.'

Hanging from a nail in the wall was a leather satchel. Quexton crossed to it, took it down and showed me what was inside. I could see it contained several parchment rolls.

'Here are some old rolls that I, as you might say, borrowed. I felt able to do so as none of them is alive, by which I mean none is still active, the tenancies having been closed. One of these is the lease relating to what was formerly Brabner's Farm.'

He removed a roll, checked its identity and handed it to me. I put on my spectacles and laid the lease flat on the table. It began in the usual way, and I could see the identity of the property it related to, the 'howse communly knowen as Brabiner's Farm'. Further on I could see it laid down the ancient conditions of the holding. The details were obscured here and there by spots of damp and holes in the material, and were in any case very hard to read, with the words crammed together with minimal space between.

'From what I see here, Brabner had worked strips amounting to some six land yards or roods.'

'That's right,' said Quexton. 'When the last tenant died, Ted Brabner's father that is, the farm was of paltry value. The tenancy holding itself was not much. A couple of acres, distributed across several strips. It was not so small that the Brabners were destitute, and not so large that they were able to grow a surplus. Only enough for a man and his family to survive year by year.'

'And what happened when old Brabner died?'

'The Squire, through Martin Mansfield, applied what he said were the tenancy conditions. These were that the property would revert to the manor unless Edward Brabner Junior, his son, made payment of the heriot demanded. In the event that he could not pay heriot, he would be turned out.'

I looked up and down the parchment.

'And the amount of heriot is fixed?'

'Not according to the Squire's interpretation of the lease. He claimed the right to increase heriot, and in fact did so six-fold over the usual amount for the property of thirteen shillings and fourpence.'

'So when old Brabner died, Lumsden demanded what – four pounds in heriot?'

'Exactly.'

'Which he did not receive, I take it.'

'He did not, with the result that Brabner the son, with his family, faced a summary eviction.'

'So what happened?'

'The farmhouse was burned, the family barely escaped.'

'Who burned it?'

Quexton looked steadily at me for a moment, then said, 'It is put about that Brabner did it himself, out of hatred and desperation. But if so it is strange that one of his children burned to death.'

I bent closer, squinting at the script.

'I am looking for an option by the landholder to increase heriot, but I see only the specific figure of thirteen shillings and fourpence.'

'You won't find an option to increase, Mr Cragg, because it is not there.'

I was astonished.

'Are you saying the Brabners need not have been turned out?'

'Not if they could raise thirteen shillings and fourpence, the fixed sum. I guess that would have been within their compass.'

'Then Brabner was cheated.'

'He was. But what could he have done to prove it? When Mansfield showed him the roll he had no idea what it said, and no means of reading it for himself.'

'So however much the farmer might cite customary rights, he had no choice but to believe Mansfield when he told him the written deed overrode custom, even though it didn't.'

'This is the point, Cragg: the lease actually confirms custom. Therefore, we may be sure that this farmer lost his livelihood through fraud.'

'What happened to him?'

'He left the parish with his family – an old mother, a wife

and the surviving children – all except one boy who remained here with relatives. I don't know where Brabner is now. He has not been heard from.'

I stood up and prepared to leave. I had the information I'd hoped for. I thanked Quexton for it, but asked one more favour.

'I would like to borrow the Brabner lease. May I?'

'I am afraid not, Cragg. I cannot let it go out of my hands.'

'But it has lapsed and no longer operates. It is only a piece of parchment now.'

'I prefer to keep it for the time being. But will a copy transcribed on to modern paper satisfy you?'

Quexton opened the table drawer and, searching around inside, brought out a single sheet written in a modern hand. He presented it to me with a flourish. I placed it alongside the original lease on the table and looked back and forth between the two. It was a true copy.

'Thank you,' I said. 'This will do quite well.'

I found Furzey in Mrs Booth's parlour surrounded by paper. I had given him the names of the jurors Miss Hart and I had recruited and he was compiling a list of them in his inquest ledger.

'Furzey, I am glad to find you here.'

'Where else would I be? I am working on the case.'

'I am glad to see it. Meat feeds the stomach, work feeds the brain, is it not so?'

'Whoever said that was not a lawyer's clerk.'

I laughed but Furzey would not be humoured. He continued writing as if I was not there. I said, 'Will you leave off for a few minutes and listen to me, if you please? You must tell me what you have found out about John Lavenham. You said that you had smoked him out.'

I hooked him under the arm and brought him to his feet.

'Come and sit by the fire. I want to hear it all.'

We were no sooner disposed on either side of the fireplace than Luke Fidelis came in.

'If I have to spend another two hours with Mrs Lumsden I will be stark mad. That woman would drive the mother of God to distraction.'

'Calm yourself and join us here for a moment. Mr Furzey is about to give me some intelligence of great value about John Lavenham. It *is* of great value, I hope, Furzey?'

Furzey merely gazed with a look of steady seriousness into the flames.

'Come on, man, out with it,' I said. 'What have you found out about Lavenham's appearance at Bow Street?'

Furzey cleared his throat and, after a further pause worthy of an actor in Drury Lane, held up two fingers.

'Two times. Two.'

'Two times? Please, construe a little.'

'It's the number he's been up. Twice. In the dock.'

'How do you know?'

'Lord Lonsdale's man of business was in Preston with a suit at the Palatine Court. I happen to know that his clerk is the brother of one of the clerks at Bow Street, so when I got your letter I went over to speak to him. Oh yes, he told me, he'd heard all about the notorious Lavenham. And he gave me a deposition of exactly what he knew.'

'What was Lavenham notorious for?'

'Suspected of passing false documents. In short, forgery.'

'What sort of documents?'

'He was accused of trying to sell some dubious East India Company certificates. And of writing some antique deeds of gift that weren't true.'

'Yet he remained at liberty?'

'Such matters cannot always be proven. On the matter of the certificates, Lavenham claimed he handled them without knowing they were wrong. The deeds were supposedly older than human memory, so there could be no human witness against him in that charge.'

I looked at Luke Fidelis.

'So they were not unlike . . .?'

'The heap of rolls inside the Ingolside Manor Chest,' said Fidelis.

'Exactly,' I said. 'Now listen to me, both of you. Here is the significant thing. When I interviewed Mr Moorhouse junior earlier today, he told me Martin Mansfield had recently showed him a roll which, he claimed, had just come to light. This roll gives the Squire the right, so he said, to set the amount of heriot payable when a tenancy passes from one generation to the next, and to evict any tenant who fails to pay said heriot.'

'A convenient piece of parchment indeed, and just at the moment when heriot will become due upon old Moorhouse's shuffling off.'

'There is more. I have here a lease – the wording of it, not the lease itself – which emerged from the documents chest two years ago. It was used in exactly the same way after the death of old man Brabner, the sitting tenant at Brabner's Farm. Brabner the son was told by Mansfield that Squire Lumsden now required heriot of four pounds, whereas it had previously been thirteen shillings and sixpence. Brabner couldn't pay and was then burned out. One of his children died. I have seen the farm and it is tenantless, blackened and a ruin. I do not suppose Arthur Lumsden is very bothered by that, so long as the land is engrossed into his estate.'

Furzey took the paper and looked through it.

'Well if this is a true copy, the bailiff was lying to Brabner,' he said. 'There is no such provision here. The rate of heriot on Brabner's Farm is confirmed at the traditional amount.'

'I thought the same, Furzey, when I looked through it. I must admit, though, the language in these old parchments is damned difficult to make out.'

Furzey was huffed. He frowned up at me.

'I was reading such documents at my Daddy's knee, Mr Cragg.'

'Very well. But I question the matter because poor Brabner did not have your advantage. He was faced not even with a transcript, but the original parchment, having to contend not only with the language but the antiquated script. Unable to read the lease for himself, he could only take Mansfield's and Lumsden's word on its contents.'

'He could have taken legal advice.'

'A man who cannot find four pounds cannot afford a lawyer. But I wonder if that indeed was a part of Lavenham's role in all this. To play the lawyer. To read, or appear to read, the old documents and give the result not just to Lumsden but to the tenants. What they might not believe in the familiar mouth of Mansfield, they would take from that of the fellow from London.'

Fidelis shook his head.

'Remember you have found evidence that he was capable of doing more than read the old leases. He could also *write* them.'

'Not easy to prove,' said Furzey. 'The rumours about his activities in London are all very well, but there must be a witness to say he was doing something similar here.'

'There may be physical evidence,' I said. 'And, while you get back to your clerking, that question is part of my business this afternoon. Will you accompany me, Luke? We are going to Lakeside Lodge, for the ostensible reason that it is time we took away Lavenham's body. I hope you will supervise the removal. It will be a foul, stinking job I fear.'

Fidelis's face brightened.

'I welcome it, Titus, if it means I can escape dancing attendance on my patient for a few more hours.'

# FIFTEEN

Leaving Furzey to his list making, including a new schedule of the witnesses to go alongside the names of the jurors, I went out with Luke. I led the way to the market place where, as it had been market day, people were still doing last-minute business even as the tradesmen were beginning to dismantle their stalls. I saw a drowsy carter lounging beside his donkey and cart. As he seemed to have no business in hand, I approached him.

'There's sixpence for you if you'll come with us and carry back the corpse of John Lavenham from Lakeside Lodge to the Dissenters' Hall.'

'A body, is it?' he said. 'That'll be worth ninepence of any bugger's money, will that.'

I agreed the sum and we three set off.

'So if Lord Lonsdale's man is right,' I said as we went along, a few strides ahead of the carter, 'Lavenham was something of a fraud monger.'

'Suspected,' said Fidelis. 'Nothing proven, but he's certainly a plausible suspect.'

'He had a quite a way with him, I've heard. Seems men and women liked him equally. He was generous with cash as well as words, according to Mrs Greenhalgh.'

We did not find Wilkin Tree at home but Lizzy Duckham, who came to the door, was pleased to see us.

'If it's to get that corpus out of here, there'll be no one more tickled than me.'

Fidelis took the carter around to the row of outhouses, where Lavenham's remains still lay, and I invited myself into Mrs Duckham's kitchen.

'I would like to make another short visit to Mr Lavenham's room,' I said. 'But first I wonder if there's anything you can tell me about what he was doing. Did he talk about it? Did you happen to go in there when he was at work?'

'Many's the time he locked himself in. I would knock and he'd shout to come back later, or else he'd unlock and say I must not disturb his desk.'

'And when you went in, what did you observe on the desk?'

'I don't know. A lot of papers, with writing things like pens and ink. But I didn't take much notice as I was forbidden touching owt there. I just went about my work airing the room, sweeping and picking up his dirty clothes.'

'You said papers. What kind of papers? Were there any rolls, or scrolls? Of parchment I mean, not paper.'

'Rolls? Yes, I remember he had some. Was that parchment they were of? He often had one held down by these stones he had.'

'You mean, he'd unrolled them and the stones stopped them rolling back?'

'Aye.'

'And were the rolls written on already? Or was he writing on them?'

'I couldn't say, Mr Cragg. He wouldn't do owt while I was with him. I'll tell you what, though. I can read and write, no trouble, when it's your usual handwriting or printing. But from what I could see of his rolls of parchment, I could never read them.'

'Were the letters and words crowded together?'

'They were that. You wouldn't know where one stopped and the next started. And they were shaped different from what I call normal. Different from what they look like in my Bible at home.'

I went up to Lavenham's room, which was in the same state as I had found it before. At that time, I had taken away paper that was written on and, though I had noticed a few rolls of what I thought were blank parchments, I was then blind to their significance. I looked at them again now and, fully unrolling each, I was blind no more. There were five of these rolls. Four were indeed blank, but the fifth, when I unrolled it completely, was not. At the top of it was written in ancient legal hand the word 'WHEREAS'.

At that moment I heard my name called from below the window. Looking out over the path that ran between the house and the shore of the lake, I saw the cart and the donkey there, with the carter and Luke Fidelis looking up at me. A long sheet-wrapped shape lay on the cart bed. Fidelis beckoned to me and, quickly snatching up the 'Whereas' roll, I went down to join them.

We set off back to Ingolside and as we walked I told Fidelis what I had found at Lakeside Lodge.

'Four rolls of parchment ready to be written on, and one already started but only with one word – "Whereas".'

'Why were they at Lakeside Lodge, though? He had his work room at the Manor House, where the Manor Chest was.'

'You say the Manor Chest?' said the carter, a burly man of about sixty who was leading his donkey immediately behind us.

'I do,' I said. 'What do you know about it?'

'I had that on my cart two times. The chest.'

'You did? When?'

'After those two Londoners first came. Once I had to take it from the Manor to the Lodge as we've just been to, and again when I had to bring it back again to the Manor.'

'When was this? And who gave you the job?'

'Squire gave it me. We had to bring it at night, he said, and to not tell anybody.'

'So you did it in secret?'

'I did. And nobody knew, except those of us that lifted it. It's a heavy great box, I can promise you.'

'So why you are revealing this now, to us?'

'Seeing as we took it back, it doesn't matter no more, does it? Chest's back safe where it should be and Mr Lavenham is no more.'

'What is your name, may I ask?'

'Harry Jolliby.'

'Would you be ready to repeat what you have just said in public, Mr Jolliby?'

'I don't mind.'

'Then please come to the Dissenters' Hall on Thursday in the morning.'

I jerked my thumb back to indicate the body of John Lavenham.

'I am enquiring into that. How it happened. Your statement will be of great help.'

\*   \*   \*

'In what precise way will you benefit from Jolliby's evidence?' asked Fidelis after we had deposited the malodorous body at the Dissenters' Hall and the carter had left us. 'Do you imagine he can tell you anything about Lavenham's death?'

'I want to establish just what Lavenham was doing, and how he was doing it here in Ingolside. The removal back and forth of the chest is an important element in that. My finding of the "Whereas" parchments at Lakeside Lodge is another. Once the old documents were taken back to Manor House for him to work on them there, there was a separation of duties. Lavenham read and copied in the room at Manor House, and worked on the blank parchment at Lakeside Lodge. In both cases, it seems the Squire required him to work in secret. But I wonder if the secret was kept. Tree was threatened with death: I wonder if Lavenham was too.'

'You have found no evidence that he was?'

'Not yet. In any case, I want to find out more about the local feeling over the work he was doing.'

'I take it you *are* trying to end up discovering how John Lavenham met his death?'

'You know I am.'

'Well I would say you're taking a long road to get there. And I very much doubt you will, by that route, not by the day after tomorrow.'

'Oh?' I said, a little stiffly. 'Then what route would you suggest?'

'You should be looking for the shortest way – and you will only find that, you know, by understanding what happened in the interval between the destruction of the Three Horns inn and the discovery of his body three days later.'

He spoke in a strangely reserved way, as if hiding something from me. I almost always valued Fidelis's advice, but I sometimes became irritated when he played me like this.

'As you know, Luke, I like to be methodical. In fact, I am nothing if not methodical.'

'Method sometimes takes too long, Titus. Flying quickly by intuition is often the thing. Where do you go now?'

'Being methodical, I shall consult with Furzey again. And you?'

'Being intuitive, I shall visit the brewery, Mr Gillow's premises.'

'Not a social visit, then?'

'A visit born from passing curiosity. Let us meet tomorrow. I shall call at Holloway's house early.'

'Very well,' I said. 'Until tomorrow, early.'

I left him and, having stopped at Mrs Booth's to inform Furzey that I wanted Jolliby on the list of witnesses, I went on towards Holloway's Farm. As I walked I reflected on what I had insisted on to Fidelis – my methodicalness. As any attorney preparing a case does, one must always seek every detail, so that nothing appears missing. One must fill in all the spaces in the brief, so that everything is neat, tidy, complete. Fidelis was not like this. He was quick, impulsive, and mistaken almost as often as he was right. Suddenly I was reminded of John Gay's story of the careful slug and the quick-witted grasshopper. The latter got along much faster but was quite unable to find his way home.

'Lizzy, Lizzy!' I said, hurrying in to my wife, who I found in the Holloways' parlour writing a letter to our girl Matty in Preston. 'I have found another pertinent application of a fable from Gay, to go with your three philosophers. It helps speak of the difference between me and Luke: I am the dull slug – d'you see? – and he is the madcap grasshopper. Have you read that one in Miss Hart's book?'

'I have. But oh! If you are the slug, you are surely the most lovable and handsome of the species.' And she gave me a kiss.

Later, as the air was warm and still, we strolled together along the western shore of the lake. I told her about my discovery that the Manor Chest had travelled to Lakeside Lodge – which we could see across the water – and then back again, and that I could not understand why.

'I think I can guess,' she said.

'Tell me.'

'Consider how we were talking earlier of the difference between yourself and Luke, but then think of the difference between you and this man Lavenham.'

'How is that to the point?'

'At the beginning, Arthur Lumsden was content to let Lavenham

do his work over at Lakeside Lodge – indeed he at first preferred
it as it is well removed from the Manor House. Therefore, he
sent the chest to the Lodge where Lavenham had it at hand for
his work. Only later did the Squire see that having Lavenham at
a distance did not progress the work fast enough. Lavenham
needed close supervision. So Lumsden set aside a room at the
Manor House and sent the carter to fetch the chest back again.'

I took Elizabeth's hand.

'I am sure you are right. So why was Lumsden so secretive
about where John Lavenham was working?'

'I think it is because he didn't want any of his tenants knowing
that the old documents were at a place more easily approached
than the Manor House. He didn't want any of them forcing their
way in and reading their own leases while Lavenham was
consulting them.'

'They could not have read them, surely.'

'Someone else might. Then Squire would no longer be able
to lie about the contents of the leases. He is certainly a man of
very bad character. Did he not once offer a young girl a paper
bag full of sweetmeats to go into a haystack with him?'

'You told me so.'

'It is a good thing she refused for the bag contained nothing
but pieces of gravel, the blackguard.'

We had walked some distance under the green canopy of trees
that lined the path. Now we came to a clearing, with an uninter-
rupted view across the lake and up the steep, dense woodland
on the opposite side. The water's surface was smooth except
where a few water birds quarreled and made ripples and, further
out, a fish here and there came to the surface for a fly. The air
was quiet and the light growing dim when, in a pause between
the birds' chattering, a sound came to our ears from high up in
the far-side woods, an echoing, ululating howl.

And I thought of Quexton's characterization of himself: a lone
wolf.

# SIXTEEN

True to his promise, Luke Fidelis arrived early on Wednesday at Holloway's Farm, just as we were eating breakfast. He was evidently excited.

'I have something to show you, Titus, which is very much to the point.'

'Is that the point which you mentioned yesterday? The one you were aiming for. Have you arrived there?'

'Not quite. However, I have made good progress.'

He put his hand in his pocket and brought out two papers folded to form small packets, one appearing flat and the other a little bulkier. He took up a clean plate, opened the fatter of the two packets and poured from it a heap of little yellow granules, resembling coarse sand, on to the plate. He indicated the granules.

'What do you think this is?'

Elizabeth leaned over to look at them for herself.

'Are they seeds?'

'They are not,' said Fidelis.

'They look like some sort of spice,' I said.

I put my nose down and found they indeed had an indefinable spicy aroma. Then I took a pinch between finger and thumb and rubbed them together to feel the granular texture of the residue.

'Put some on your tongue,' Fidelis said.

I did so. The bitterness of the tiny granules was distinct.

'Is this in connection with your visit to Mr Gillow's brewery?'

'It is.'

'Some part of the hop plant, then?'

'Excellent, Titus. They are the grains that adhere around the ears, or cones as they're called, of the hop fruit and they give much of the flavour to your ale. This has all been explained to me by Mr Gillow when he gave them to me yesterday when I visited him. Now, let's see what is in this second packet.'

He very carefully opened the flatter of the packets and

showed me a very small sample of what looked like the same granules.

'They appear identical,' Elizabeth said.

'I have inspected them through my microscope and, yes, they are identical.'

I asked, 'Can you tell us what is their significance?'

'That lies in where I found this second smaller sample.'

We waited for him to tell us, but he outwaited us and I was driven to say, a little testily, 'Which was, Luke?'

'On the dead man, Titus. I first noticed them outside Lakeside Lodge as Jolliby and I were lifting the corpse on to his cart. I brushed some of it out of his hair, finding it mainly in the back of his head, and then later I came across small amounts more in the seams at the back of his coat which is why I took them to Mr Gillow. You realize what this must mean?'

'I suppose he must have been in contact with hops, perhaps in the brewery's hop store.'

'Yes, but we can be much more precise. Now consider, Titus. Lavenham did not customarily wear a wig.'

'He had two. I have seen them in his room.'

Fidelis smiled patiently.

'Perhaps for his appearances in court, Titus. But these traces were in his natural hair at the back of his head and in his coat, as if he had been lying on a pile of hops.'

'Taking a nap, while drunk?'

Luke shook his head.

'I think not, judging by the state of his shoes.'

'His shoes?'

'There were none of these granules on the soles. John Lavenham did not walk on his own pins into the hop store. I conclude instead that he was carried there and laid down on his back.'

'Perhaps he was hoisted in drunk, and left to sleep it off,' said Elizabeth.

'Either that or he was already a corpse when he was laid down among the hops,' I said.

'I cannot think why anyone would do that,' said Fidelis. 'But I have no time to go into it now. I must go to Mrs Lumsden and poultice her bed sores.'

He left and we went back to our breakfast.

'Whoever took or admitted Lavenham to the hops store must have been part of the brewery,' I said. 'A brewery is not left unlocked at night. A key must have been used to get him in there, or else he was let in by someone who worked there.'

'As a dead body?' said Elizabeth.

'A murdered body, if so. Why try to conceal a natural death?'

'But who could have murdered him?'

'Someone wrote the note that was delivered to Tree, saying he must leave if he wanted to live. Perhaps Lavenham had a similar note. And whoever wrote that—'

'May be the same who wrote the note you told me about, the one Squire Lumsden got. Fetch both of them down, Titus, so that we may compare the two.'

I brought the anonymous notes down and we laid them side by side on the breakfast table. Both were written on nondescript paper such as might have been torn out of a notebook. The handwriting was not unlike – painfully formed letters, not linked with those before and after but each scribed individually.

'The writer is either barely literate, or pretending to be,' Elizabeth said.

After breakfast we parted. Elizabeth was engaged to take a drive with Miss Hart, while I had final preparations to make for the next day's inquest. It was of prime importance to manage the examination of witnesses and therefore I reviewed Furzey's list and wrote the names out again in the order I would call them. It had occurred to me before I began this exercise that the list would now have to include yet another new witness, Oswald Gillow, who I had previously had in mind as jury foreman. Now his name would have to shift across from the list of the jurors to that of the witnesses. I then remembered with a little distaste the name of the alternative juror: Curly Berry, the landlord of the Dog and Drum inn and persistent purveyor of pickled eggs.

My next task was to bundle all the documents in the case together. I had Quexton's transcription of the ancient lease of Brabner's Farm. I had the letter to Lavenham from his woman friend in London and the affidavit collected by Furzey from the clerk of Lord Lonsdale in Preston, and the threatening anonymous

notes posted at Manor House and Lakeside Lodge. I also had
the plain sheets of parchment I had collected from Lavenham's
room, together with the one sheet that had been written on and
then abandoned.

Leaving Holloway's Farm, I walked along Street to find Furzey
and we sat together a long time, going through the case, the
witnesses and the written evidence. We dined with Mrs Booth
and later walked up to the Dissenters' Hall to make sure it had
been made ready. We found the room arranged just as I had
planned, with Ben Bennett sitting there on the raised platform
in what during the proceedings would be my chair. He was
surveying the room, as if trying out the role of Coroner for
himself and, taking a view of him in this role from the floor, I
was satisfied with how everything looked. A great many of my
hearings took place at country inns, where space was cramped
and the formal dignities such as one hoped to enjoy on these
occasions were difficult to maintain, with a higher risk of disorder,
contempt for the proceedings and even fights between members
of the attending public. In the Dissenters' Hall, dignity inhered
of itself, exactly as it should.

As Elizabeth and I supped that evening with Mr Holloway and
his niece, the farmer asked me to explain the whole inquest
process. I told how the jury must inspect the corpse, and then
hear how it was found. If there is any further evidence – documents, eye-witness reports and any hearsay evidence that I could
accept as pertinent – this is then examined or heard. Finally, the
jurors must deliberate together, if necessary advised or assisted
by myself, and agree a finding of fact which they deliver as a
verdict.

'But what is the use of it?' said Holloway. 'The man is dead.
Nothing can bring him back. Surely he should be buried and
done with and we would not have all the expense laid at the door
of the parish, nor the peace of this place disturbed.'

'Don't be so hasty, Mr Holloway,' I said. 'There are two
considerations which, taken together, make the inquest essential.
One is a material question: has a murder been committed? If so
and the culprit is named, then he (or she as it sometimes is) must
in the end forfeit not only their life but everything they own. The

title Coroner is sometimes called Crowner. It means I am the crown's representative, charged with determining whether there has been a murder, and whether a murderer's property is owed to the King.'

'Ha-ha!' laughed Holloway. 'I see, then, you are more or less a tax assessor, Mr Cragg.'

'My father, who was Coroner before me, sometimes said that. But the confiscation of property is also a terrible part of the punishment. In addition to the gallows there is the prospect of his family, who may be quite innocent, being thrown into destitution by having all their goods confiscated.'

Elizabeth, sitting beside me, put a hand on my arm. It was Miss Hart, though, who broke the silence.

'Mr Cragg, you said there was a second consideration. What is that?'

'It is quite simply serving the truth, Miss Hart, and with the truth, justice. When a person is found unexpectedly to have died, and there being no honest witnesses, it's necessary to know as exactly as possible what occurred. Now, if there has been wickedness behind it, then of course the wicked must be caught and justly punished. But equally, when wickedness is absent, this too must be asserted, so that rumour, false accusations and malicious gossip are suppressed.'

'It is very true,' said Miss Hart. 'Those things are great disturbers of harmony in families and between neighbours.'

She rose from her chair.

'And speaking of harmony, I have been learning some new pieces of music which I would enjoy playing for you. Shall we go through to the music parlour without more ado? I should not mind if you gentlemen wish to puff your pipes while you listen.'

The music was even better than on previous evenings and the performer's dispensation with regard to our smoking made for an agreeable after-dinner hour.

It must have been while we were enjoying this musical interlude at Mr Holloway's house that a phaeton pulled up at the Dog and Drum inn. Its driver and sole occupant was a woman who, having jumped down from the box, strode into Mr Curly Berry's premises and demanded food and accommodation for the night. Faced with a bare offer of pickled eggs, bread and cheese, she refused the food and insisted on joining the Berrys at their own table. Here she ate heartily of soup and broiled lake trout after which, being tired, she asked to be taken to her bedchamber. The damp and chilly room offered to her had no appeal so she demanded in imperious tones that Berry show her his own quarters. On seeing these she declared them satisfactory to her needs and waited while Berry and his wife collected their night clothing and scuttled out, leaving the guest in possession of their marital bedroom.

The woman's name was Mrs Françoise Siran du Bressac. I knew nothing of her arrival or of her significance until my inquest was in session, the next morning.

# SEVENTEEN

At half past eight, after an early breakfast, I walked once more with Elizabeth to take some fresh air down beside the lake. The hearing was due to begin at ten o'clock, giving us time to stroll along the western path. As the sun broke through, the dark lake water sparkled beside us. Ducks and ducklings paddled about, upending themselves from time to time to pluck food from the bed of the lake. A heron flapped attentively from one peninsula to the next. Further out on the deeper water fisher boats bobbed in the light breeze.

'Hey! What are those two doing?' asked Elizabeth, pointing further along the path. 'Not dancing, surely.'

About two hundred yards ahead of us the path was overshadowed by a great elm. Beneath it, Elizabeth had seen the same two figures as I had noticed on my first morning in Ingolside. Now, as then, they had laid their hats on the ground and were dodging around each other on their toes, while pummeling the air between them.

'You are quite right, they are not dancing,' I said. 'They are fighting, or rather sparring. You have heard about the great boxing bout to be held on Saturday?'

'Only a little. Miss Hart is excited, I think, though she will not admit it. And Mr Holloway too, in his bluff way.'

'The big man is one of the fighters, Johnson by name. The other is Quexton, his trainer.'

'Quexton? You told me he came here to prevent enclosures.'

'He leads a double life. He is partly the agitator against the removal of popular custom and right, and partly a boxer's trainer. Quexton in my opinion is the real reason why John Lavenham came here.'

'Because?'

'Remember you said the tenants might find someone to read their leases if they could get their hands on them? That is Quexton. His reputation came before him and Lumsden knew he was a man capable of reading old documents and exposing his lies.'

'So he sent for an experienced forger to create new documents.'

'Yes.'

'It is very opportune that a prize fight was to be staged here, wasn't it? From Quexton's point of view.'

'I suppose he arranged for Charlie Johnson to meet the Ripon fighter as part of his scheme. It gives him a pretext for being here.'

'Well, I am glad Johnson is training hard. From his name, his opponent's strength must be alarming. The Rockbreaker.'

'I have had a word with Johnson,' I said. 'He claims he can outmatch the Rockbreaker. And you know it is just a name. He is called that not because he can break rocks with his fists, but only to strike awe.'

Elizabeth laughed.

'I know that, Titus. In my opinion it is only cockfighting but bigger, and without the feathers.'

We drew nearer to the two men. Seeing us approach, Quexton spoke a word to the fighter and, breaking away, approached us. He used his neckerchief to mop the sweat from his face.

'Mr Cragg,' he said. 'I am happy to see you.'

His eye glanced at Elizabeth, betraying the surprised admiration that was usual in men looking on her for the first time.

'This is my wife, Elizabeth,' I said. 'Elizabeth, Mr Quexton.'

Quexton gave her a deep bow.

'I am charmed.'

'I have heard marvelous good things of you, Sir,' she said. 'That you are a friend to the poor and go around righting their wrongs wherever you find them.'

'I try. I do not always succeed.'

'You must make many friends.'

'Some, and some enemies too.'

'Oh, I suppose that must be so. It is dangerous to deal with people of evil intent, for they may turn that intent on you. Perhaps you are even subject to violent intimidation, Mr Quexton?'

'Yes, the threat of it from time to time.'

Quexton smiled modestly, as if he were admitting reluctantly

to some quality or talent in himself. He nodded in the direction
of the prizefighter, now propped up against the tree and breathing
deeply.

'I am lucky in having the services of a stout bodyguard in Mr
Johnson over there,' said Quexton. 'He is professionally qualified
to answer violence with the same, if called upon. But speaking
of violence, Mr Cragg, you inquest the death of John Lavenham
this morning, I think.'

'We do,' I said.

'There is much interest in it locally.'

'So I understand. Will you be there?'

'I would not miss such a spectacle for worlds. Can we expect
to be shocked by the outcome?'

'I don't know the outcome. No one does, any more than anyone
knows who will win your fight.'

'On the balance of probability, we will win, though it may be
a fight of many rounds before Charlie comes out on top.'

'One may bet on your man, then?'

'One may.'

'Do you bet on him yourself?'

'I do not, Sir. I bet on his opponent.'

This astonished me. The bet seemed a betrayal of everything
Quexton and Johnson had been working so hard to achieve.

'You have just told me Mr Johnson will probably win. Are
you not sure of it after all?'

Quexton laughed.

'It is impossible to calculate exactly. Therefore we hedge
against defeat and in that way we are able to feed and clothe
ourselves. You may call it betrayal; I call it pragmatic.'

When we arrived at the Dissenters' Hall, the public were already
taking their places, or at least putting their hats down. Elizabeth
spotted Miss Hart who was keeping her a seat. On the platform
Furzey was ready in his chair at the right side of mine, counting
the jurymen one by one as they arrived. We proceeded to swear
in each of them, of whom the last was Curly Berry who was
now serving in Mr Gillow's place.

Once they were all sworn, the landlord of the Dog and Drum
began speaking with great animation to his fellow jurors,

convincing them of his superior knowledge of the law informed
by the many times he had, as innkeeper, played host to lawyers,
and in one case a judge, and conversed with them on matters of
legal procedure. The result, when I came to ask them to nominate
a foreman, was that they gave me Curly Berry's name.

'Berry is a very unlikeable person,' I said quietly to Furzey.

'Certainly he is.'

'And I don't appreciate the way he has inserted himself into
the jury. He previously harassed me to include him and I gave
him the reserve seat as a sop. He is now foreman of the panel.
How did this happen?'

Furzey was no lover of country juries, regarding them all as
bumpkins of low intelligence and malign intent.

'We must watch him,' he muttered in my ear. 'But it's too late
to remove him now.'

With a sigh of resignation, I rang my bell and announced we
would inspect the corpse in question, which lay waiting for us
in the adjoining room.

The naked remains of John Lavenham were by this point in
a deplorable condition. Quite apart from the smell, one could
see the decay in the ghastly hue and the spongy damp texture of
his flesh. In consideration of this I gave the men a very rapid
tour of what lay on the table before us, indicating the neck wound
and the hole in his chest, and explaining how the sewn-up inci-
sion from belly button to breastbone had come about in the course
of Dr Fidelis's investigation.

Two of the jurors vomited into the bucket that Furzey had, as
usual, set in the corner of the room for the very purpose. Curly
Berry wrinkled his nose and said, 'As Scripture sayeth, let the
gorge of the righteous rise and discharge itself in the face of
unrighteousness.'

Biblical quotations are in my eyes the lowest form of wisdom
as they pre-empt reasoned discussion.

'I suppose you can give chapter and verse, Mr Berry,' I said.

This wiped the smirk off Berry's visage as he could not do
so. I then gave the men the instructions – sententious instructions,
but necessary ones – that I give privately to any jury led by men
of Curly Berry's type.

'These proceedings are not for jollity. Nor is there room in them for prejudice. We decide what we decide soberly and on the evidence alone, or rather on the facts as we judge them to be, having heard the evidence.'

The jurors nodded like automata. I did not feel confident that they knew the difference between judgement and prejudice, but this was not the time to try to enlighten them. I led the way back into the hall and, as the jury settled into their places, rang my bell again. I was about to call the body's first finder to come to the witness chair when a stir rippled around the hall. This was caused by the arrival of a female stranger, wearing a brocaded riding dress and a hat from which a profusion of feathers sprouted. She spotted a bench less fully occupied than most and, raising the riding whip she carried, pointed at it imperiously. The people shifted along to give her room and she sat.

When the room had settled I said, 'I call Charles Bowden, being the first finder of the deceased.'

The gamekeeper was dressed up in Sunday best clothes for the occasion, with a starched stock visibly constricting his neck. This made the weathered ruddiness of his features more obvious, but also increased his evident discomfort at the prospect of being questioned in public, on an unfamiliar stage. I outlined to him and the court all the events that had occurred on the night Lavenham was found dead, and asked him to tell us what his role had been. Looking a little more at ease, he cleared his throat.

'The Squire asked us to walk up and see if Street was quiet.'

'When was this?'

'About fifteen minutes after they'd all gone from the front of the Manor House, the mob of them.'

'What did you find?'

Bowden stuck a finger behind his stock and jiggled it.

'There was nobody about in Street. Unusually empty, it was.'

'And when you got to the Market Place, what did you see?'

'He were lying on the steps, John Lavenham that is. We reckoned he was drunk. Then Martin put a hand on his shoulder, to pull him up maybe, and he rolled over and down the steps until he was spread out on his back. We knew he was dead then. There was blood on his shirt, and on his back and a hole in his chest.'

'What did you do?'

'I went and fetched Squire and he came out with Mr Tree and

had Jolliby's cart brought up. They took the body away to
Lakeside Lodge where John Lavenham was living – when he
was living, if you take my meaning. It was the last I saw of it.'

'Thank you, Mr Bowden. Please stay in the room in case I
need you again. I now call Dr Fidelis.'

Fidelis came forward and, listened to intently by the whole
room, described the condition of Lavenham's body and clothing.
After he had detailed the chest wound, I said, 'And when you
opened him, did you find a bullet?'

'I did.'

'Was it this bullet?'

I had the bullet in a paper envelope, which I unfolded. I handed
the bullet to Furzey who passed it in turn to Fidelis.

'Yes, I believe this is the one,' he said. 'It had struck a spinal
bone and had become deformed in just this way.'

'Will you show the bullet to the jury, Mr Furzey, if you please?'

The bullet went from hand to hand along the bench and I
continued my questioning.

'Can you tell us anything about the firing of this bullet?'

'It passed through the right ventricle of the heart and shattered
the spinal column. I believe it was fired at extremely close range.'

'Why is that?'

'Because there appeared to be some residue of burned powder
around the wound. This would have been emitted from the gun
barrel at the same time as the bullet.'

'If he was cleaning a pistol and it accidentally discharged, as
some have been saying, that would certainly have been at point-
blank range.'

'Yes, if he were doing that. But I know he wasn't.'

'How do you know?'

'Because he was already dead when he was shot. A dead man
cannot clean a pistol.'

I asked him to be more specific and he told the court what he
had earlier told me: if Lavenham had been shot while his heart
was beating, the wound would have produced an enormous gush
of blood. There was no evidence for this inside the body, or on
his clothing, and only doubtful residual evidence around the site
where he was discovered.

'He might have died somewhere else,' I pointed out.

'Wherever it was, his clothes would still have been soaked in gore. I found that they were only soiled with blood rather than saturated in it.'

'Very well, let us turn to his clothing, because you found something in them that you believe to be significant, did you not?'

'Yes.'

He told the court about the dust from the hop cones that he had found adhering to Lavenham's clothes though not to his shoes.

'What conclusion do you draw?'

'That Mr Lavenham, or his corpse, had lain among hop cones.'

I looked out and caught sight of Oswald Gillow. He was whispering urgently to one sitting beside him, who by his appearance might have been his brother.

'If we must rule out the gun shot as the cause of John Lavenham's death, let us address again the most important matter before us. How and when exactly did he die? Was it on the same day? The day before? The *week* before? Can you give us an estimation of the time of his death?'

'He was found dead on the evening of Saturday the thirtieth of April,' Fidelis stated. 'And I can say with some certainty that he was alive seventy-two hours earlier.'

'And how do you arrive at that statement?'

'Because the evening of Wednesday the twenty-seventh was when the fire at the Three Horns inn took place.'

'Please explain, Doctor.'

'I have since seen patients here in Ingolside suffering from the effects of that disastrous fire – mainly coughing, wheezing and shortness of breath – and I have examined their expectorations which my microscope revealed contained much soot. Then, having taken samples of mucus from Mr Lavenham's lungs, I microscopically inspected these in the same way.'

'You told me of an experiment you would perform. Is this it?'

'Yes.'

'And what did it reveal?'

'That the dead man's phlegm was polluted with the very same sooty deposits as my patients. I concluded that he had been inside the inn when the fire was burning, and that he had breathed in the smoke, as the patients I mentioned had also done. I must add that it is more than possible that Mr Lavenham, in breathing in the smoke, was in fact breathing his last. To inhale fire smoke is often fatal.'

'Yet you cannot say for certain that John Lavenham died in this way, by breathing smoke?'

'No. As I mentioned, I have seen several people as patients who were in the inn at the time, some of whom are present in this room, and they are still breathing, although with difficulty.'

A few of the public laughed.

'Dr Fidelis,' I said, 'does anything else about the state of the corpse speak of when the death occurred?'

'As I have said, we know he died some time between the twenty-seventh and the thirtieth of last month. When I examined the body, two weeks after its discovery, it was in a state consistent with that. The flesh had begun to stink and to attract clouds of flies, its tinge showed signs of darkening and there were the first indications of bloating. Yet the hair was still firmly in place and there was as yet no beginning of liquefaction in the body's organs.'

A sudden high-pitched sob pierced the air and all turned to look around the hall for its origin. It came from the stranger who had earlier made such a dramatic entrance. I saw that she was pressing a handkerchief against her face and shaking somewhat. It was clear that Fidelis had completed his evidence so I excused him and stood. As the people began to chatter and speculate about the woman, I jumped from the platform and walked along the side of the hall until I stood beside her. I knelt on one knee to be at her level and said in a low voice, 'Madam, they are all wondering who you are, and I myself am wondering if you can assist this enquiry.'

She raised her face from the handkerchief to look at me and whispered with a distinctly French inflection, 'May we speak privately, Sir?'

# EIGHTEEN

The only room in the building, aside from the large one we were in, was where John Lavenham's remains were lying. So, having told the company that there would be a fifteen-minute delay, I took the foreign woman into the open air. We crossed over to the Green, which was encircled by a path, and set off to walk around it. She had by now regained her composure and, far from being woebegone as she had earlier seemed, became forthright and voluble in her speech.

'Perhaps you will begin by telling me your name and where you are come from.'

'My name is Françoise Siran du Bressac. I have come here from London.'

'From your speech and your name, I think you are French.'

'Yes. But I have been in England for fourteen years. I came with my husband the Comte, to avoid his imprisonment in the Bastille. He had insulted the King.'

'I see. It was a fortunate escape. I have heard tell of what it is like for prisoners in the Bastille. So, since then, you have lived in London?'

'We have, Sir. The Comte fell into drunkenness and debt, then left me to live with a trollop in the part of London called Alsatia. Do you know it?'

'A sanctuary where debtors go to avoid being arrested, is it not?'

'That's exactly the reason why the Comte my husband lives there. He left me with hardly a penny.'

'But you don't reside there yourself?'

'My God, no. It is all filth and poverty and everywhere dangerous. I live in the Covent Garden.'

'What is your connection with the dead man whose death we are enquiring into?'

'I lived with him. Nine days ago I had a letter in London from a man whose name I did not recognize: Martin Mansfield. He wrote that John had died in this place in Lancashire and asked if there were any close relations who should know of this. I decided to find everything out for myself since I do not have faith in other people to act on my behalf. It has been a long and wearisome journey.'

'I have reason to think that Mr Lavenham's death was a consequence of the work he came here to do. My task is to find out more – to know just how and why he died, which is still a mystery. Therefore I am holding a trial, called an inquest, to see if we can get at the truth.'

She turned to me with fierce flashing eyes.

'That is what *I* want! That is why I have come.'

'Then perhaps we can assist each other, Madame du Bressac. Will you come back inside and speak to the inquest? Will you tell everything about Mr Lavenham to help us to know him? I think that may help us in our search for the truth behind his destruction.'

'Yes, Sir,' she said in a strong voice. 'I will speak about him.'

I took her back into the hall and told her to wait until I had called her. Then I returned to my seat and told Furzey that there was to be a new witness. He sighed and put the witness list in front of me.

'In that case will you kindly insert her name here?'

When I had done this clerkly task, I rang the bell and asked Madame du Bressac to take the chair. Her appearance, in full view of everybody for the first time, caused a noticeable stir and a flurry of talk among the people. It was not because she was so handsome – though that was a fact – but her strength, her air of command, made the audience lean forward in expectation of some kind of display.

I swore her in and asked if she and John Lavenham were husband and wife.

'Certainly not,' she said. 'I have already a husband. Mr Lavenham was my protector, on whatsoever occasion in which I could not protect myself.'

This resulted in a new round of speculative whispering in the audience.

'And when did you meet Mr Lavenham?'

'I have known him for three or four years. He made it possible to open a basket-making shop in Covent Garden. He is my partner in the enterprise as well as my lover.'

Another wave of comment – scandalized comment – murmured around the room.

'How did Mr Lavenham make his living in London during the time you knew him?'

'In any way he could. He was skillful at reading very old papers and parchments. He sold his services to attorneys and people like that who needed to understand certain old contracts or charters, but who lacked the skill to read for themselves.'

'Do you know why Mr Lavenham came here to Ingolside?'

'Only that he was invited to come and read many old legal papers. A letter came from someone. It invited him to travel to this place as his knack to read was required here.'

'Who wrote this letter?'

'A man named Mansfield. I think a powerful man.'

'Did Lavenham say anything more to you about the nature of the work Mansfield asked him to do here?'

'No. But John expected it would be cozening work.'

'Did you say "cozening work"?'

'Yes. A bit of pulling wool over eyes, to tell you his own words. He did not say it would be dangerous, or that he might die doing it, however.'

'Was Mr Lavenham an honest man?'

She raised her perfectly shaped eyebrows.

'I do not know what you mean, Sir?'

'Did he break the law?'

She shrugged.

'To break the law is normal. All people break the law if they can gain something by it and not get caught.'

This provoked renewed murmuring. The witness looked around, coolly meeting people's eyes, challenging their disapproval.

'Perhaps that is more true in London than it is here,' I said. 'But what I am asking more specifically is this: did Mr Lavenham do more than read old documents? Did he perhaps also sometimes *write* them?'

'He was highly skillful in writing them. He could make a replica of any old manuscripts you want.'

'Did he make forgeries ever?'

'He was accused but he never was caught doing that. Never. He told me for forgery a man can be hanged. He did not wish to be hanged.'

'Thank you, Madame du Bressac. You have been very helpful to this inquest. You may return to your place.'

Telling the court that it was time to learn more of John Lavenham's work, I called the carter Jolliby to give evidence, which he did quite readily and easily.

'Aye, I did transport the Manor Chest from Manor House to Lakeside Lodge. I did it at night so nobody'd see. I was told to do this because Squire didn't want anybody bothering him with wanting to look at any of the documents for themselves. Then Squire told me to go back and fetch the chest again back to Manor House. A couple of weeks later that was. I was told Mr Lavenham had got a room there for his work. Copying he told me when he was riding up along with me.'

Squire Lumsden, whose turn came next, was, much as expected, one of those blustering, half-scorning witnesses. He said, in his replies to my questions, 'I engaged John Lavenham as a reader and a copier. Our country, our nation, demands improvement. I am determined to raise the arable and dairy yields of the farmers here, and also to newly produce meat for the market. I therefore must replace many of the old feudal relations between myself and my tenants so that I can weed out the unproductive, unimproved tenancies. That is what I am striving for. No, Sir, improvement doesn't mean altering the terms of any leases and charters in the Manorial Chest. I deny that and I will fight any man who gainsays me.'

After this performance it was time to call Martin Mansfield to the chair. He came up looking wary. He had heard enough from the mouth of Madame du Bressac to sense danger, and now after Lumsden's evidence he had got a sense of where my questions might lie. I noticed as he approached the chair his eyes were flicking birdlike, this way and that.

Mansfield's first tactic was to launch questions at me, rather than the other way around.

'All these matters about leases and heriot,' he said. 'Where is the relevance? Why do you go so far beyond your brief, Sir?'

'I shall decide the limits of my brief, Mr Mansfield.'

'What right have you to be pushing your nose into the affairs of the manor?'

'Because I am the Coroner, a representative of the King, conducting a serious enquiry.'

Mansfield flushed with anger.

'It is shameful. You come here uninvited and—'

'Mr Mansfield.'

'You put all in a stir with your questions about what is only an accident with a pistol. What are you playing at?'

'Mr Mansfield,' I repeated, 'we have already established there was no accident with a pistol. Now, I will ask the questions, if you please. Did you invite John Lavenham to come to Ingolside by letter, as we have just heard described?'

He looked scowling up and down the room, until his eye rested on the comfortable high-backed chair that had been brought in particularly, and on Squire Lumsden who occupied it. I thought the Squire's hand moved a fraction, upon which I saw Mansfield's face relax. Hereafter he became a little more pliant.

'Yes, I did,' he said.

'Would you tell us how you described the work that you hoped Mr Lavenham would be doing here?'

Mansfield was thinking, calculating.

'I don't remember exactly how I put it,' he said after a moment. 'If you could show the letter to me, that would assist my memory.'

It was a clever reply, like a defensive move at chess. Mansfield didn't know if the letter he'd written still existed. Madame du Bressac might well have found it in London and brought it with her; she might indeed have handed it to me. Either way Mansfield needed to know if there was any prospect of the letter being produced in evidence.

'I must ask you to rely on your own recollection, if you please, Mr Mansfield.'

He screwed up his face, as if making an intense effort to remember.

'I wrote that we were putting the old documents of the manor in order, and that Mr Lavenham's name had been recommended to us as someone who could assist in the task. Or something like.'

'Did you mention that he might be required to write documents?'

'I . . . No, to the best of my recollection, no.'

'But in fact that is what you wanted him to do, isn't it? To copy certain papers, or parchments.'

'Oh! Yes, to make transcripts. Yes, of course we did, if that is what you mean.'

'Well, you know, I don't just mean transcripts, or copies. Did you invite John Lavenham to come to Ingolside to create any *new* ancient documents? I mean counterfeits, Sir. I mean documents which would, as we have heard Lavenham himself once put it, pull wool over eyes.'

This mention of counterfeiting gave the audience fresh cause to prick up their ears. Everyone knew that counterfeiting was among the most serious of crimes.

'No, that is not true. That was Lavenham's fantasy.'

'So you are telling me Mr Lavenham did not produce any false documents while living here in Ingolside.'

'If he did, I never asked him to, and I never saw such a document.'

'What about the lease on Moorhouse's Farm?'

Mansfield, who had had his eyes fixed mostly at the floor, now looked sharply up at me.

'What do you suggest by that question?'

'Did you accurately describe to Thomas Moorhouse the terms of his lease? That is what I want to know.'

Mansfield mumbled something indistinct.

'Speak up,' I said.

'I don't . . . I don't know. I couldn't read the old script very well. No one here could. It is why we employed Mr Lavenham.'

'Did you know at the time that he had been suspected in London of fraud, and of passing false documents?'

'No.'

'Do you know why he had blank parchment sheets at his disposal, and old-fashioned reed pens as well as quills?'

'No, I don't.'

'I see.'

This statement by me – 'I see' – commonly has many meanings, but when used by an interrogator it carries one prime sense.

It means not 'I see what you are saying', but 'I see what you are *not* saying' and is useful when trying to unnerve the person under question. I make no apology for this. In a legal setting it is the questioner's task to get at the truth.

I heard the church clock striking twelve. I picked up my watch from the table before me to confirm the time. I said, 'I think we might all benefit from a pause in these proceedings, in order for those who wish it to have a bit of refreshment.'

The jury certainly wished it, exchanging glances and nudging each other in anticipation of food and drink. I rang my hand bell.

'We shall have a recess of one hour.'

# NINETEEN

I led the jury out into the open air, which was bright now with sunshine and the warmth and cheer of early May. They went ahead of me, hurrying across the road to the Dog and Drum, their minds filled with thoughts not on a man's rotting body lying on a table, nor of parchment, heriot, gunshots and hop cones, but on ale, bread and cheese and perhaps also, if they were familiar with Mr Berry's table, on pickled eggs.

Luke had arranged that I, with Elizabeth and Furzey, would eat at Mrs Booth's. Spears of asparagus had been got — I presumed by Luke Fidelis — and a ham boiled with caper sauce and many trimmings. At the end, when we had all complimented Helen Booth on her food, I turned the conversation to the drink.

'This ale is excellent, is it not? But what do we know about the man who brewed it? Mr Gillow seems a law-abiding, prosperous and hard-working person. Did he know that Lavenham's body lay in his hop store at some time after his death? I will have to examine him on that point.'

'I find Gillow amiable,' said Fidelis. 'When I showed him the tiny grains I found in Lavenham's clothing, he readily confirmed what they were.'

'Did you tell him why you were interested?'

'No. I didn't tell him where I got them.'

'Do you think he suspected?'

'I have no idea.'

'What about the man himself? Is my summary of his character accurate, Helen?'

'I know him only as a neighbour, a fellow villager. He is regarded as a devoted husband to his wife, who is sister to Ben Bennett's wife. The two couples were somewhat estranged, though, since Bennett and his wife fell under the spell of John Wesley and became stringently opposed to ale-bibbing. Irrespective of that, Gillow appears to be an honest dealer.'

Fidelis lifted his ale jar.

'And an excellent brewer. But how did the dead body of Lavenham come to lie in his premises? We have been thinking it was possible Lavenham died because the farmers hated him and his work here. Gillow is not a farmer and it seems unlikely he had a grudge against Lavenham on the same score.'

'Mrs Gillow might have, though,' said Mrs Booth.

'Mrs Gillow?' I said. 'How's that?'

'Gillow's wife is a Brabner, sister of the evicted farmer. She had great cause to resent the treatment of her brother's family.'

'And Gillow is devoted to his wife?'

'As I said, famously.'

'Good,' I said. 'Very good. Then perhaps her cause became his cause also. At last, then, there's a chink of light in the darkness, and a new hypothesis.'

I did not go straight back to the hall, but deviated via St Silas church. I needed to widen the chink of light Helen Booth had opened. My hypothesis – as my more intelligent readers will have already guessed – was that with Lavenham's body at hand in the hop store, Gillow or his wife had attached the note to it, before displaying it in the Market Place. But without the note itself this conjecture would be hard to prove. Still, I had an idea for how I could find it.

In the church, as I'd hoped, I found Mr Cumberledge. He was humming to himself while putting hymn books out for Evensong. What I wanted to ask him couldn't damage Mr Cumberledge himself and would therefore with luck get an answer.

'You did not attend the inquest we have been having this morning, Sir,' I said when we had exchanged polite greetings.

'Well, you know, it would not be right for me to go into the assembly room of the Dissenters, even for a secular event. Have you reached a conclusion by now on the matter?'

'Not yet, but I think we are close. I have a question for you, however. You told me that on the night of the riot you came up behind Martin Mansfield and Gamekeeper Bowden in the Market Place, just after they had found John Lavenham's body. I wanted to ask you about the paper that was on the body. It seems to have disappeared.'

It was a shot at a closed door. Who could tell if anything lay

behind it? If anyone, the Rector could. I waited while he looked
up towards the roof. What was he thinking? He could not know
but perhaps he was trying to work out how I had heard about
this supposed paper, or who had told me of it. But then I realized
that the Rector was not calculating at all. He was simply trying
to remember.

'Oh yes,' he said at last. 'I do recall it now. The paper. How
remiss of me. It was pinned to his coat just over the heart. I took
it off, as I was curious about it. I put it into my pocket, I believe.'

'And have you still got this paper?'

'Oh, I . . .'

He thrust his hand into the left-hand pocket of his coat, drew
it out and immediately explored the right-hand pocket. He then
patted his coat and tried the inside pockets.

'I am sorry, Mr Cragg, it appears I do not.'

'Perhaps you were wearing a different coat?'

'Ah! Yes, perhaps I was. Mrs Cumberledge will know.'

'Would you be so kind as to go with me into the Rectory that
we may look in your other coats?'

As my father had counseled when I inherited his job, there is
nothing worse for an inquest than a drunken jury. A mildly
inebriated one is bearable – indeed almost inevitable as you
wouldn't find many a man willing to give up a day's work without
the offer of food and drink at dinner time. On the other hand,
drinkers often come in strong when the ale's free, so that the
timing of the dinner-time recess is a delicate matter. Too short,
and they return unsatisfied and uncooperative. Too long and
they're half-seas-over. As we now gathered again in the Dissenters'
Hall, I scrutinized the jurymen. Most had taken a drink at the
Dog and Drum, but were only mildly bousy.

I rang the hand bell and beckoned Martin Mansfield back into
the witness chair. The bailiff came forward wearing a face that
registered something between resignation and resentment.

'To continue,' I said, 'we must now turn fully to the cause of
our being here: Mr Lavenham's death. Did you with Mr Arthur
Lumsden and Charles Bowden confront the crowd of villagers
on the night of Saturday the thirtieth of April, when Mr Lumsden
read them the Riot Act?'

He confirmed it.

'And did you see John Lavenham in the crowd?'

'No.'

'You were armed with guns, I believe. Sporting guns from the gun room at the manor, were they not?'

'Yes.'

'And you had occasion to fire these guns.'

'Guns were fired, yes. In the air.'

'Did you fire your piece?'

Again, Mansfield hesitated. I reckoned he was not so much trying to remember what happened, but what he had earlier told me.

'Yes.'

'When we spoke of this a few days ago, you said you had not fired.'

'I was misremembering. I've got it straight now. What I meant was, I did not fire at the crowd.'

'And the other two, Bowden and Mr Lumsden, did they also fire?'

'Yes. But if you're trying to make out that any of us caused the gunshot wound in Lavenham's chest, the one the doctor was talking about, then we couldn't have. We all three fired into the sky.'

'So what happened after the mob dispersed?'

'After some time, when things seemed to have become quiet, Squire told myself and Bowden to reload and walk up Street. He wanted to make sure the people had really gone away to their homes.'

'What happened when you reached Market Place?'

'It was deserted except for a man sitting on the steps of the stone cross. He was propped against its foot. Bowden went ahead of me and saw it was John Lavenham. I reached the place just as he was touching Lavenham, who immediately fell down sideways. We saw then that he was dead.'

'What did you do?'

'Bowden went to fetch Mr Lumsden, who when he came gave directions for the body to be taken to Lakeside Lodge where Lavenham had been living.'

'Did you reflect on Mr Lavenham's death?'

'Well, I—'

'Do you know, for instance, of anyone who wished Mr Lavenham ill?

'No.'

'Will you look at these?'

I picked up the two anonymous notes, the one sent to the Squire and the other to Wilkin Tree.

'Will you read them out aloud?'

Mansfield read the two anonymous notes and told us that he recognized the longer and more violently expressed note as having been sent to the Squire, but hadn't seen the short note before.

'That one was received by Mr Wilkin Tree at Lakeside Lodge. Do you know if John Lavenham, who also lived at that address, was the target of anything like it?'

'Not that he mentioned to me.'

I took the notes back.

'And do you recognize the hand in which either note is written?'

'No.'

I gave the notes to Furzey who passed them to Curly Berry who read them and passed them down the bench. While the jurymen were each reading, or at least having a look at the notes, I said, 'And was there a similar note on, or rather attached to, John Lavenham's body when you found him?'

Mansfield hesitated, taken aback.

'I . . . don't know. I don't know what you are talking about.'

I took from my pocket a folded piece of paper, the one that I had only minutes earlier received from Mrs Cumberledge in her husband's dressing room at the Rectory.

'I am talking about this.'

I handed the paper to Mansfield. On one side were the printed musical staves with accompanying words. More significantly the back had words written by pen.

'Will you please unfold it and tell us what you see?'

Mansfield's hands were shaking as he opened the paper and held it up to the light.

'It is a hymn entitled "When I Survey the Wondrous Cross". It has the words and music printed on it.'

'Look on the other side, if you please, and read out what is written.'

Mansfield turned the paper and looked it over.

'It's very badly spelled.'

'Read it out as clearly you can, if you please.'

'It says: *Squire: Now you know what may happen when folk make leases and old documents that be not, er, anywise old but . . . but newly made, and lying and all in what they say, just so as you can take the land for yourself and leave us poor folk starving.*'

He handed the note back and I passed it to Furzey who handed it in turn to the jury for their examination. I then asked Furzey to give me the scrap of paper with the pin inserted in it. I held this up in the air for all to see.

'I must tell you,' I said, 'that when Dr Fidelis and I examined the body of John Lavenham, we found this scrap of paper attached with this pin to his coat. As the jury will see as they examine that hymn sheet, a small portion of its upper margin has been torn off. This scrap I am showing you exactly matches that missing portion, so we can be sure that the hymn sheet was attached to the coat of the deceased. Mr Furzey, will you show the torn scrap to the jury so they can verify this?'

While this was going on I excused Mansfield.

'Will the Reverend Cuthbert Cumberledge please come to the chair?'

I had thought beforehand the Rector might be reluctant to give evidence but, once we got started, he seemed rather to relish it. Like most clergyman he enjoyed an audience.

At my request he told how he had come into the Market Place behind Mansfield and Bowden, found the paper on Lavenham's coat and torn it off.

I gestured for Furzey to hand him the paper.

'When did you first see it?' I asked.

'Not until I turned the body over. He was lying on his front when I came up.'

'So you turned the body over?'

'Yes. The gamekeeper had gone away to fetch the Squire. Mansfield was standing back. I can picture him. He was trembling with shock, I can tell you. But I wanted to get a look at the corpse, because I didn't know who it was.'

'And it was then that you saw the paper, as you turned the body on to its back?'

'Yes. It was pinned there, on his coat.'

'And what did you do?'

'I pulled it off.'

'Why did you do that?'

'I suppose I wanted to know what it said. But then people were running up to us and so on, so I put it in my pocket and then, you see, well, I forgot all about it.'

'And did Mansfield see you do this?'

Cumberledge paused, screwing up his eyes.

'He was standing . . . yes, I am picturing it. He was standing a few feet away behind me. Perhaps he didn't see what I did as my back was to him.'

'And you put it in your pocket, you say?'

'Yes.'

'And will you confirm that is the paper?'

'Yes, I believe it is.'

'At the time you took possession, did you see what was on it? Did you see it was a printed hymn?'

'A hymn? No, I don't think I saw that at all, though I see now it has printed music and words on it. But I took no notice of that. What caught my attention was the handwriting on the other side. It appeared remarkably uneducated.'

'Did you read what it said?'

'No. I meant to read it at my leisure.'

'Why didn't you tell anyone about it?'

'I didn't mean not to. That is to say, I *must* have meant to tell about it, but then the whole thing slipped from my mind. I probably imagined I had, you know, in fact given it to Mansfield, or perhaps the Squire himself. My wife will tell you. I am growing forgetful, with my age being what it is.'

'And the printed hymn, Mr Cumberledge. Can you tell us what sort of hymn it is?'

He peered at the paper, his lips moving as he read the title and authorship of the hymn.

'Dear me!' he said, looking up. 'It's entitled "When I Survey the Wondrous Cross". Nothing wrong with that, of course, surveying the cross I mean. But this hymn has the mark of Enthusiasm running through it: thorns, flowing blood, dwelling on vanity and pride. It is all characteristic of Dissent. And look!

I see it's by that notorious dissenter Isaac Watts. So the case is complete.'

'It is not a hymn that is sung in your own church?'

'Good Lord, no! On no account at St Silas. I shudder at the thought. Yet you may probably hear it being sung in this hall, by the Dissenters who come here.'

'I thank you for your testimony, Mr Cumberledge. You may resume your previous place.'

# TWENTY

My watch told me that I should parcel up the evidence within the next hour, or we would not reach a conclusion before the end of the day. I looked over the list of remaining witnesses and asked Thomas Moorhouse to come forward.

I had previously seen Moorhouse only in his own home. Now in public his manner was an enlargement of what he had been there: a man of forceful opinions, with whom one would not enter an argument lightly.

'Mr Moorhouse, if I may enquire,' I said. 'How is your father?'

'He is very poorly, Sir, and not expected to live.'

'And if the sad event of his death should happen, what becomes of your farm?'

'I've been told I have to pay a tax in an amount that I never knew I must pay.'

'Do you mean the tax called heriot?'

'That's the one.'

'It is due when the tenancy changes, am I right?'

'Yes.'

'And did John Lavenham, and then Squire Lumsden's bailiff Martin Mansfield, both visit you to tell you about heriot in case your father died?'

'They did. I've told you this.'

'Will you kindly repeat it for this inquest?'

So Moorhouse recounted the story of how he was informed that the heriot payable when his father died would be the great sum of eight pounds, whereas Moorhouse believed only the traditional sum of six shillings and eightpence would be due. He spoke of the document then shown to him by Mansfield who told him that, by its terms, the Squire anciently had the right to set the rate of heriot himself and that if he chose to charge eight pounds, so be it.

I asked the witness if he himself had read the document, but Moorhouse, although he knew his letters, had not been able to make head nor tail of Mansfield's parchment, being written as it was in the old style.

'And did Mr Mansfield say what would happen if you did not pay the full eight pounds?' I asked.

'He said we would be kicked out, my wife and me, just like Ted Brabner and his family, which is what will happen because truly I can't pay it. If there's any comfort it's that we never got kids of our own, not like Ted.'

'May I ask, Mr Moorhouse, about your religious affiliation?'

'What's that got to do with this?'

'It has to do with the handwritten note we have heard read aloud just now by the bailiff.'

'I still don't follow you.'

'That note refers to leases that have been falsified in order for the control of the land to be returned into the Squire's control, does it not?'

'So it appears. That's got no religion in it that I can see.'

'It was written on the back of a hymn sheet. The hymn is one used by dissenting sects such as the one that meets in this hall.'

'I don't know, except that's what the Rector was saying.'

'Do you attend worship here, Mr Moorhouse, in this hall or meeting house?'

'I have done, yes.'

'And have you sung the hymn "When I Survey the Wondrous Cross"?'

'Yes, I have, but—'

'And is, in fact, the hymn sheet yours, on which you wrote the threatening note on the back of it and pinned it to John Lavenham's corpse? Is it, Mr Moorhouse? And did you?'

I may have put a little extra vehemence into my question. Moorhouse, anyway, was undoubtedly alarmed and his confidence was momentarily shaken.

'Why are you asking me that? No! No, I did nothing of the kind.'

'What about those two other threatening notes, sent anonymously to the Squire and to Mr Wilkin Tree? Did you also write them? You had reason enough to want rid of Tree as well as Lavenham, and you had every reason also to hate Mr Lumsden.'

Moorhouse took a deep breath, gathering himself. He stiffened his neck, straightened his back and looked me directly in the eye.

'No, Coroner, I did not. I have had nothing to do with any of this secret letter writing.'

'I also want to hear about the fire at the Three Horns inn. Were you present when that fire broke out?'

'I was. Along with forty others.'

'What did you do when you saw the flames?'

'I got out into the street double quick.'

'You were unhurt?'

'I was.'

'Did you breathe the smoke?'

'Hardly at all.'

'And did you then assist in helping others who were still inside the burning inn?'

'I did. I wet a cloth and put it around my face, like a few of us, and went back inside. We couldn't stay long for heat and smoke.'

'How many did you bring out?'

'A couple before I had to give it up.'

'Was one of them John Lavenham?'

'No.'

'Did you see him when you went in there?'

'No. The smoke was that thick. It was hard to see past the end of my nose.'

'It's a wonder you found anyone at all, Mr Moorhouse.'

At this moment a boy came into the hall and asked for a word with the witness. I beckoned him to my side.

'Who are you, boy?'

'We're Mr Moorhouse's neighbours on Elm Tree Lane and Mrs Moorhouse has sent me to tell him his dad can't be woken.'

'Are you saying old Moorhouse is dead?' I asked.

The child raised and let drop his shoulders. While listening to the boy I had also heard the audience and jury murmuring amongst themselves. They were speculating about what I had myself already decided: that Moorhouse had a clear motive to threaten the Squire, and as a victim of John Lavenham's deceitful practices, a motive also to kill him. Not only that, he was there at the Three Horns when, as seemed likely, Lavenham died.

I rose from my chair and went over to the witness.

'The boy says your father has been taken very badly. You had better go home. You might take Dr Fidelis with you in case he needs a doctor.'

Thomas Moorhouse got up and hurried away, collecting Luke Fidelis on his way out. I was frustrated. I felt we were on the edge of hearing some conclusive evidence.

Of the witnesses only the Widow Greenhalgh, Wilkin Tree and Oswald Gillow were still to be heard. I called Goody Greenhalgh next, and asked her to tell what happened on the night her inn was destroyed by fire. Many in the room, and some from the jury, already knew what she was saying because they had themselves escaped from the flames on that night. The cause of the fire which nearly took their lives was of no certain cause, but the most likely was that the chimney had caught fire; that John Lavenham had been inside the inn when fire broke out and was fairly raddled by drink; that Mrs Greenhalgh herself was carried to safety by, as she thought but was not sure, Ben Bennett. She ended her evidence by telling the inquest that the handsome Dr Fidelis had given her the best advice of her life in prescribing seawater baths, and that if it had been Ben Bennett that carried her from the fire then he was an angel of heaven and that it should not be held against him that he dissented from the Thirty-Nine Articles of the Church of England and its Book of Common Prayer.

When she had finished, I called for Wilkin Tree to come to the chair. He did not appear. I called him again but Tree was not in the hall and, as no one present knew where he was, I called the next, and last name on the list, that of Oswald Gillow. To my surprise this call too was without answer. I knew that Gillow had been in the hall earlier, but now he had slipped away. The last two witnesses had absented themselves and could not be heard.

'You don't need them, Sir,' said Furzey in my ear, as the whole room buzzed with speculation over where the witnesses were. 'We all know who is guilty by now.'

'Do we?'

'Everyone in Preston shares my opinion that you can be remarkably slow of wit, but even you must see the truth by now.

Thomas Moorhouse murdered Lavenham. He killed him in the fire under cover of the smoke. He himself said no one could see in there. It's as plain as the time on the church clock.'

'The bullet in the chest? Is that plain?'

'We all heard the doctor. It was done later, so it's irrelevant to the murder. It's just a fallaxity. Do your summing up and direct them. You'll get the right verdict.'

'There is no right verdict, man, except the one the jury delivers. I cannot tell them what to find. I can tell them where to look, but they must draw their own conclusion. Else this entire process is meaningless.'

I spent a few minutes collecting my thoughts. Furzey's argument was highly persuasive. We were here to decide how Lavenham died, and not to investigate what happened to the body afterwards, however interesting that may be.

I called the room to order and addressed the jury. I told them to concentrate on the evidence we had heard relating specifically to the death. I went on to assist them by going over in outline what had been said in the room on that subject in the course of the day.

'You may believe that you know from all this what happened to John Lavenham,' I added. 'Or it may still baffle you. There is, for instance, the fact that his body was assaulted after his death, and we are all wondering how that came about. Also that he seems to have lain for quite some time in Mr Gillow's brewery. But maybe that is not our concern. The question that principally matters, and the question you have been brought here to decide, is: has a murder or a manslaughter been committed? If it has not, that is all I need to hear. If it has, and if you know the name of the culprit, tell me. If you do not know the culprit, tell me that. Now, I ask you to confer amongst yourselves and arrive at a just verdict. Do not give me one that just *might* be true. You must be sure of it.'

The twelve men rose from their bench and formed a huddle in the open space behind my chair. Meanwhile, uneasy about my absentee witnesses, I went out into the room and asked if anyone could tell me when Wilkin Tree had left the hall. Someone said it was well before the dinner break. Another stated that Oswald Gillow had gone out after Moorhouse's evidence.

Cornelius Quexton came up to me and took me aside.

'You were hard on poor Moorhouse, Cragg,' he said. 'There are other members of the Dissenters who might have had that hymn sheet.'

'I know there are. But it remains the case that he has the strongest motive to write the warning to Squire Lumsden, and he had very good reason to be angry about the projected agricultural improvements. This convinces my clerk, for one, that he may have murdered Lavenham.'

'And are you convinced of it?'

'No, I am not entirely. Experience has taught me that writers of threatening letters are rarely killers. I put my trust in the doctor's evidence that Lavenham might have died from inhaling smoke.'

'Your doctor friend is a clever fellow and has come near to the truth.'

I had been looking back to where the jury were arguing together, with Curly Berry to the fore in the debate. I turned sharply back to Quexton.

'Are you telling me you know the truth?'

Quexton showed me the palms of his hands.

'I claim no special or particular insight, Cragg. My remark is intuitive.'

At that moment, in the edge of my vision, I saw that someone had burst into the hall, calling out in excitement. Leaving Quexton I hurried over to shush him, saying the jury's discussion must not be disturbed and finding that the new arrival was Daniel, Ben Bennett's nephew. I had previously seen him as an almost silent presence but now he was gabbling. Following him as usual was his mastiff, whose huge doleful eyes provided a passive contrast to his master's animation.

'Henry Moorhouse is dead, he's dead,' he was saying. 'The doctor's said so, and Tommy Moorhouse's got a long, long face and Mrs Moorhouse that's so pretty, any road I think she is, she's crying and howling and all's in a scrow at Moorhouse's.'

The boy's news had moved many of the people in the hall to shake their heads. Not only had old Moorhouse had been well-liked, the probable fate of the younger Moorhouses, which had been well advertised by the Lavenham inquest, was causing both sympathy and outrage.

'It's not right,' I heard someone say.

'They'll be turned out sooner'n a goose egg's coved and cracked,' said another. 'It's gone beyond reason, has this, never mind its unkindliness.'

The spirit that had already brought a crowd of Ingolsiders out before the Manor House was rising up once more. The Squire's name was being muttered. The spirit of revolt was in the air again.

'We should do summat.'

'I'd like to break his head.'

'I'd do worse but he's got the guns, hasn't he?'

'Mr Cragg! Mr Cragg, Sir!'

It was Curly Berry's voice calling me from the front of the hall.

'We've got a verdict for you here.'

I went back to the platform and my chair. Many of those who had been milling around also returned to their seats, while others remained standing, some edging nearer to the front to hear better what would be the outcome of the day's proceedings.

The jurymen were standing in a disorderly knot below me. I told Furzey to disperse them to the jury bench and rang my bell. As the audience's babble receded, I asked the ritual questions of Curly Berry and his men.

'Have you reached a verdict on which you are all agreed?'

'Aye, we have that,' said Berry, and went on in a low voice, 'though it's not the one you wanted.'

I let this go by and said, 'Very well. Take a slip of paper, if you please, from the clerk, write your verdict on it, put your signature and hand it back.'

Berry came to our table, took the printed verdict form from Furzey along with a pen dipped in ink. He laid the slip on the table and bent over it, writing two lines of script and signing his name. He took up the sand shaker, scattered sand across the wet ink, blew it off again and handed the paper to Furzey, who gestured him back to his seat.

I then asked Furzey in the usual form of words to read out the verdict. In any inquest this was Furzey's favourite moment. He swiveled like a guardsman to face the people, cleared his throat once, and again, and holding the paper in front of his face intoned in an unnaturally deep voice: '*Accidental death by reason of suffocation from breathing in smoke from a blazing public house that he was inside of at the time. Signed Curly Berry, Jury Foreman.*'

He then folded the paper once and presented it to me.

'Fools,' he murmured. 'They have it wrong. It was foul play, plain as the face of the church clock.'

'No, Furzey,' I said. 'If anyone understands the form, it should be you. Whatever it was we were thinking beforehand, from this moment Lavenham's death is as they say it is. And by the way your announcement is a success down there.'

I nodded towards the many Ingolsiders present in the hall. There were cheers being raised as well as snatches of song and shouts of 'Victoria!' and 'Go on!' Despite their discontent over the prospective eviction of the Moorhouses, when they heard the verdict most of them made it a cause for celebration.

# TWENTY-ONE

However ignorant or dimwitted they are, and however doubtful their decisions, the jury (as I had just had cause to remind Furzey) is my ultimate master. I can persuade, reason with, cajole, entreat or bully them, but it remains for them to have their way with the truth. It is they who mould it, shape it and declare it, and this I must accept.

In the present case the decision they had handed down was superficially a perfectly good one: I had known for some days that Lavenham probably did die in the fire, and whether this was with or without human help seemed very difficult to determine. Calling it an accident was therefore the safest and easiest choice. But there was a wider view of the process of inquest. Lavenham's body had been mutilated by a gunshot, hidden for some three days and then put out on public display, and when there is evil done in a community, evil of such magnitude and by unknown persons, it is like a boil in the skin, swelling and burning. An inquest can hope to lance such a boil by revealing the whole truth behind a death, but here that hope had been frustrated. The malice of the boil was not drained away.

As the audience went on its way, Furzey and I gathered up the papers and items of evidence and began to get them into order. Meanwhile, Daniel had fetched a broom and, now less agitated, was brushing the floor between the seats, where people had scattered nutshells and fruit pips. Carrying our bundles to the door, we found the dog Limer lying across the threshold. He showed his prodigious teeth at our approach.

'Jesu!' said Furzey. 'I'll go out after you, if you don't mind.'

But Daniel had seen our dilemma. Dropping his besom, he ambled over to us and without any word of command, or no audible one, he had the huge dog lumbering to his feet and out of our way. I thanked both boy and dog, and we went out.

As we walked into Street I was thinking over the exchange I had just had at the hall with Quexton. He was aware that I understood his hatred of enclosures, and of other 'improvements'. Now he had deliberately planted the idea that he knew more of the truth of what happened to Lavenham than I did. He was like a player at cards suggesting he held a Gleek and expected to win the hand. But what strategic reason did he have for doing that? Was it true, or a card player's bluff?

'What do you think of Cornelius Quexton?' I asked Furzey.

'I suspect him of atheism,' Furzey said. 'And of being a bomb maker.'

'To blow up what?'

'Anything you like. But eh, I am glad all's finished and I can go home. This place gives me the shivers.'

'Oh? Why is that?'

'Well, for a start, I haven't heard one jest since I came here.'

We carried our burdens to Mrs Booth's, finding her in front of her house standing in conversation with Elizabeth, Mr Holloway, Miss Hart and Luke Fidelis. Their conversation was on the merits of the inquest verdict. For Fidelis and his landlady it was unsatisfactory, while Holloway and Miss Hart both found it just. Elizabeth asked me what I thought.

'I have a degree of disappointment,' I said. 'It's a reasonable verdict, I know, and a safe one, but . . .'

'You wanted a more revealing decision, Titus,' said Fidelis.

'Of course. I don't have to tell you that there's more to this than a lungful of smoke. However, I should not have allowed Curly Berry to become the manager of the jury. He knows where his advantage lies.'

I told them how on my first visit to the Squire I had met Berry coming away from Sarah Lumsden's room with a bag of money.

'He is her creature,' said Mark Holloway. 'By paying him she makes sure of his loyalty. John Lavenham was working for her son, whose very reasonable project she objects to and will do anything she can to stop. I say it is in her interest to have the unfortunate Lavenham out of the way, but not in her interest to have the whole affair smelling of foul play.'

'She may find it profitable that the only alehouse left in Ingolside is hers,' said Fidelis. 'That would be the case even if Lavenham had not died.'

Mrs Booth said, 'But happen not for long. I have heard that

Squire is already promising to repair and re-open his inn before
the end of the year.'

While she was speaking, Madame du Bressac came up.

'We were talking about the verdict of the jury,' I told her.
'What is your opinion, Madame?'

'It is disappointing, Mr Cragg. I want to know more about it.
An accident, they said. But caused by who? Did someone from
malice light the fire? And who also made the outrage more
complicated?'

'What do you mean by more complicated?' I said.

'Didn't someone shoot a bullet into him after he was dead?
Of course, I can suspect that person wanted to make a demonstration. Even to make people afraid with showing what a shot
in the chest looks like.'

She gave a dry, ironic laugh.

'But it's a terribly quaint thing they have done to my friend.'

'I am surprised you would consider it quaint,' said Mrs Booth.

'*Pas comique, je vous assure*,' said Madame du Bressac. 'I
mean it is cunning, and terrible too. But to talk about this is not
the reason I have come. Mr Cragg, please tell me, can I do his
burial in the village here? I think it is better to make it in the
place where he died. To travel the corpse to London, I cannot
do it.'

'You will need to see Mr Cumberledge, the Rector at St Silas
church,' I said. 'It is for him to read the service. And also for
the sexton, who will dig the grave. He will probably expect an
honorarium. A small gift of money for his spadework.'

I turned to Mrs Booth.

'What is the name of the sexton here?'

'He's old Lewis Parsley. His son Tibby helps him with the
graves. They live in a cottage close by the church.'

'Oh, will you come with me, Mr Cragg?' said Madame du
Bressac. 'I do not know the country way of doing this.'

'With pleasure, Madame. We must go immediately, however,
as now that my business is done we will be leaving Ingolside in
the morning. Do you object to a few minutes' walking?'

'Oh no, Mr Cragg, I adore to walk.'

Elizabeth said she would go with us and we set off together
up Street.

'Titus, must we leave in the morning?' said Elizabeth as we went along. 'We shall miss the Whit celebrations. Remember we are invited to the Rectory tea party. And then there is the big fight. Surely you want to see that.'

She was right. I do not, in the general way, enjoy blood sports, but I felt involved in this contest through my slight liking of Cornelius Quexton. I did rather want to see the outcome. Beside that, I would have to see about Lavenham's possessions. That duty would often fall to me in cases of a death far from home.

'Would Holloway and Miss Hart object to our staying a few days longer with them?'

'I think they will be pleased. I will have a word with Amelia.'

Elizabeth then asked Madame du Bressac if she was comfortable at the Dog and Drum.

'I know how to make myself comfortable, Mrs Cragg, although today the house is in a brouhaha because the prizefighter from Yorkshire is expected. The Berrys have been trying to make his apartment fit. People are saying they have had the carpenter in to make the bed more strong. They have brought in much food too, though it is also said the fighter travels with his own food as he is very particular of what he eats.'

'That's very wise if he's staying at Curly Berry's,' I said.

'And you?' said Elizabeth. 'There will only be the usual fare, which Titus tells me is disgusting. Would you therefore like to sup tonight with us at Mr Holloway's? The house is kept by my cousin Amelia and she will be sure to enjoy having you. Let me ask her and I will send word.'

At the Rectory we found Cumberledge overseeing the last stage of the erection of a sailcloth pavilion on his lawn.

'It's to prevent us getting soused in case the weather turns inclement,' he said. 'I have ordered down a large packet of the finest tea from Percival Cherry's grocery in Kendal, at considerable expense. I cannot allow it to go to waste in the rain.'

It was only when Madame du Bressac spoke to him that the Rector seemed to register her presence and was, indeed, a little stuck for an answer when she asked him about the burial of her lover.

'Well now, ah! You are French and therefore a, um, a Roman

Catholic, I take it. So it would be irregular, very, to inter a man like that in our Anglican churchyard.'

'Mr Lavenham was not a Catholic, Sir. He was an Englishman.'

'Was he? Ah, yes, I see. Then I suppose we can hold his funeral after all. I would suggest under the circumstances that there is the minimum of ceremony. Ah! Here is Parsley, our sexton. We shall certainly need to bring him into the discussion.'

Lewis Parsley was an old man bent by rheumatism. He was dragging with great effort a hay bale after him.

'Where do you want the seating, Rector?'

'Line the bales up in the centre of the tent, where it is driest, if you would. But Parsley, I have a different matter you must attend to. What day would be best for the burial of John Lavenham, do you think?'

'That dead London feller?' said Parsley. 'Could do it tomorrow morning if we like. Tibby'll dig out his grave first thing, same as he'll be digging one for Henry Moorhouse. And likely as not, he'll be making a third grave, soon enough an' all.'

'Who will that be for, Mr Parsley?' I asked.

'That's for Charlie Johnson, I reckon. He might last twenty-five rounds if he's lucky, but if it goes past that he'll find that the Rockbreaker's a killer, no two ways.'

He gave a bleak laugh. A sexton's laugh.

We called at the carpenter's shop on the way down Street and found that he had a readymade coffin, very plain but a close enough fit for Lavenham. I then went to Jolliby's yard and ordered the cart to meet us at the Dissenters' Hall in the morning, and to pick up the coffin on the way.

Farmer Holloway was a little wary of having Madame du Bressac under his roof but Miss Hart told him she would enjoy hearing news of the fashionable world, and other curiosities of London life, so he assented to her dining with us. Talk of the metropolis absorbed most of the conversation at table, so that it was not until the end of the meal that I wondered if she would like to see where Lavenham had been living and, if so, Elizabeth and I would be happy to walk her down to Lakeside Lodge.

'You will perhaps meet the surveyor who was also employed

by Mr Lumsden in his project of agricultural improvement. His name is Wilkin Tree.'

'Wilkin Tree,' said Madame du Bressac. 'I know him, of course. John introduced me to Wilky one evening in Covent Garden. I cannot say I am much in love with the man.'

'Are you saying Tree and John Lavenham knew each other before they came here?'

'Of course. They were great friends, and partners in crime more than once.'

'What crimes?'

'I don't know. You will have to ask Wilky. I do know they went many times drinking and whoring together, until finally I had John à *l'attaché*.'

'But for some reason that I don't know, Tree denies this,' I said. 'He claims he met Lavenham for the first time here at Ingolside.'

'He is lying, *tout simplement*.'

But to my mind the matter wasn't quite so simple. Tree had gone out of his way to make me think not only that he and Lavenham had been strangers before coming to Ingolside, but that they did not much like each other.

'Why would they pretend not to know or like each other?'

'Perhaps for safety,' said Elizabeth. 'If the criminal past of one should come to Mr Lumsden's attention, the other would not be tainted.'

'You are astute, Mrs Cragg,' said Madame du Bressac. 'I am sure they did it for their better security.'

'To avoid the crime of association, then,' I said.

It was still light after we had eaten, so I proposed we take the walk down to the lakeside immediately. Madame du Bressac, who had already declared her love of walking in the air, was delighted by our excursion. She told us she was brought up a country child in Savoy, close to the great lake of Annecy, a body of water a few times larger than Ingolmere but not, she said, unlike it. She told us the French names of some of what she called the 'noble' trees, as well as those of the birds on the water – the teal being a *sarcelle* and the crested grebe, which performs an extraordinary head-shaking nuptial dance, is known to the French as the *grèbe houppé*.

When we arrived at Lakeside Lodge the evening light was well on its way towards dusk. We nevertheless found Wilkin Tree coming out of his door, wearing an overcoat, field boots and gaiters and carrying his gun and a game bag. Madame du Bressac hung back as I asked him if we could detain him for a few moments.

'I cannot dwell long,' he told us. 'I'm joining Mr Bowden the gamekeeper on his rounds. Mr Bowden's been kind enough to let me go out with him from time to time. A bright full moon is in prospect, so more than likely we'll be having a look around the warrens, and then go up to the ridge to see if that wolf's got into one of his traps.'

'Do you see yourself in the guise of a gamekeeper?'

He laughed. 'I would rather catch poachers than be one. But mainly it is for the sport. I like to shoot game but cannot do it without risking fines or transportation – unless I have the keeper with me.'

'Then before you hurry away, I have brought someone to visit you,' I said.

Tree's face twitched, like a man expecting to hear ill news.

'Who is that?'

'Don't you remember me, Wilky?' said Madame du Bressac, now stepping forward.

Tree turned and looked at her in slack faced amazement.

'Well, my——! Is it . . . Frankie?'

'The same.'

'But I last saw you in the metropolis! What, may I ask, are you doing in Ingolside, of all places?'

'Ingolside is not "of all places", when I have come to see the place where my poor John has died.'

'A place that is very far from the wickedness of town.'

'Wickedness, Sir? I hope you shall not make a libel against me.'

'I shouldn't dare do that, Madam.'

'Will you not invite us into your house?'

'I regret, Bowden's boy brought word to me to meet at eight. I must be going.'

He turned as if to leave us. I put my hand on his shoulder.

'You left the inquest early. You should not have done that, you know.'

Tree swung around.

'I am a busy man. I have a job of work to do.'

'We wanted to hear your testimony.'

'But you did not need it. I have nothing to tell but what was already said in the morning by others.'

'Only you yourself could have told of your friendship with John Lavenham: a friendship that you had previously concealed.'

By this time Tree was looking shifty, his eyes flicking between each of our faces. His deceit on the subject of his association with John Lavenham was now exposed and he must have been looking for a way to cover it again. He could think of nothing. Instead he hoisted the bag to his shoulder.

'As I have already said, I must be going.'

'Would you unlock the house before you go? Madame du Bressac would much like to see Lavenham's room.'

He brought out a key, unlocked the door and suggested we leave the key under a stone on departure. Then, without another word, he headed up the path and through the trees.

Lavenham's room had not been touched since my last visit. Elizabeth, who had not before been there, exclaimed at the disorder.

'It's proof of all that I said to you, Titus. A most unmethodical, chaotic fellow was Mr Lavenham.'

'He was that in every way except with his pencraft,' said Madame du Bressac. 'There he was precise and orderly. The results were beautiful.'

'If not always according to the law,' I said, glancing at her for a response.

'Well, he is dead so it does not matter if I say it,' she said. 'John was a master of facsimile. A *faussaire*, as we call it in France. His most difficult commission was to make a copy exactly of the Magna Carta, paid for by a very high nobleman. He did it in the perfect secrecy and ever since his Magna Carta is taken for one of the originals. No one doubts it. So you see, when this man Arthur Lumsden summoned my John to work for him, he was sending for the very best.'

Madame du Bressac began moving this way and that around the room, lifting and folding John Lavenham's abandoned clothing, collecting his shoes and wigs, his snuff box, smoking accoutrements and writing materials. Soon a neat heap of his belongings lay on the floor and when she looked up from it her eyes were wet. Elizabeth touched her arm in sympathy.

'Will you pack his things and take them away with you?'

'No, because they are not mine. We were never married. But I would like to have a keepsake.'

'What would that be?'

'Perhaps his signet.'

She picked up an engraved silver seal from Lavenham's desk. Legally speaking, unless it was specified in his will, she had no right to it. But I could not see any harm in her taking it.

'Why not?' I said. 'But on this subject, tell me who were Lavenham's closest living relations? It will fall to me to send all this to them.'

'He never told me that he had any.'

'Did he make a will?'

'I can't say.'

'Well if there is no family living, and no will, all this must be sold for the benefit of the Crown.'

We walked back as the last of daylight faded from a clear sky above the lake. Shortly there would be only the bright disc of the moon hanging above the water and the surrounding fields and woods, just as Wilkin Tree had predicted.

# TWENTY-TWO

The burial of John Lavenham was to take place at mid-morning. Elizabeth and I walked up to the inn, as previously arranged, so that we could attend the corpse to the churchyard in company with Madame du Bressac.

All Ingolside bustled around us with preparations for the Ales. A boat had been out on the lake, setting buoys to mark the course of the boat races, which would be rowed in the morning. Along the length of Street ale tents were going up at intervals. Coloured pennants were being strung from house to house along and across the road, while trestles and tables were being brought out of the shops and houses, and tasseled awnings to cover them. Mugs and glasses, bowls and plates, bottles, jars and carving boards were coming out in quantity. Men rolled beer barrels and women carried trays of pies and cakes.

At the inn, just inside the door, we found Curly Berry sitting on the boot catcher's bench, like a man on watch. As soon as we appeared he leaped to his feet, pressing a finger to his lips.

'Shhh! Make no noise! The Rockbreaker is here. He is sleeping.'

He shooed us into the dining room and sent the maid to tell Madame du Bressac we had arrived.

'The Rockbreaker must not be disturbed,' he insisted, 'or it will put his training quite out. He must sleep until ten, and then shave, after which he rope-skips for half an hour. He has a great breakfast consisting of porridge, bread, butter, eggs, forcemeat balls, bacon, chops, potatoes, roots, cheese and so on. Then he rests, after which he runs around the marsh for what's called a sweat. Then he comes back and spars and lifts heavy stones, and eats his dinner, which is much the same as his breakfast, and rests again for an hour, and spars and lifts stones for another hour in the inn yard, then he rests for another spell and finally goes out again for a sweat. You see, it is all intrinsic and by design. In other words, it is all philosophical.'

'Do you have an opinion on the fight?' asked Elizabeth. 'A prediction?'

'With all his training, the Rockbreaker cannot fail to prevail,' said Berry. 'He is a giant – strong as a bear, nimble as a squirrel and clever as a cat. The southern fellow has no hope.'

Jolliby's cart was waiting for us at the Dissenters' Hall. Together the carter and I laid Lavenham gingerly in his box, nailed down the lid and heaved the box on to the bed of the cart. We set off walking on either side of the donkey's head, with Elizabeth and Madame du Bressac forming the rear of our simple cortège.

'What are people saying about yesterday's inquest verdict?' I asked Jolliby.

'Up and down Street they support it,' Jolliby replied. 'There're too many outsiders' opinions over that man's death, too many folk coming in with their ideas. Ingolside is happy to keep it simple. Accident, and that's it.'

'What have you against "outsiders"?'

'Not me, Mr Cragg. I'm content with you, I am. But then I've been all over, seen it all. I was a soldier forty year ago with the Duke. By Christ, he made us march. They say he was a great man but I'll say he was a hard one. We were once marching on this road in the Low Countries when—'

But Jolliby's memoirs of the War of the Spanish Succession, however charming, would lead us far off the point. I interrupted him.

'But tell me this, Jolliby. If people all agree that Mr Lavenham died accidentally in the fire at the Three Horns, what do they think happened to him after that, and before his corpse was found in the Market Place?'

'He disappeared, didn't he? And turned up three days later, like another certain person did that I won't mention. Some have got the idea Mr Lavenham was flown all the way up to heaven by an angel, but when they got there Saint Peter wouldn't let 'im in. They argued it for three days then Saint Peter packed 'im off back to earth. Finally this angel was found not to be an angel at all but a witch who disguised herself. And here's the proof. He had a hole right through 'is chest, did Mr Lavenham, when they found 'im.'

'What is that the proof of?'

'For the carrying of 'im, up and back again. The witch's besom stick went through the hole, see?'

'Ah, yes, now I do see. Have you ever thought of writing a book of fables, Mr Jolliby?'

The Reverend Cumberledge must have been keeping watch for us. Just as we reached the gate of the graveyard, he shot from the church in his cassock and stole, with book in hand, and took his place ahead of the cart. His face wore a fixed expression of a man doing his duty but not enjoying it. So we processed to the grave, freshly dug by Tibby Parsley, who stood in readiness beside it along with his father. Also waiting there were Luke Fidelis and Helen Booth, the only other mourners. Waving his hand, the Rector indicated that the coffin be taken from the cart and lowered into the ground. The Parsleys, Jolliby and myself managed it between us while Cumberledge waited with an air of impatience.

'I shall employ my own shorter version of the Burial of the Dead. I do not depart from the Rubric but I skip over some of the longer prayers and readings. I am the resurrection and the life, sayeth the Lord . . .'

The air was pleasant and the sun shone. A bird sang heartily in one of the tall yews strung along one side of the churchyard. A faraway dog barked. A woman shouted for her children to come to the kitchen door. These were comforting sounds to set against the uncompromising sonorities of the Prayer Book.

'I was dumb with silence,' read the Rector. 'I held my peace even from good and my sorrow was stirred. My heart was hot within me. While I was musing the fire burned.'

I tried not to dwell much on these words, nor on the madness of the witch tale Jolliby had told me. I didn't wonder whether Lavenham's soul was saved or damned, or the fire burned on him in death as it had at the end of his life. I had performed my own duty by him as best I could. An inquest had nothing to say about a man's life after death.

The earthly deaths of others were the common currency of my work, but in doing it I am rarely reminded of my own death. Funerals, though, have the opposite effect and on this day I was no different from most mourners who stand by a graveside: I was thinking about myself and my own future demise.

'Then spake I with my tongue, Lord make me know mine end and the measure of my days.'

Would it be good to know exactly, by what accident or other
means, that one will die? I did not think so.

I looked into the freshly dug grave, with the earth still moist
in its side and the coffin containing the remains of Lavenham
lying mute at the bottom, waiting to be covered.

'For all our days are passed away in thy wrath. We spend our
years as a tale that is told.'

Perhaps that was better. 'A tale to be told.' The ending of a
tale is natural and expected and nothing to be feared.

As we cast earth into the grave, dust to dust rattling on the
coffin lid, I was aware of an unexpected hand taking part in the
proceedings. I looked up. The latecomer was Cornelius Quexton.

Cumberledge read the Lord's Prayer and the last Collect before,
in tones of wearisome relief, he pronounced the blessing. I handed
the old sexton his fee and, as we walked away, Elizabeth took
my hand for a moment and pressed it. Behind us we heard the
slide and shuffle of spades as the Parsleys, father and son, began
to fill the grave.

Quexton was walking by himself. I fell back behind the others
until I was in step with him.

'Von Schplifflerghun tells, doesn't he, of how he vanquished
the force of Snezhkovsky at the battle of the Black Valley and
his rival was beheaded by the sabre of one of Schplifflerghun's
Pandurs. When he heard that the headless body was to be buried
near Brno, Schplifflerghun rode up to the graveside carrying the
head in a sack and threw it into the grave. A colourful story, but
I suppose that is one of the four-fifths of fictitious matter in his
book.'

Quexton shook his head.

'No, it is quite true. He sent men back to the battlefield espe-
cially to recover Snezhkovksy's head. He wished to play the
magnanimous victor.'

'When I read the story, I thought he was acting more in
contempt than magnanimity.'

'You were right, of course. Men like Schplifflerghun are never
truly magnanimous. When they pretend to be doing good it is in
reality an aggression.'

I was wondering if Quexton had come to John Lavenham's
graveside in the same spirit – to make the burial complete and

final – when Françoise du Bressac caught up with us. Quexton turned and gave her a courteous bow.

'Ah, Madame!' he said. '*Je veux bien exprimer mes condoléances.*'

Quexton left us to return to his lodgings, where he meant to use the last hours before the fight to (as he put it) further tickle-up Charlie Johnson's fitness for the task ahead. As his way home took him past the Dog and Drum, he offered to squire Madame du Bressac back to the inn.

Elizabeth and I parted from Fidelis and Mrs Booth at her door and went on to Holloway's Farm.

'Mr Quexton and the Frenchwoman seem friendly,' said Elizabeth as we arrived at Mr Holloway's front door. 'I wonder what they might have to say to each other.'

'And in her own language,' I added.

Hearing us come into the hall, Amelia Hart emerged from the parlour with a folded piece of paper, a note addressed to me. It had, she told me, been dropped through the door at some time in the last hour. Seeing the handwriting on it, I quickly stuffed it into my coat pocket unopened. Elizabeth looked at me curiously but said nothing.

But she had plenty to say when, later in our bedroom, I finally unfolded the piece of paper and read it to her.

*Coroner, thast faylt to find hoo kilt Jon Lavnam. Tha wilt find nowt more now so get owt of way else weel naw what to do. Yaw laf's in ower hands tha naws. Git back to ya hawm and si nowt. A frend.*

'A friend!' I said. 'He is threatening my life. "Your life's in our hands" – I don't like the sound of that.'

'What does it mean, Titus?'

'I suppose it means what it says: go away!'

'Is it the work of the same people who wrote anonymously to the Squire and to Wilkin Tree?'

'Possibly, I reckon, but these things can spread like the scarlet fever, with people catching on to the idea and starting to do it for themselves. But someone doesn't like me, that's evident.'

# TWENTY-THREE

ngolside awoke next morning infused with new vigour. Now at last the Whitsun Ales were upon us, and the day looked set to be dry. Fiddle music and song were in the air. In Market Place the stalls set up the previous evening were loaded with tawdry lace and many gewgawish things for sale. All sorts of shies and skittles had appeared with toys or toffee apples for prizes, as had the sellers of iced cakes, custards and syllabubs. The ale tents that sprang up at various locations along Street had been plentifully supplied by Oswald Gillow. Competing stands selling rum and port wine, as well as others specializing in lemonade and sugared drinks for more refined refreshment, had also been opened.

By ten o'clock the last rowing race had already been won. Later there would be athletic contests and, in the evening, dancing on the Green. But the main event of this afternoon was the fight, which was due to begin at two in the afternoon. Possible outcomes were the subject of furious debate. Some shouted for the Rockbreaker on the grounds that, although a Yorkshireman, at least he was north country while Johnson was a detested southerner. Others, however, favoured Johnson on the basis that anyone who opposed a Yorkshireman, no matter where they came from, must be fiercely encouraged and supported.

At breakfast Mr Holloway and his niece had not changed their allegiances, with the farmer becoming heated on the side of the Rockbreaker and Miss Hart more gently hoping for the success of Charlie Johnson. The discussion was interrupted by a boy who had run from the Manor House with a message for me. I was commanded to attend Mrs Lumsden.

We rose from our meal and Elizabeth and Amelia put on their best bonnets, with fresh flowers tied around, and went out with me. They were to join up with a party of ladies at Mrs Booth's to make a tour together of the various attractions. Leaving them at Mrs Booth's door I returned down Street where I found, directly in front of the Manor House, a gang of men preparing the ground on which the trial of fists would be held. Under the supervision of a portly bearded man they had defined the boxing area with a rope laid down in a ring, approximately twenty feet across. Outside this was another rope ring, marking the edge of the spectators' area, leaving a margin of two yards at most. The boxing ring had been laid with sand and sawdust and men were now scraping a line in the ground running from one edge to the other while passing through the ring's centre. This, in pugilism, is referred to as the Scratch. They were also defining a new inner area about a yard across at the centre of the ring, known as the Square.

To my surprise, I found Mrs Lumsden out of bed and sitting in a bath chair. She had been wrapped in woollen shawls and wore a quilted cap.

'I greatly enjoyed the rowers' contest,' she said loudly as I entered the room. 'I had a capital view from the windows of this room. The young men were splendid in strength and endurance, as they have always been going back further than the grandfathers of their grandfathers' grandfathers. However, now we have something never seen before here at Whitsun: the fist fight! I am looking forward to it. We will watch it from our front windows and I bet my life that Quexton's man will prevail.'

Her manner was that of one addressing a whole gathering of people rather than just myself. I had never seen her so animated. Then as soon as she had properly registered my arrival she reverted to her more usual self. I gave her a formal bow, noticing that she had not offered me any refreshment.

'What may I do for you today, Madam?'

'You may, if you please, explain to me your conduct of yesterday's inquest. I am very displeased by it. You as good as accused young Moorhouse of doing away with the fellow Lavenham.'

'Mrs Lumsden, you have formed that opinion somewhat arbitrarily. You were not, as far as I know, at the hearing.'

'I was not, but I've had a thoroughgoing account of it from the foreman of the jury himself. He said you bullied poor Mr Thomas Moorhouse and you then tried to make the jury give you a verdict of murder by him.'

'Madam, I assure you, I—'

'The Archbishop of York himself is more likely to commit murder than Mr Moorhouse.'

'He seemed to me when I met him to be a very passionate sort.'

'The Archbishop? Passionate? I doubt his wife would agree. And now I hear Tommy Moorhouse's father is dead and he and his wife will be sent headlong packing on the road to nowhere. What can I do to stop it, Mr Clogg?'

'That is difficult to say, Mrs Lumsden. Authority here is in the hands of Mr Arthur Lumsden, your son.'

'Who should be ashamed of himself.'

'You know, at least, that Moorhouse was not in fact found liable by the jury for Mr Lavenham's death.'

'It is a small comfort, and it doesn't take away my disappointment in you, Mr Clack.'

In the hall on my way out I met Fidelis impatiently staring at the clock while he waited to go up.

'Your patient is out of bed and intermittently full of cheer, Luke. Have you been giving her an elixir of some kind?'

'The elixir is this afternoon's fight, Titus. She is extraordinarily excited by it.'

'So she told me. And she is also excited – to anger – by my examination of Moorhouse at the inquest. In her opinion I have acted as a satanic prosecutor, whereas she is sure the man is innocent of all wrongdoing.'

'Did you mention his fame as a poacher?'

To leave the sick room and go into the air was perfect refreshment. The sweetness of the spring-scented flowers dressing the windowsills all along Street struck me forcibly, along with the cheerful smell of fresh bakery and roasting meat. I stopped to take a glass of bumbo at a stall served by Lizzy Duckham.

'How do, Mr Cragg?' she said.

'Well, thank you, Mrs Duckham, and good health to you. May I ask, do you have an idea of the discussion amongst the jurors yesterday? Perhaps your husband told you something.'

'You do not know yourself, Mr Cragg?'

'It is frowned upon for the Coroner to be present at the jury's final discussion and I abide by that. It is rare that I find out much of what was said, excepting the verdict itself.'

'Duckham says it was Curly Berry who talked them into it. There were those, Duckham included, who thought it was a murder.'

'Had they formed an idea of how it was done?'

'They were saying Mr Lavenham was knocked on the head on purpose when the fire was well set. But Berry told them there was nothing sure in that and that he was hit by a falling timber, so they better give you an accident for a verdict.'

I drained my glass and walked on. The Ales entertainments were already fully under way and Street was busy with people running here and there giving and receiving instructions, fetching and carrying. Others were ranging about in jovial groups, looking for pleasure, laughing and jostling. They went in and out of the ale tents, where Gillow's specially brewed, specially strong Whitsun ales were cheaply available. They took a try at skittles, or tumble-hen, or any of the other games that were offered. Pie men and cake sellers wandered among them with their wares on small portable tables, which they set down to serve customers.

Glancing up and down Street, I felt exposed. Someone, perhaps someone in this miscellaneous crowd, and probably more than one, wanted me out of Ingolside. Those people had let me know of the fact and also that my life was at their disposal – 'owr hands', they had said.

At the entrance of one ale tent I came upon Cornelius Quexton, with a small audience of drinkers. Listening intently to him, they were the quietest knot of people anywhere on Street. Having never heard Quexton giving out in public, I stopped to listen with them.

He spoke like a seasoned campaigner, a street-corner Cicero, telling his listeners – now that yesterday's inquest had brought to light how Squire Lumsden had been re-writing the old documents to suit himself – they must be ever doubtful of claims from the Squire.

'From this day forward,' Quexton said with the deepest, sincerest ring in his voice, 'let no word of the Squire's be trusted. Every charter, every lease or contract written on parchment and plucked supposedly from the parish chest, you must read and test. How, you may ask, will you tell the true lease or contract from the false? It is simple. It is the true document that affirms the ancient rights of the people. It attests to a universal truth, which is that the ancient lore is the truest for all humble ranks of people. Yes, the new ways, the ways of Squire Lumsden, will make rich men even richer. As they seize more land, stealthily, parcel by parcel, always in the lying name of improvement, remember that it only makes them more powerful and further removed from the needs of you the people, the poor people, who will now be rendered weaker and poorer by cruel degrees. And be in no doubt that you – who need your strips of plough, and the common woods and marshes to keep yourselves warm and cook your food, and keep your pigs alive – you will have them taken from you, in the way I have said, by slow degrees until at last you are cast out of your very cottages and little farms. For these, needless to say, the Squire has no use. He wants only the land. So then, abandoned, you must fend pennilessly for yourselves. And what will you do? Why, you will have no choice but to flock to the towns and become slaves in the manufactories that already grow monstrously there. Do you want that? Do you truly want that?'

There were murmurs of 'Nay!' and 'Heck as like!'

Quexton used a gesture beloved of orators everywhere: he raised his index finger and shook it at them.

'Then beware, that is my warning, beware of your Squire and his doings. And resist! Resist, in every way you can.'

He raised his mug of ale, and his lips split in a broad smile.

'Good, my friends! Very good! Here endeth the lesson!'

As his listeners applauded, cheering and slapping their hands furiously together, I slipped away. Yet I dwelt for some time on what I had heard. Had those been seditious words? It all depended on how you viewed the rule of Squires and how you thought about the working of God's world. If the squiredom consists of nothing but men like any other men, except they happen to have climbed to a higher rung of the ladder, then so be it. But if Kings and nobles be in any way ordained by God, as being parts of a fixed order for society, which some do still believe they are, then might not the squire be the same? If so, words against him might be construed criminal and liable to punishment. A large part of me knew quite well that Lumsden was not appointed by direct decision of the Almighty. But I was still uneasy listening to

Quexton. This was the spirit of Wat Tyler, Robert Aske and Gerard Winstanley. That spirit made for an unstable commonwealth, one of disorder, conflict and violence. It made for many of the things I stood against: attacks, blows and killing, bullying and, yes, insidious letters threatening murder.

I noticed Luke Fidelis entering an ale tent. When I caught up with him he was talking with brewer Gillow, but he broke off as I approached and took my arm, guiding me out of the tent.

'What were you discussing?' I said, as we walked along together.

'The best way to keep ale so as to delay its souring as long as possible. I have some ideas on the matter. I suggest, for example, the addition of slaked lime. He resists the idea, naturally. It is exasperating, the eternal fight between making things better and keeping everything the same.'

'This is precisely what I myself have been thinking about, Luke. I have just heard Quexton addressing a group of Ingolsiders on the subject. The death of John Lavenham has exposed a great crack in the order of society here, and it is the self-same argument as you describe. My only quarrel might be with your suggestion that the poor wish to stop things getting better. They may well be trying to prevent everything becoming worse.'

'No, Titus, no. What rubbish you talk sometimes. In my practice, people are unreasonably retrograde, terrified of change and of what is new, babbling about bloodletting, auspices, the touch of a hanged man – the stupider the better, they seem to think. Mrs Lumsden herself is the Devil's work to persuade there are better medical means than empirics and superstitions.'

'From what I can see,' I said, 'the poor people are afraid for their livelihood, afraid it will be overwhelmed in the tide of improvement. It is a fear not wholly misplaced, Luke.'

'It's a dispute we must settle on not settling, then. Speaking of fights, will you see Johnson and the Rockbreaker go at each other?'

'Elizabeth and I are engaged to attend at the Rectory at two, for a tea party. Damned inconvenient timing.'

Fidelis laughed delightedly.

'Tea! The elixir of sobriety! I wish you and your wife well of it.'

We strolled up Street and on to the Green where the furious mixture of commerce and jollity was in full spate. We went into the thick of it and I soon found myself caught up in the excitement. I was shying at a row of wooden balls placed on a shelf in egg cups when a horn blast and the furious rumbling of wheels caught my attention. I turned to see a coach and four coming in to rest in front of the Dog and Drum. It was crammed with gaily dressed passengers, inside and on every possible outside perch. The board on the side of the coach showed that they had come from Ripon, bearing Yorkshire men and women whose object was to get around the boxing ring and shout for their fellow. Within the next hour, a further six similar coaches had thundered into Ingolside and disgorged more loads of roaring young people into the town.

# TWENTY-FOUR

The Cumberledges' two o'clock tea party, their counter-attack against the excesses of the Church Ales, was due to begin simultaneously with the attraction being put on at the other end of Street. By consequence, those interested in the latter event, including the Squire and Mr Holloway, stayed away from the Rectory. Mrs Cumberledge was unable to grasp the reason.

'I wonder at the small number of adult people attending our garden party. It is not at all the great success of previous years. Our greatest number of guests this time are children, it seems. They are being entertained by our own dear daughters, Hetty and Lucy.'

Hetty and Lucy, both in their teens, had thrown themselves heartily into the organization of garden games, including blind-man's buff, quoits and Scotch-hopping. They had also engaged Bennett's nephew Daniel to offer rides to the smallest ones around the garden on the back of his great dog, Limer.

I had told Elizabeth as we arrived that I would slip away after an hour or so and go down to the boxing ring, in the hope that Johnson and the Rockbreaker would still be going at each other and I could see the end of the bout. In the meantime, I took possession of a cup of tea and a piece of plum cake while having a few words with Mrs Cumberledge ('The Rector is so pleased you have come'), Martin Mansfield ('I never take strong drink') and a few others from the respectable and abstinent company. Finally I found myself talking with Mr Bennett at the entrance of Mr Cumberledge's pavilion. I thanked him for the use of his hall the day before.

'It is not my hall, Mr Cragg,' he said. 'It belongs to the Dissenters' Society, who will be glad of your fee when it comes.'

I said that of course it would be paid.

'Our running costs are modest,' he said, 'as it is not an old building, but there are always payments to make. We like to give a twelvepence now and again to my nephew for his sweeping and cleaning.'

'He is a conscientious boy.'

'And secretive with it. I never know what he's thinking. He confides more in that great dog of his than in any person we know.'

At this moment Robert Furzey joined us. His cheeks were rosy-red, his manner was uncharacteristically excitable and his speech was slurred. In short, Furzey had sneaked in here from the alehouse, in direct contravention of Mrs Cumberledge's rule, and to make this worse he was far gone in drink, which invariably made him quarrelsome. So it was merely a question of whether he would pick his fight with me, or with the leader of the Dissenters. As it happened, it was with me.

'Why are you so pack with that Question fellow?' he said. 'He's an agitator, in my regard, and disturber of the peace, as well as being an atheist.'

'He is a likable type of man, Furzey, not an agitator. Not a violent man. And I think you may even be wrong about his religious views.'

I said this, though not two hours ago I had heard Quexton calling for resistance to Lumsden and his projects. But resistance takes many forms, I was thinking, peaceful as well as aggressive.

'He is?' said Furzey, planting his feet wider apart, which was a sure sign he was preparing to press the argument over many rounds. 'Don't you know he trains that tub of brawn Johnson to punch other men's heads in?'

'That is different.'

'He is a politician and his politics is the kind that leads to broken heads.'

'How so?'

'He raises false hopes among the people. When they're disappointed, which they're bound to be, those people will turn to fighting and arson and Heaven knows what. Where is your tranquility then? The burning of the Three Horns alehouse is fresh in the memory. Unsigned letters carrying threats have been received – we have seen three of the kind ourselves.'

I had not told him about the most recent example of epistolary abuse, the one aimed at myself.

'Mr Quexton had nothing to do with those.'

'Who's to say? Who's to say he's not, indeed, a murderer?'

'Now, Furzey, have a care. You are letting your tongue run wild.'

My clerk poked my chest with his finger.

'Did Question not come here to stop Mr Lumsden's very necessary improvements?'

'It's Quexton, Furzey.'

'And is not John Lavenham, who came here to further those improvements, now dead? So tell me, what better suspicion is there than the one pointing to that fellow Question, who makes himself so agreeable but is a viper.'

'Calm yourself, man!' I said sharply. 'You jump too high to that conclusion. And for the last time, his name is Quexton.'

Bennett, standing beside us, was bemused that I had allowed this altercation between myself and my employee to run on.

'I've seen him,' cried Furzey. 'I've seen him on Elm Tree Lane chucking the cheek of that orphan Brabner boy. I've seen him pick-thanking and currying favour with the Widow Booth and the Widow Bradshaw, and any other poor widows he could practise on. According to my lights he is a whited sepulchre and all pretence.'

'Calm yourself. This is unworthy.'

'I'll tell you what is unworthy. I'll tell you . . . But what's the use?'

Abruptly he broke off and with an impatient snort turned on his heel, marched unsteadily out of the tent and, with a dismissive wave of his arm, out of the Rector's garden.

'I deeply regret that you had to witness that outburst, Mr Bennett,' I said. 'Robert Furzey is usually the model of sobriety, wedded to rectitude and the law. However, when in drink, which is rare, he is apt to pick a fight.'

Bennett pursed his lips and shook his head.

'I am sorry to see him intoxicated. I had high hopes of him, as he is very sound on Predestination.'

By now the conversation in the Rectory garden was being regularly punctuated by distant roars, cheers and choruses of 'Up! Up! Up!' from the direction of the Manor House. They indicated that Johnson and the Rockbreaker were hammering away at each other with serious intent. I found myself itching to go down there, as were some others, judging by their faces and the way they turned their heads at each eruption of the crowd.

It was another twenty minutes before I could get away, and even then Mrs Cumberledge was unhappy.

'You are leaving so early, Mr Cragg.'

'My Elizabeth will stay on awhile,' I said. 'But I am promised elsewhere, I fear.'

My white lie was regrettable but necessary under the circumstances. Elizabeth seemed not to mind being left behind.

'Go on and revel in your punches and bloody noses,' she whispered to me before I left. 'As long as I do not have to see it, I will be happy.'

As I arrived the uproar around the ring was intense. The crowd was mixed, men with women, and jammed together. They jostled and elbowed continually to see the action better while the noise of their factional support – I reckoned it was close to half-and-half – rose and fell according to the rhythm of the contest. Sitting on chairs in the margin between the ring and the crowd were the judges and timekeeper while, in the ring itself, was the referee, a man wiry of build compared to the two mountainous fighters. In addition, each contestant had a pair of seconds: grizzled and burly veterans for the Rockbreaker and, to my surprise, Luke Fidelis standing with Cornelius Quexton behind Johnson. Fidelis was holding a bucket and a sponge.

Battle had been joined little more than forty minutes before, having been preceded by preliminary matters – a couple of unprized three-round contests between likely young men of the region, and then the naming of the referee and the two fighters, with the prize they would fight for, followed by the reading of the rules by the chief judge – the large bearded man I had seen supervising the arrangement of the ring – the introduction of his two fellow judges and the timekeeper.

Broughton Rules were in use. These allowed for the boxers to wear thin leather gloves tightly fitting their hands, which gave to their knuckles some protection (though very little to their opponent's face). The Rockbreaker was wearing a pair of these but Johnson's hands were merely bound with leather strapping.

Both men showed evidence of blows received but neither was bleeding and they seemed equally fresh and game. They went up on their toes or bent back, played feints, ducked under a fist swinging from out wide, then swung one back, or tried to frustrate the other's duck with a high hammering blow coming down on the top of his head.

Shortly after I'd arrived, one of these aerial punches from the Rockbreaker made Johnson stagger and, before he'd recovered, a second punch to the side of his face put him down on the sand. Running to him, Quexton and Fidelis each went on one knee. Standing next to me was a man who, seemingly familiar with the many finer points of pugilation, had been commenting on the proceedings throughout in a loud voice. He had me marked as a novice spectator and explained to me that the seconds were not permitted to lift a downed fighter, but only to give him encouragement while the timekeeper called the count.

'He will rise again,' my informant told me. 'He is only taking a breath for half a minute.'

Johnson rolled over until he was on his knees, levered himself back to his feet and joined his opponent centre ring inside the Square, with the referee between them, while the timekeeper counted a full thirty seconds. At the command 'box on!' the two men went at each other once again.

When the bell rang for the end of the three-minute round, the fighters went to their stools for sixty seconds of respite. Fidelis plunged the sponge into the bucket and mopped Johnson's face and naked upper body. Quexton knelt before his man talking to him, encouraging him, giving tactical instructions and pointing out flaws in the Rockbreaker's defence. I noticed a rosy swelling the size of a conker had appeared above one of Johnson's eyes, just on the rim of its socket.

The bell sounded for the next round, the twelfth, and the boxers sprang to their feet and went up to the Scratch, giving every appearance of eagerness. A second bell set them going. This time, after only a minute, Johnson landed a blacksmith's blow on the Rockbreaker's chin, to a mighty cheer from roughly half the crowd. The Ripon man seemed to tip over backwards on the hinge of his heels before crashing to the ground. It was like the demolition of a barn. But his trainer quickly roused him and he heaved himself up before shambling to the safety of the Square for the completion of the count.

It went on like this, with fluctuating urgency, for round after round. There were more knock-downs, some being genuine bone shakers but some only convenience falls, to let a man take a breather of thirty seconds in the Square. From time to time the action became frenzied – and so did the crowd – particularly when the Rockbreaker and Johnson grappled, trying to heave each other over, while bringing knees and furious kicks into the other's body. The referee would allow this to go on for a time before ordering them to break and so they began circling around, again looking for openings while getting in a punch when they could.

It was in the fifteenth that first blood was drawn, and it was Johnson's blood. The Rockbreaker had been trying to find an angle to land on that swelling above Johnson's eye, and finally he got one, delivering a slashing strike that brought a gush of blood. With this pouring into his eye, Johnson was inconvenienced to the extent that he spent the rest of the round running away, while the Rockbreaker stalked him this way and that across the ring. When the break came, Johnson reeled towards his stool. Fidelis mopped the wound with a cloth, then produced what looked like a ball of wax which he pressed to it. This was a styptic preparation Fidelis had discovered (he later told me) during a journey to France some years before. Holding the back of Johnson's head, he kept the pressure on the cut until the bell rang for the next round. As Johnson got up I saw that Johnson's bleeding had for the moment been staunched.

Round after round passed. In some there was little enough aggressive action, but rather a display of feinting and dancing as is seen when a boxer trains. But in others serious bumps were delivered. In round twenty-one, Johnson moved in to pummel the Rockbreaker's body, like one seeking to tenderize meat. In the process he took some blows around the ear, but I could see that his tactic of close fighting, as well as undermining the Rockbreaker's strength, was helping him to protect his own injured eye socket.

As round thirty passed, my advisor next to me turned and chopped my shoulder none too lightly with a loosely bunched fist, then pointed at the contestants.

'Watch their legs, man! This is when the legs begin to wobble. Not much to see yet but in two or three rounds they'll look more like a pair of brawling drunkards than artists in pugilation.'

And so it happened. By round thirty-six both men were struggling to maintain a consistent vertical posture, which brought about the paradoxical phenomenon of the two opponents depending on each other to stay on their feet. For a few rounds, ignoring the crowd's jeers and cat calls, they leaned against each other while padding about in a mazy tour of the ring, giving each other half-hearted slaps to the body.

Round forty began. Neither fighter danced now, and neither spent much time on his toes. They were a pair of flat-footed shufflers and their blows continued for the most part to lack conviction. Slumped on his stool at the round's end, I saw Johnson receiving a tirade from Quexton. He seemed to be saying 'stand up and fight', and a lot more beside. Fidelis, who had had little to say to Johnson throughout the fight, now leaned in to say a few words of his own in Johnson's ear. Tired as he was, Johnson reacted with a sudden whipping glance towards Fidelis. His lips moved. Fidelis drew his head back and continued his work with the sponge.

At the start of round forty-one my confidant turned to me with another prediction.

'Time for the second wind,' he said. 'Things will hot up again now.'

My admiration for the man increased greatly when precisely this happened. For the next few rounds Johnson showed renewed fire, perhaps in response to his seconds' encouragement, while the Rockbreaker was equally reinvigorated. I knew how an exhausted athlete can unaccountably recover his wind when all seems lost, but I was struck by my informant's ability to name the round in which it would occur. Accordingly, in the forty-sixth round, the Rockbreaker got a hold around Johnson's neck and, cinching his head in the bend of his arm, delivered a stuttering rain of punches on to the forehead, followed by two savage under punches to the heart. Johnson went down on one knee and took a thirty-second count, breathing heavily. Then he rose with a contemptuous grin, slipped the Rockbreaker's next punch and launched a furious attack of his own. With the regularity of a

striking clock he landed as many as eight straight left-hand
punches on the area around the Rockbreaker's mouth and chin,
to a chorus of mighty cheers from his supporters. He might have
gone on to land eight more had the bell not interrupted him.

In the break before round fifty, I asked my new friend for his
assessment of the state of affairs.

'Both men still look strong but we are coming now to the
decisive phase in the fight. It will be won and lost in the next
three rounds.'

'Who will prevail?'

But now the fellow's experience failed him. He widened his
eyes and shook his head.

'I cannot tell you. But mark my word, we'll know in no more
than three rounds' time.'

# TWENTY-FIVE

The fiftieth and fifty-first were close-fought rounds. Neither boxer strained less than the other to dispatch his opponent, but their movements could no longer be likened to a dance. On the contrary, they had all the purpose and fury of battling bulls. They punched and grappled, barged, kicked and elbowed, while the sweat flew off them in gouts, and blood flecked the sand they stood on. Both were bleeding from the nose and the wound had re-opened above the eye of Johnson, who had in turn gashed the Rockbreaker's lips, the upper as well as the lower.

It was not merely my neighbour who sensed it; the crowd as a whole felt the fight was coming to a climax. They hooted and roared, whistled and shrieked, the men and the women equally. The energy of the fighters was hoisted further by the cacophony. The blows had lost the last remnants of skill and dash, but not all of their effectiveness as the two men's fists crashed and crunched into each other's bodies.

The end, when it came, was extraordinary. The Rockbreaker flung himself towards Johnson, his fists thrashing and his chin thrust out. With a nimbleness that after half a century of rounds seemed incredible, Johnson ducked and the Rockbreaker's fists connected only with the air. Then, from a lower position relative to his adversary, Johnson boomed a punch directly upwards on to the point of the Rockbreaker's chin. Still being propelled forward, his toes were the last part of his body touching the ground as the Rockbreaker passed over the crouching Johnson's head and shoulders and landed on his opponent's back. Thereupon Johnson stood up straight, causing the Rockbreaker to slither down, over his buttocks and head first to the ground. Without so much as a cry or a curse, his head hit the sand and he turned a forward roll before sprawling limply on his back.

The count was taken up by the whole crowd, which seemed to last twice thirty seconds, but the Ripon Rockbreaker never moved. The fight was over.

Half the crowd were surly, disbelieving and sore. Many had lost cash in bets, and all felt the sharp descent from drunken cheering to the crapulous misery of defeat. The other half were jubilant. The head judge's chair was seized and Johnson, looking dazed, was planted on it, hoisted to shoulder height and carried, in a triumph worthy of the Caesars, up the whole length of Street to the Green and back again as far as Market Place. Following them, I caught sight of Cornelius Quexton on the other side of the road. He wore a serene smile of contentment.

On his return, Johnson was brought to the steps of the Market Cross, where two gentlemen stood waiting for him – Arthur Lumsden and another even more portly figure, who held in his hand a small well-filled leather bag. Soon this gentleman's name was being whispered around the crowd: he was Richard Elcock of Newby Hall, and he was carrying the purse containing the prize of one hundred guineas. Johnson was let down from the chair and left to stand next to Elcock and Lumsden. Elcock turned to him and was seen to make an inaudible speech in which he may be assumed to be congratulating the fighter on his victory and wishing him well in the course of his future professional life. He then raised up the purse so that all could see it, Johnson put his two battered hands together palms up and Elcock placed the purse on them with a flourish. The people gave a mighty cheer and immediately began chanting demands for Johnson to give a speech. With head swaying, he stood looking around him through one eye, its swollen counterpart being now quite closed. He seemed bemused at the people as they jumped up and down and cheered for him. Fidelis mounted the steps. Holding his head in both hands and raising the eyelid, he looked intently at the wounded eye. He spoke a few words, which Johnson answered with even fewer. Then Quexton arrived and Fidelis stepped back with a nod of his head. Quexton, breathing hard from the effort of getting through the tightly packed crowd, shook hands warmly with Elcock and, more coldly, with Lumsden. He turned to the people, holding up a hand to command quiet.

'Ladies, gentlemen – and you others!' he called in a ringing voice.

This raised a happy cheer.

'I know you will understand,' he went on, 'if Mr Johnson,

after his fatiguing exertions this afternoon, does not attempt to address you. It was indeed a heroic contest in which both men gave their best – but the best of the best was that of the man standing beside me. Before I invite you to express your delight, and your unbounded and whole-hearted admiration for him, give if you please a cheer for Mr Richard Elcock who put up the purse and made possible this great display of courage and skill.'

The crowd called huzzah, more out of duty than respect for the gentry, after which they were invited to give three cheers for the Ripon Rockbreaker which they answered with only a little more enthusiasm. They were waiting for a chance to give more climactic cheers. Quexton gave it to them. He went up to Johnson, hoisted one of his arms in the air and shouted out in a triumphant voice: 'I give you Mistah! Charlie! Johnson! The warrior, the fighter, the victor and now the Champion of all Lancashire and all Yorkshire – and indeed, my friends, the Champion of the entire North Country.'

The delirium of the crowd reached a new crescendo, and continued at that pitch for the next five minutes. After this Johnson was brought away by Quexton, so he could come to his senses and have his wounds tended in the safety and quiet of their lodging. The two sponsoring gentlemen also left the stage to repair to the Manor House, while the lingering crowd went on singing and giving ragged cheers to show they were not yet ready to disperse and break the triumphant mood. But this excited press of people were in no way expecting the very unusual spectacle that now appeared before them.

'Make way! Let me through! Urgent! Urgent business!'

These shouts came from one who I soon saw was Thomas Moorhouse. He was pulling his young wife behind him as he shouldered his way with difficulty through the throng and towards the stone cross. On reaching the cross, he climbed the steps and tugged Alice up by the hand. He then placed himself in front of her and, with his fingers on her shoulders, showed her just how he wanted her to stand. He then put two fingers under her chin to raise up her face.

'Look what she's wearing!' someone called out.

It was not the mob cap Alice Moorhouse wore that had attracted attention, nor the plain blue dress with a belt around the waist, and over it an apron. Nor was it the clogs without hose on her feet. What they were looking at was the halter around her neck, on the end of which a leather loop hung down.

'He's not selling her? My God, he is! He's selling her!' shouted another.

'How much d'you want for her, Tommy?'

Others in the crowd started calling out and laughing.

'How much! How much!'

Moorhouse held up his hand.

'Listen to me. Listen!' he shouted. 'We're doing this proper. And be in no doubt, any of you, this is no jest or passing fancy.'

The hard, grave look on his face quietened them and they settled down to hear what Moorhouse would say next. A wife in a halter at the Market Cross was not something seen every week, or even every year, but they had all heard of it from time to time. A man would tire of his woman, or find himself unable to support her, and so put her up in the old country way haltered at the public market, and deliver her after selling to the highest bidder.

'Very well, now you all understand me,' thundered Moorhouse. 'Gather round, then, you men, you bachelors. Use your eyes. You can see what she is, healthy and pretty and only twenty-three years old. She's handy in the kitchen and the dairy but I'll not say about the bedroom, as the man who takes her on must find that out for himself. Now I'll show you her as she walks. Make room there, please. Make room.'

There was a general shuffling back to leave a space on the ground all around the cross's plinth. Moorhouse guided Alice down and, holding the end of the halter, led her in procession around the cross once, twice and then a third time before leading her back up the steps to the foot of the cross itself. Alice's expression was solemn, her eyes blank.

'This is barbarous, Titus!'

It was Elizabeth's voice. I had been so distracted and incredulous that I had not noticed her arrival at my side.

'I can hardly believe it,' I said. 'We have heard tell of such things, have we not? But I never thought I would see it.'

'Well can't you stop it? Can't you intervene?'

I thought about her question. Yes, I could intervene. I could try to talk Moorhouse out of attempting to sell his wife. I did not think that I would succeed.

'Moorhouse hinted to me that he might seek a desperate remedy against the Squire's eviction of him. This must be it.'

'But, Titus, she is a woman, a person. She is not a cow or a sow or a sheep, to be sold at market like any beast.'

'Shh!' I said. 'He's speaking again.'

Touching Alice's shoulders, Moorhouse now turned her towards him so that they faced each other squarely. He addressed her in a ringing voice. 'Woman, do you freely consent to be sold according to old custom under this Market Cross? Speak so that all can hear.'

She was standing very straight, her head slightly tilted back so that her chin was prominent. She looked into her husband's eyes and spoke in a firm and definite voice.

'I do.'

Moorhouse turned to the people below them.

'Did you all hear? Did you mark that? Good. So we are ready to begin now. Who'll give me a bid? And let it not be a stupid one. It must be a top price.'

There were some hoots of laughter and someone shouted, 'Top price? She's skinny as an elver.'

Another grinning fellow raised his hand.

'Aye, she's a groat's worth at best. I bid a groat.'

Moorhouse was visibly furious. His face was rigid as he pointed in warning at this last shouter.

'Is that your opinion, Oswald Smethwick? And you with a wife already, who'll slap your teeth into your brains when she hears you've been giving out such lip.'

The crowd roared with laughter at Smethwick's discomfort, then quietened again to listen to Moorhouse.

'Now come on, friends, this is in earnest and we are doing it right, by the country custom. So is there in this mumpus of people no bachelor or widower who wants a bit of comfort in his life? This is a pretty young 'un who'll look after you, you may be sure of it, for she's willing and biddable and there's not a bit of a shrew about her.'

'If she's so good, why've you spent the last five years beating her? Is it because she's barren?'

'Or has she got the scab under that dress?'

Some laughed hoarsely, as there were still many in the crowd who were taking a leering pleasure in the bizarre proceedings.

'She's healthy, I say,' Moorhouse shouted. 'But me, I am away for America. That is all the reason I do this, for though my heart may break, I cannot take her with me.'

He looked around, hawk like, his head thrust forward. Most of the crowd were beginning to find it discomfiting, in proportion as they were realizing Moorhouse was deadly earnest.

'Leave off, Tommy Moorhouse, this is not seemly,' shouted someone near the back of the throng. 'You married her. You spoke the vows. Till death, Tommy. Till death.'

'This *is* death, curse you. No, it's worse than death. Remember the Brabners. The farm lands taken off them. Beasts slaughtered. House burned out. And that's my fate an' all, cast out like Cain only to cry and to wander. If that is not worse than death, I would like to know what death is.'

The throng appeared to be mostly silenced as Moorhouse stood there, legs wide apart and hands on his hips, eyeing them, swaying his head and louring.

He raised up an arm to the sky, where the sun was now down to the rooftops and the air was cooling.

'Bid for her, damn you. Bid!' he shouted again. 'For she must sell, or else I'll not be answerable for what I do.'

He did not get as far as specifying what he might do, as now a voice was heard at the very back of the crowd.

'Oh well, if no one else wants her, I'll bid. I'll take her.'

This came from the side of the Market Place opposite to where Elizabeth and I stood. It was a shrill challenge, a decisive call, and it came from a woman's mouth.

'Who's that?' said Elizabeth. 'A woman? What woman would ever take part in disgraceful doings like these, Titus?'

I could now see the woman in the middle of the throng, pushing towards the cross. To be more precise I could see her hat and the plumes rising from it.

'It's Madame du Bressac,' I said. 'I don't suppose Moorhouse knows anything about her, but I know that this might not bode well for Alice Moorhouse.'

The Frenchwoman reached the cross at last and mounted the

steps. She caught hold of Moorhouse's coat to indicate she was speaking to him, but called out loudly and boldly for everyone to hear.

'I will give you four guineas for this woman and I will then take her into my keeping. Are we agreed on it?'

# TWENTY-SIX

The people around the cross were at first dumbfounded, with even the last ribald remnants standing in silence. Then, around me, I heard a few doubtful murmurs, and a debate began. Some were saying that such a transaction was not in keeping with custom, and that the purchaser of a wife in a halter should always be a man desiring, for one reason or another, to become a husband. Under no known interpretation could Madame du Bressac be so described.

There were others saying different. Moorhouse's speech had had a strong effect and many were thinking, if they were Alice Moorhouse, they would be better out of the clutches of Thomas her husband, who likened himself to Cain and would not be answerable for what he might do if he didn't sell her. This woman would take her to London, give her shelter and find her employment. As to the true nature of the employment she might offer, they were too innocent of city ways to imagine.

Attached to her belt, Madame du Bressac carried a purse not unlike, though not as full as, the one Charlie Johnson had just taken away with him. She pulled the drawstrings loose and shook out four golden coins, which she placed on the flat uppermost surface of the cross's plinth.

'I put my money down,' she said. 'Will we shake hands?'

Moorhouse for the first time appeared unsure. He appealed to the crowd once more.

'I am bid four guineas. Is there, if you please, any other bidder?'

Elizabeth tugged my sleeve.

'Titus! Can't we stop this? Surely it isn't lawful.'

'This is not our village, Lizzy. And remember it's the Whitsun holiday, when the common people hold sway. They believe it's their right to do as they please at Whitsun. The Squire himself could not rule these proceedings out, I think.'

'Then who can stop it?'

I nodded to all those standing around us.

'It's up to Ingolside to stop it, or allow it. For the time being Ingolside itself is the law.'

'It is hateful to be impotent in face of wrong.'

'Impotence is impotence, however, and wrong has many faces. Let us see how this comes out.'

Moorhouse had paced up and down for a minute, perhaps two. He did not look happy, but then he never did. Finally, there being nothing like a counter bid coming in, he went up to Madame du Bressac and put out his hand. She shook it. The deal was done.

For the rest of the evening and much of the night, Ingolsiders would be staying out, having fun among the amusement stalls, ale tents and fortunetellers' booths on the Green or along the length of Street. Almost all of the people were drinking, the younger ones were dancing and love-making while the older ones smoked at their doors, or plied their knitting needles, or played at cards, shuffleboard and skittles. Children sat in circles around storytellers, or in front of the Punch and Judy show on the corner of Elm Tree Lane. I happened to be passing this when I noticed Furzey watching the play from the back of the audience. I went up to him.

'How do, Furzey. Do you feel better now?'

'I do. I am more myself now.'

It seemed any ill feeling between us had dissipated along with the effects of Gillow's extra-strong ale.

'Did you see the fight?' I said.

'Not me. The only battles I like are courtroom battles. So I had forty winks instead and I'm a new man.'

'What about what Tom Moorhouse did? You saw that?'

'Getting rid of his wife? I've heard of it.'

Furzey pointed at the show.

'We could re-name this the Tommy and Alice show now. She's the better off without him, if he beat her as bad as Punch beats Judy.'

'Is that the settled view of the matter?' I said.

'From what they're saying.'

But I wondered if Moorhouse was more than an angry man who beat his wife and then rejected her. Was he in fact John

Lavenham's killer? And was the real reason he was quitting Ingolside for America simply his fear of the gallows?

Now Luke Fidelis came up and we all three repaired to a coffee stall on the Market Place and sat smoking and drinking our coffee. There was something I was itching to know from my friend.

'However did you get the job of medical assistant to Johnson?'

'Quexton's idea. He came to Mrs Booth's early in the morning and asked me. He had been ready to go into the fight as his man's sole second, but somebody had put it to him that I might be of use.'

'And you *were* of use. You said something into Johnson's ear, after the fortieth round, that had quite a strong effect. What was it? I saw him give you a savage look after.'

'I only told him to fight for his mother. Fight for her and to hell with the rest.'

'What do you know about his mother?'

'Nothing. But everyone has a mother, and everyone will fight for her. I don't quite know why I said it but, as you say, it seemed to work.'

Our talk turned to the extraordinary aftermath of the boxing match, the sale of Mrs Moorhouse.

'I didn't see it,' said Fidelis. 'I was tending Johnson's wounds and have heard only the bare facts. You must tell me how it happened.'

I gave a full account of the auction.

'Did the crowd not object or try to stop it?' Fidelis asked.

'At first they didn't know whether to be entertained or appalled. But Moorhouse appealed to customary right and, as it went on, the majority seemed to accept that.'

'Do you have no idea of why Moorhouse did it though, something so extreme as that?'

'For practical reasons,' said Furzey. 'He wants to travel alone. He might need to take another name, go wherever and do whatever he likes. To have his wife along would only be a nuisance. That is purpose one.'

'And is purpose two,' said Fidelis, 'to get the money he needs for his passage to America?'

Furzey tapped the table with his index finger.

'You are right, Doctor. She was his most valuable asset.'

'Then the question is how did he think he would get away with it?'

At this point Elizabeth put her head into the tent, looking for me.

'Come and join us,' I said. 'Will you drink a cup of coffee?'

Elizabeth sat down with us but said no to the drink. I told her what we were discussing.

'That is exactly what I want to know,' she said. 'Is it not a crime in this country to sell another person?'

I thought for a moment, then said, 'It might not be, I think, but Furzey understands the intricacies of common law much better than me.'

Furzey cleared his throat. When asked to elucidate a point of law, he would habitually address the question as a judge might to his court.

'It is customary in these remote country areas for marriage to be regulated differently from what is usual in a town. *Nota bene*, many couples in the country do not even marry in church, but simply exchange vows in front of an innkeeper or a blacksmith, in a form which everyone agrees makes a true marriage.'

He raised a finger.

'Now, though wife-selling may not happen as often as a blacksmith marriage, it is by the same token the poor countryman's way of divorcement. Once a husband's exchanged his woman for money and delivered her in a halter, his duties to her are, by the consent of all, discharged. The marriage is over. It is not a mere separation, *a mensa et thoro*, but *a vinculo matrimonii*: that is, absolutely abolished, allowing both parties to go their separate ways.'

'That is very clear, Furzey,' Fidelis said. 'And so, if you are right, and the sale is done in the accepted form, it will not be opposed by the community.'

Elizabeth closed her eyes and sighed.

'Many people did believe he knocked her about,' she said. 'Perhaps they thought it the best answer for her.'

But, listening to this, my thoughts were moving along quite different lines.

'I wonder if he had another reason,' I said. 'Suppose he did murder Lavenham during the fire at the Three Horns, as I have rather suspected. He might have hit him on the head and left him in the smoke, before coming back to carry him out in the pretence of saving him.'

'And?' asked Fidelis.

'Suppose also that Alice knows her husband killed him – maybe he told her, or she found out somehow – and so he must be sure she is packed off to London with Madame as soon as possible, and will never come back to make statements against him.'

'But he would be safe, wouldn't he?' said Elizabeth. 'A wife may not testify against her husband.'

'But Moorhouse's action in selling her would suggest he and Alice had only a blacksmith marriage in the first place. An assize court might allow such a wife's evidence. He could not run the risk.'

Furzey had another question.

'How, then, did he know Alice would be taken away to London? How could he know Madame would buy her?'

'Oh, that is easy,' said Fidelis. 'The entire sale was rigged in advance. She wanted the woman for her own reasons and she fixed it with Moorhouse.'

'And we know,' said Elizabeth, 'or think we know, what those reasons are.'

'Basket making?' Fidelis suggested.

'It is not a matter for humour,' said Elizabeth. 'Poor Alice would not be the first country girl to be cozened into a ruinous way of life. I think we all remember the case of poor Fanny Kirby.'

We sat for a moment in silence remembering that spirited girl who had occupied so much of my time two years earlier.

'He may also be afraid of her gossiping,' said Elizabeth. 'That might bring other witnesses forward. We know what happened in the inquest and how suspicion against him was raised. It would not be surprising if he's taken steps to protect himself. Yet his callousness is enormous. He is one of those who calculate everything so that their own interests come before every other human life – and that is why I agree with you, Titus, in thinking he is capable of a murder.'

'What reinforced my own suspicion that Moorhouse is a

murderer,' I said, 'was when he spoke in Market Place of how he was going into exile. He said it was just as Cain had been exiled to the Land of Nod. I wonder if he understood what he was implying when he compared himself to the world's first murderer.'

'He is going west of Eden, not east,' said Fidelis. 'But perhaps America really is Cain's Land of Nod. I must go there and find out.'

'Before you do, I suggest we try to find Alice Moorhouse and see if the suspicion is true that she knew Moorhouse was a murderer. She is likely at the Dog and Drum with her new mistress.'

'This is not a matter for me, Coroner,' said Furzey. 'I have engaged a horse at the livery stable and I will leave here in an hour for home. This place has lost its charm for me.'

'By what road do you go?' I asked.

'To Kendal and thence to Preston. There is an overnight coach which always has a last-minute place.'

We all shook hands with him and wished him a good journey.

# TWENTY-SEVEN

T he Dog and Drum was bursting with rowdy customers. 'I've not seen such a ruck as this in here,' said black-haired Maggie. 'They're tossing it back as never before. The boys are sicking it up against one side of the house, and the old 'uns are pissing it out against t'other. It's the best Whit Ales we've ever seen.'

I asked for Madame du Bressac.

'The Frenchie woman, that bought Alice Moorhouse for four pound? Never heard of the like, me, but my father says a wife was sold for a servant seven years back in Carlisle, so it's happened before.'

'Where is the Frenchwoman's room?'

'She's been stopping in the Berrys' private apartment. You go up those steps and it's behind the door you see right in front of you.'

Following these instructions, we went through and presented ourselves at the door. Elizabeth said it might be best if she spoke with Alice privately, and this was agreed. I knocked and a muffled voice called out what I took to be 'Come in'. We did.

We passed into a small lobby with several doors, one of which lay open. It was a bedroom and on the bed lay two large travelling boxes. Under her new mistress's supervision, Alice was packing them.

Madame had been in residence here for just forty-eight hours but she had already strewn the Berrys' rooms with a great assortment of clothing and clutter. Alice was now putting this profusion of day clothing, underclothing, night clothing, hats, shoes, wigs and cosmetics into tidy piles and filling the boxes with them. Madame's directions were precise as to where everything should go, and Alice's cheeks were red with the effort of getting it right.

As soon as she saw us enter, Alice looked alarmed. As Françoise du Bressac greeted us with a cold smile, Alice scurried into a room beyond and shut the door.

'You are leaving Ingolside, Madame?' I said, nodding at the boxes.

'I have reserved places in one of the Yorkshire coaches, which will leave before morning, I am told. It gives us time to get ready.'

'Everyone is surprised about the transaction you completed with Thomas Moorhouse,' I said.

'I did it, as any Christian would, to save her. Moorhouse was a brute to her. She comes with me to a better life.'

'May I have a private word with Alice, Madame?' said Elizabeth. 'We have been friends and I should like to bid her farewell.'

Madame waved towards the inner door through which Alice had retreated.

'Go in if you like. She is there.'

After knocking, Elizabeth pushed it open and went inside, closing the door behind her. Madame went to the box Alice had been working at and picked out a bodice, which she refolded and replaced. Fidelis spoke first.

'I wonder, did you perhaps know beforehand that Mr Moorhouse intended to sell his wife? Or was it accidentally that you happened on the sale?'

He adopted a pleasant conciliatory tone, not wanting to antagonize her.

'I knew of it before. Of course I knew. I avoid always the *étourderie*.'

'So you agreed the price with him in advance?'

She spoke sharply. 'I did not say that. And this is a business matter, Doctor. It is a thing only between me and Monsieur Moorhouse, and nobody else.'

There was an imperious quality to her, a way of speaking that invites a man to quail rather than contradict her. It was her aristocratic nature, I supposed.

Finally, I broke the awkward silence that followed.

'I am surprised you do not wait to take your leave until morning, Madame.'

'I have important business to attend to. I have left notice of my wishes with Reverend Cumberledge regarding the gravestone. It will give John's full name, when he was born and died, and

the message *Au Revoir Mon Cheri*. It means I will see him again,
you see, for I believe there is destiny in the next life, if not in
this one.'

We spent a little more time talking about her coach journey
back to London, where she would stop on the way and suchlike,
until Elizabeth came back to us and we all said a final farewell
to Madame du Bressac.

The light had all but dwindled away. Across the road from the
roaring inn, and compared to it, the Green was now a relatively
quiet retreat. It was lit by paper lanterns and ringed by benches,
no doubt for the viewing of cricket on an ordinary Saturday and,
finding one that was free, Luke and I sat down with Elizabeth
between us to hear in the twilight her account of her chat with
Alice Moorhouse.

'The room had been used for Madame's dressing and keeping
her dresses and gowns,' she told us. 'She must have brought a
score of them with her.

'Alice was kneeling on the floor folding one of them so I knelt
down with her to put her at ease. It didn't work, though. She
was very nervous and possibly frightened and chiefly answered
me with single words – yes, no, and happen – and wouldn't look
me in the eye. She said nothing against her husband – I should
say her former husband. I wondered about this and asked if she
is happy or sad to be parted from him. She said she was neither
one nor the other. I tried gently to warn her of the sort of work
– if that is the word – that Madame du Bressac would likely
have for her, but she only hunched her shoulders. She told me
she was ready for anything and that anything was better than the
life she had had.'

'Did you put it to her that she knew the truth about the death
of John Lavenham?' I said.

'I mentioned it. She only looked at me and said, "Maybe I
do, maybe I don't. It doesn't matter now." She wants the whole
business done with and is thinking only about the future. In
spite of everything, I think she has reserves of spirit and determination in her, which she will need when she gets to Covent
Garden.'

'You think she goes to London willingly?' said Fidelis.

'Sometimes a person can be so bullied that they lose their free will.'

'I don't know that she was bullied,' said Elizabeth. 'She agreed publicly to be sold when she stood with Moorhouse at the cross. She wanted rid of him.'

'We have nothing else to go on but her own words,' I said. 'We may wonder what she really thinks, but wondering does not lead anywhere.'

It was the lawyer in me speaking, slow-moving and cautious. But even Fidelis couldn't see the matter otherwise. He sighed and said, 'By the way, what is *étourderie*?'

Elizabeth laughed.

'It is the action of the grasshopper. It is what the slug never does.'

'What is it then?'

'Impulsiveness, Luke, and not taking care. It is chasing after the setting sun, which in the end gets you hopelessly lost far from home.'

She sprang up from the bench.

'So, what shall we do now? Would it be impulsive of me to suggest going to look for a syllabub?'

Extending the day in pleasure-seeking is wearing as you get older. At nearly fifty I already found myself, on occasion, longing for my bed at nine o'clock. On this night, by the time we'd had syllabubs, walked once more around the Green and watched a group of Morris men dance a stag hunt, it was near eleven. So, leaving Fidelis about to compete with a drunken Yorkshireman in a game of arm wrestling, Elizabeth and I headed back down Street to Holloway's and went straight to bed.

Lying next to my wife, it suddenly occurred to me that I had quite forgotten I was under sentence from an anonymous letter-writer. Indeed, I had only thought of it once, and that was in passing. Elizabeth had thought about it more seriously.

'Shall we leave as soon as we can, Titus?' she said. 'I do not like this anonymous threat against you. You have completed your business so there is nothing to keep us here.'

'There isn't. We must enquire about the best way to travel but it won't be until after Whitsunday.'

'Good. I hate to think of you being assaulted by someone whose spelling is so atrocious.'

Elizabeth picked the book by Gay from the bedside stand and began leafing through it.

'Oh! Here is the verse, Titus. *The Slug and the Grasshopper*, just what we were speaking of earlier. It is the very demonstration of *étourderie* matched against good sense, the exact different characters of yourself and Luke. Let me read it to you.'

I stopped a yawn and blinked my eyes.

'Please do. I know it, I think, but to be truthful I'm not sure of the details.'

And so she began: 'A slug called out to a grasshopper, "Ho!" . . .'

I tried to stay awake, but never heard how it ended.

# TWENTY-EIGHT

Whitsunday broke warmer and brighter than any previous day of the year. Deciding to go out and down to the lakeside before breakfast, Elizabeth and I found the air so fine and pure that by taking deep breaths we cleared away much of the cobweb left in our heads by yesterday's indulgence.

We first called at the house of the postmaster, whose name was Oystern, to enquire about how best to travel home. He had (as he should) a comprehensive knowledge of routes around the region.

'Your best and easiest idea's horseback across the bay at low tide,' he told us, 'and to ride thence to Preston, or take the coach from Lancaster. To have you safely across the sands and give enough time to catch the coach, you need the tide to be at its lowest early morning, which it'll be this week from Tuesday till Friday. Don't try it today or tomorrow because you'll drown before you get there. You could take the coach from Kendal, but there is none going south on Sundays and Mondays.'

'Is there not a ship that goes to Preston from Trimbleby?' said Elizabeth. 'I came here on the *Jennifer.*'

'She'll not be here until end of the week, and there's no other ship that I've heard of.'

'Shall we stay until Tuesday, then?' I said as we walked down to the lake's shore. 'And take the route across the sands to Lancaster and from there the coach home?'

'I should like it much better than six hours in the coach from Kendal.'

'Very well. You'll be bouncing Hector on your knee by Tuesday evening.'

We had completed a little of our favourite walk along the western bank, when we heard men shouting in the woods high above the opposite shore. They were hallooing and calling to each other, though it was impossible to make out what they were saying.

'Are they out shooting?' said Elizabeth.

'I doubt it, on a Sunday. The wolf, though. I wonder if it is to do with the wolf. If they are after him they might not call it sport, but something else.'

'What else?'

'A wolf is always considered a threat, in all societies. It is less of an animal than a kind of boggart, intent on tearing the throats of lambs and calves in the fields, gobbling up little children and haunting the graveyards with its howling.'

'But this one is real enough, Titus. We heard it howling the other evening.'

'We did. Or thought we did. Anyway, what I'm saying is, that to go after the wolf is of the nature of making war on it and everybody knows wars do not stop even for the Sabbath.'

Elizabeth was holding my arm and I felt her shudder.

'I don't like such talk, Titus.'

I shook off her arm and waved at the sky.

'But look at the day, Lizzy. What evil thing can possibly happen on a day like this?'

At the Whitsunday service, the Reverend Cumberledge preached on drunkenness to a church full of sore heads and crapulous regrets. It made a receptive congregation and when, after near an hour's homily, he came in his most resounding voice to the climax, there were not a few cries of supplication from the dry-mouthed and throbbing heads before him.

'Will ye not therefore renounce the gross intemperance of strong ales?' he challenged.

'Aye. On my life. Amen. Amen.'

'And will ye also abjure once and for all the temptation of spiritous liquor?'

'We shall, we shall. Verily. Amen.'

'For "wine is a mocker, strong drink is raging," saith Scripture. "And whoever is deceived thereby is not wise".'

'Yea. Make me wise, Lord. I have sinned.'

'So, my friends, resolve from this day on wisdom.'

'Amen!'

'On temperance.'

'Amen! Amen!'

'And, for the good of your souls, on sobriety.'

He descended from the pulpit with a satisfied smile. Rarely had his preaching been punctuated by so many cries of mortification and repentance.

'The Rector disparages John Wesley,' Elizabeth whispered to me, 'but that sermon might have been written by any Methodist.'

We passed through the church porch and into the sunlit churchyard with Mr Holloway, Miss Hart and, just ahead of us, Squire Lumsden. Waiting at and around the lychgate was a group of leather-gaitered men carrying guns, led by the gamekeeper Charles Bowden. Bowden's expression was grave as he saluted the Squire.

'Begging your worship's pardon, but Mr Wilkin Tree that's been living in Lakeside Lodge has vanished,' he said. 'The woman who cleans the lodge found no sign of him when she went there yesterday morning, and I went myself at seven today, and there's still no sign of him or any that he's spent the night there. We've been out as a search party in the woods, in case that wolf got him. No sign as yet. We've come down for our breakfasts then we'll go back.'

Word quickly passed through the congregation, who had gathered in groups in different parts of the churchyard. I went forward and told the Squire that I'd seen him on Friday evening before eight o'clock and that he left me to climb up through the trees, as he'd agreed to join Bowden for a night patrol of the rabbit warrens. Nobody else had seen Wilkin Tree since then.

Squire Lumsden asked Bowden if he had indeed engaged to meet Tree on Friday night. The gamekeeper shook his head.

'We said we might go out on patrol this last Friday night, being as it would be a favourable moon. We've done it before, more than once. But my wife was feverish all day Friday, so I never sent him word that it was on.'

'No message by a boy inviting him?' I said.

'No. Like I said.'

'Then what the devil was he up to?' said Lumsden.

Lumsden gave instructions for men to begin the search again, starting from Lakeside Lodge and following every path that led upwards through the trees. He said he would join them in the wood within the hour bringing his dog, who he said was a dabster at tracking.

'I had better join the search myself,' I said to Elizabeth. 'This may become a Coroner's case.'

'Oh no, Titus! Let it not keep us here any longer.'

'We must see. I will bring Luke to join us. It might be a doctor's case even if it is not a Coroner's one.'

Some of the men brought a firearm, and those without one carried a stick or a sickle (in one case a hatchet). Going into the trees, I myself picked up a long, straight piece of fallen wood, not so much to use as a weapon as to keep my footing and probe the undergrowth. Luke had brought a knobbed walking cane that would make a serviceable club if required. He had also brought a canvas haversack containing some medical equipment and a brace of pistols.

We had joined the group led by Arthur Lumsden and his much-lauded dog. It was agreed that we would start not at the lake shore but from the bottom of Elm Tree Lane, and to climb straight to the upper woods, with the lower slopes being already under search. On the way up, Lumsden accosted me and, to my surprise, he was genial.

'Cragg, I want to thank you. I may have previously had words with you about your investigation into Lavenham's death. But let me say, for my part, I am extremely content with your inquest and its finding. Extremely.'

'You should thank Curly Berry and the jury, not me.'

'Berry is a prize poltroon and, by the way, in the pay of my mother. But yes, perhaps I should thank him. Nobody in this place, not even Mrs Lumsden, wanted the death to be anything other than accidental. And so, thankfully, it was found.'

As we got in amongst the trees there was excited talk among the men about the wolf which, according to the majority opinion, must have hunted Tree down and savagely killed him on that night of the full moon. This, as everyone knew, was when a wolf – specially a lone wolf – was at its most deadly. The expectation from the beginning, then, was that we would be finding a corpse variously torn up and dismembered. A group of the younger men, along with the dog, reached the ridge in advance and ran about giving wolf howls until Lumsden puffed up the slope and gave vent, telling them to give over fooling and start looking.

The windows and door were shut tight, and no dog was barking. I walked around the house and looked into the yard. A few hens and a couple of geese were about the place, but all the doors, including the barn, were shut tight. I saw Moorhouse's dog lying in the entrance to his kennel. I thought he was asleep until I went over to him and saw the bullet hole in the top of his skull. It was then that I knew Moorhouse had left for good.

I had earlier obtained the key to Lakeside Lodge's out room where the corpse due for inquest in the morning was lying. I had also engaged the services of Harry Jolliby. Saying goodbye to Elizabeth, I now went to Jolliby's cottage from where, riding his donkey and cart, we took the path along the shore to Lakeside Lodge.

I asked the carter what gossip there was this morning about the death of Wilkin Tree.

'They're telling the old tale of Groundel and Wolloff. What they're sayin' now is that Wolloff came back and killed the stranger, him being called Tree, you see? Frighted him to death, they're saying, if that's the same as killin' him.'

'I don't know that story. Will you tell it me, Mr Jolliby?'

It turned out Jolliby was a good storyteller.

'Well, Sir, in the woods above Ingolmere there is a dead, hollow oak, exactly where I don't know, and a long time ago that oak was owned by a powerful witch woman, Groundel by name, who lived in a house in the woods nearby to it. Now, down her chimney one night there came a spirit that was called Wolloff, who coveted Groundel's power. And this Wolloff carried a great sack and into this sack he put all Groundel's spell books and carried them back up the chimney and away into the forest. When Groundel found her books a-missing she was vexed and went out to challenge Wolloff to a battle of spells at a place where stood that dead old oak. Wolloff opened the books he'd stole, but he had never learned to read so the spells in 'em were no good to him, meaning that Groundel easily won the battle. She straight away took power over him and prisoned him inside the oak, where he must stay until a new tree should appear in the full moon and bring back its life. Centuries have passed, Sir, and the new tree has not appeared so that, though Groundel had long gone, Wolloff remained prisoned. But now at last a man has come at full moon, a man by the name of Tree, and all without meaning to he's let Wolloff out of prison to roam the woods again at his pleasure. That's the story, Mr Cragg, and you can believe it or not but many're a-tellin' it around the village.'

'Yes, I can well see why they might.'

'The first witness is always the first finder. I don't know his name.'

Now, with the body of Wilkin Tree safely deposited in the side room at the Dissenters' Hall, Elizabeth and I were at Holloway's Farm drawing up summonses for the list – not a very long one – of witnesses for tomorrow's hearing.

'Herbert,' she said.

I poised my pen over the paper.

'What's his family name?'

'He's Lumsden's dog, Titus.'

'Ah! I see what you mean.'

'If only he could give testimony, that would be a wonder.'

'If he could, so could the wolf. He was really the first finder.'

'Not a she, Titus?'

'Let's not argue about that. In the folk tale, it's a he. Wolloff.'

'Wolloff?'

'Never mind. It's only something fanciful Harry Jolliby told me.'

Amelia Hart was sitting with us over her sewing. I asked if she knew the names of the two men who had reached Tree's body in the woods on Sunday, after Herbert had sniffed it out.

'I don't, but let's ask Boaz. He's a bright boy.'

Amelia Hart had recommended a boy who could be trusted to carry the summonses to each of the witnesses' houses, in return for sixpence. Boaz, when he came in, proved to be aged about nine, fairly clean, and completely unafraid of us. As soon as he came in, I had confidence in him.

'That was Stephen and Simon Winderbutt, so they tell me,' he said when I asked him the same question.

'Brothers?'

'Aye, twins. So it don't matter which of 'em you talk to.'

'No, I suppose not. Do you know where they live?'

'Aye, on Moss Lane with their mother.'

I showed him the piece of paper with the list: Lizzy Duckham, Charles Bowden, Luke Fidelis. To my surprise Boaz could read.

'Right, Sir,' he said, looking with moving lips through the names. 'I can get to the Duckhams, Mr Bowden and the Winderbutts quick as a rocket, as none lives far. Dr Fid— What is it? Is he that doctor that's been niggling with Helen Booth?'

'Niggling, Boaz?' said Elizabeth. 'Shame on you! That's not a proper word to be using. You embarrass Miss Hart.'

'Sorry, Marm.'

'To answer your question,' I said. 'Yes it is "that doctor" who stays with the Widow Booth. But you can forget about him, as he already knows he is a witness.'

Almost as soon as the boy had hared away with the three summonses, Mr Holloway came in. He had been acting as the Squire's chief deputy in the wolf hunt, supervising the line of defence on the ridge, and had since been drinking bumpers with Lumsden at the Manor House.

'Disappointing outcome to the day, very,' he said, collapsing into a chair at the fireside. 'Lumsden's plan looked a good 'un. Now that no wolf appeared, the village is full of talk about there not being a real wolf at all, but a spirit wolf or some such – a werewolf. Others are going even further and talking about a goblin or a troll, for goodness' sake.'

'What do you think, Uncle?' asked Elizabeth.

'I'm not superstitious. I don't think there are werewolves, let alone goblins and trolls. I'm sure there is an actual wolf out there. Squire's been after it for weeks.'

'We heard it howl, did we not, Titus?'

'Yes, and I believe I may have seen its footprint. I do not think footprints are left by spirits or trolls. Or wolloffs.'

'Any road, the wolf escaped our beaters somehow,' Holloway went on. 'Either it slipped through the cordon in the woods or the one up on the ridge. Or maybe it hid in a foxhole while they walked over it. They're said to be the cleverest damned beasts you can meet.'

He rose, opened the writing desk between the room's two windows, and started shuffling through a handful of papers.

'Where the devil's that printed sheet of market results from Keswick?' he said.

Boaz now returned for his sixpence.

'I would've been back sooner, only I were stopped in Elm Tree Lane on way to Bowden's by a lad, wanting to know what I were doin'. When I tell'd him I were carrying a letter for sixpence, he started telling me to give up the sixpence but I go I've not got it yet. So then he wants the letter, which I wouldn't give up, an' he tries to hit me.'

Holloway was reading the report on stock prices. He lowered the paper and took off his spectacles. 'You were attacked, boy? Who was it you said did it?'

'That Danny, that lives with his uncle, Thatcher Bennett.'

'Daniel?' I asked. 'But he's harmless enough, isn't he? And while I remember here's your sixpence, Boaz.'

'Not harmless to me he's not,' said Boaz. 'He's a bully.'

From his breeches pocket he produced a handkerchief, none too clean, and wrapped his coin in it before stuffing it back.

'But you escaped and are none the worse?'

'I dodged him. And he didn't get that letter, but I had to take a long way round, like I say, to dodge him.'

In our room as I was making ready for bed, Lizzy was again reading from the book of verses by John Gay.

'It's interesting how a person looks very different from a child's point of view,' I said. 'That Daniel seemed to me a perfectly polite, tractable boy.'

She lowered the book.

'Reassuring appearances should be looked at twice. There's a story here about a boy that goes up into the mountains where, as the people believe, all sorts of evil spirits and fantastic monsters are living. The boy only wants to play with, as he thinks, a friendly bear, but when it's the bear that kills him no one in his village will believe it. They insist it must have been an evil dragon that ate him, not an ordinary lovable old bear.'

'And your point is, my love?'

'The fearful people of this village should have that poem read to them. They might see there is no werewolf in the woods. No goblin or troll. Just an ordinary wolf.'

'Whose footprint I've seen.'

'And whose howl we've both heard.'

'On the other hand, Lizzy, I cannot see what's ordinary about a wolf preying on people.'

'Look at it from the wolf's side. What could be more natural?'

Much later, in the darkest hour, I received a prod in the ribs and came foggily awake.

'I've had an idea, Titus,' she whispered. 'Can I tell you?'

'No. Tell me in the morning.'

# THIRTY-TWO

We both overslept and then on Wednesday morning everything was a rush. Necessary things for the hearing – writing materials, the case ledger, my hand bell, the notes of questions for the witnesses that I had compiled the previous evening – all had to be taken up to the hall. Once we arrived there we were busy, with Ben Bennett's help, moving tables and seats.

'Lizzy, you haven't told me your idea that you had in the night,' I said.

She was hoisting one end of a bench, with Bennett at the other. When they had carried it to its position, she moved across to me and put her mouth near my ear.

'Not with him in the room. I'll tell you presently.'

By half past nine the jurymen started coming in. For their breakfast we had small beer with ham slices and buns from the bakery and while they were having their food Elizabeth took my arm.

'Come out for a walk on the Green,' she said. 'My idea has grown into something more than just an idea since I thought more about it in the night.'

'Very well, what is it?' I said when we had gone outside. 'Did this come to you in a dream?'

'Don't be daft, Titus. Dreams are not ideas. I was lying awake and thinking about poor Boaz being bullied by that youth, Daniel. What do we know about Daniel, except he is nasty to other smaller lads?'

'I thought he was supposed to be half-sharp. He's evidently devoted to his dog. He's been fostered up by his uncle and aunt, the Bennetts. But what does this all mean? How is it relevant?'

'I suspect him.'

'You suspect him? For what? He wasn't there at the fire in which Lavenham died, as far as I know. And it was a wolf, not a boy, who terrified Wilkin Tree to death.'

'Was it? I told myself the same but then I got thinking about the poem by Gay that I told you about last night – the boy going up the mountain to see the playful bear. No one thought the bear would kill a sweet little boy, so they blamed it on an imaginary dragon. But it was Bruin the bear after all.'

'I don't think I follow you.'

'When I asked what do we know about Daniel, what was the second thing you said?'

'He is devoted to his dog.'

'Exactly. His dog, Limer, isn't he called? The biggest dog you could find. A dog so big and so good-natured that the last time we saw him he was giving rides to four-year-old children in the Rectory garden. It is not that I disbelieve in a spirit wolf – I now think there may be no sort of wolf in the forest at all, just as there was no sort of dragon in Gay's poem.'

'And it was Daniel's Limer that frightened Wilkin Tree?'

'In a word, yes.'

I was transported by a sudden burst of emotion.

'My God, Lizzy, it makes sense! In the forest moonlight he would look terrifying. Even his friendliness might appear hostile. And the pawprints beside Tree's body, they were Limer's great feet pressing into the ground as he tugged at Tree's body by the arm.'

'Yes, and suppose he was doing it playfully, Titus, not meaning to hurt. He is a playful animal, like Gay's Bruin.'

'This is wonderful. I believe you may have solved the case. You are a woman in a million and I don't mind who knows it.'

I wrapped my arms around her and recklessly kissed her full on the mouth.

'There was no wolf, but only Limer,' I repeated. 'The biggest dog in the village.'

'In the county, Titus.'

'Well, if this is true, I know how to prove it. We must go to the Bennetts' house immediately.'

'What about the inquest? It's almost ten o'clock.'

'No matter. The Bennetts live just over there. We must prove your idea first, then have the inquest.'

A minute later I was hammering on the door of Pilling's Cottage, the home of the Bennetts and also of Daniel. Mrs Bennett came to the door.

'Mrs Bennett,' I said. 'I trust you remember me, Titus Cragg.'

'Of course, you are the Coroner. You are holding an inquest today.'

'That is why I am here. Please, may I see where your nephew sleeps? I believe there may be important evidence there. This is my wife, Elizabeth, by the way.'

Mrs Bennett and Elizabeth exchanged smiles.

'Daniel sleeps in his own room, Sir. The little bedroom at the back.'

Daniel's room was indeed small, with just enough space for a narrow bed against one wall and a large dog basket against the opposite one. The only other feature of the room was a wardrobe or cupboard built into the wall. I opened its door and put my head in, while feeling around. There were just a few clothes, a hat and a pair of shoes. I went down on my knees and peered under the bed. There were two bags there, a leather one and another made of sailcloth. The leather bag was empty. The sail-cloth one was a haversack, and it contained a powder horn, some bullets, a single leather glove and a woollen muffler. I peered under again but there was nothing more to find.

I stood and looked around again, then seized the dog basket and pulled it away from the wall. A long object of some kind lay on the floor, wrapped in sacking. I picked it up and unwrapped it until I was holding in my hand the very thing I'd been hoping – no, expecting to find. It was a hunting gun of flintlock design. The gun was fairly new as far as I could tell and in good condition. I smelled the breech but it had not been fired since its last cleaning. Then I noticed that, into the gun's cherry wood stock, two letters had been carved: the initials 'W.T.'

In a little less than ten minutes' time I was back in the Dissenters' Hall, sitting behind my table and calling order. The inquest was about to begin just a quarter of an hour late.

I swore in the jury and a shoemaker named Brook was elected foreman. We then went through the customary inspection of the corpse. I pointed out to them the cuts and bite wounds and the indented skull, and manipulated the skull to show that the neck had been severed. The men's reactions were familiar: a blend of fascination and pity, with added horror in this case caused by the state of the dead man's face. Everyone knew the circumstances of how Tree had been found. Looking at the torn and bloody hand, I heard some muttering and the word 'wolf'. Or was it 'Wolloff'?

The audience in the hall was by no means as packed as it had been for John Lavenham, although, as we returned, some were still coming in and taking their seats. On my calling up the first finder, the Winderbutt brothers both stepped forward, two curly-haired young men who appeared identical to the eye of anyone except perhaps their mother. One of them sat on the chair while the other stood behind him, resting a hand on his brother's shoulder. The standing Winderbutt gave his name as Stephen, while the sitting one said he was Simon. When I asked them to swear in as witnesses, they did so in perfect unison, and when I said this was an unusual thing, not before seen in my court, they answered me again in unison.

'It is natural to us, Mr Cragg,' they said, 'as we are twins, and we think as one.'

'I can tell.'

I looked at Elizabeth, who mouthed, 'Why not try it?'

I thought the same, though aware that Furzey would never countenance two witnesses speaking together as if they were singular.

'Very well,' I said, 'we shall see as we proceed how comprehensible it is.'

It was extremely comprehensible, as the words were clear and much more audible than was usual. The brothers told how they had been to the fore in the search party, with the Lumsdens' spaniel Herbert. The dog had run ahead in the fading light and disappeared from view. Hurrying on they found him in the gully, whining and nuzzling a shape, which they could not identify until descending to its level. There they saw it was a man. His face was so terribly injured that they did not recognize him. It was not until the body had been brought up from the gully that everybody agreed it was that of Wilkin Tree.

Luke Fidelis then gave his account of the state of the body and what could be inferred from it. He explained how the sever-ance of the neck was caused when the top of the skull was stopped by striking the sharp projecting stone. The forward momentum of his body over this would have instantly broken Tree's neck and paralyzed him. In almost all such cases that he had known, in animals and people, death was nearly instantaneous as the heart and the breathing would both stop.

I asked him about the frightful injuries to the face.

'They are due to animal predation *post mortem*,' he said.

'Many people are discussing the idea that this was a predatory wolf. What do you think, Doctor?'

'The animal might have been a wolf, but I wouldn't exclude any other woodland flesh-eater.'

'And what about the injured hand and forearm?'

'It is a lacerating injury which looks like the work of a large animal. I would say it was trying to pull the body out of the gully where as we've heard it was found. I noticed the paw prints of a large dog-like animal, which could have been a wolf, printed in the ground in front of the body. I presume it was this animal that had been pulling on the body.'

After that Bowden came up and told the inquest that he had previously, more than once, invited Wilkin Tree to go out with him on his gamekeeper's rounds. They had walked through the woods looking out for poachers and, more recently, the wolf that was reported to be in the area. He had not however done this last Friday, nor had he sent any message to Mr Tree on that night.

'When you would go out with Mr Tree, did he carry a weapon?'

'Yes. His own hunting piece.'

'And if he considered he was to meet you in the woods on Friday night, do you think he would have been carrying his hunting piece?'

'Undoubtedly.'

'And was it found anywhere in the vicinity of his body, when it was discovered on Sunday?'

'No, Sir. It was not.'

Mrs Duckham now came up. She spoke about Wilkin Tree as she had known him, a tidy man, a reader and a map drawer who also liked to go shooting sometimes. I asked if Tree knew about the wolf that folk were all talking about. She said yes, he had mentioned it to her and asked her if it were true. He had more than once told her he was afraid of it.

I thanked her. The jury were whispering together, already

deliberating, as if they had heard and seen enough. The foreman approached me.

'We've heard enough, Mr Cragg. Accident, we all think, when running away from a wolf. Can we finish it with that?'

'Wait, Mr Brook,' I said. 'I have something more to show you which may change your mind.'

I asked for the boy Daniel to come to the witness chair.

As soon as he started to speak there was no doubt that his speech was impaired. He recited the oath as if his tongue was too big for his mouth, which tended to muffle his words. He was subject also to attacks of uncontrolled blinking. I questioned him with exaggerated care.

'Daniel, how old are you?'

'Sixteen.'

'Did you know Wilkin Tree?'

'Yer. Not to talk to.'

'Did you never talk to him?'

'No.'

'And did he ever see your dog Limer?'

'I don't know.'

'Do you live with your uncle and aunt Bennett, at Pilling's Cottage?'

'Yer.'

'Do you keep a gun there, Daniel?'

'You what?'

'A gun, a hunting piece.'

I could see he was thinking. Despite appearances, Daniel was no simpleton. He was put on guard by my question.

'No,' he said at last.

The gun was lying wrapped in its sacking under my chair. I leaned down and picked it up, letting the sacking fall away.

'Do you not recognize this gun, Daniel?'

'I . . . No. No, I don't.'

'Then you may be surprised to hear that about forty-five minutes ago I found it myself at Pilling's Cottage. It was in your bedroom, wrapped in sacking. Can you read, Daniel?'

'What?'

'Do you know your letters?'

'Aye.'

I handed the gun over to the jury foreman and asked him to pass it to the witness.

'Look at the stock, that's the wooden part you press against your shoulder when shooting. What can you read on it?'

'Letters. A "W" and a "T".'

'So, "W.T.", carved with a knife or chisel. What do you think that might stand for?'

'D'know.'

'Wilkin Tree, perhaps?'

The boy said nothing but quickly thrust the gun back into the hands of the foreman. I signaled for him to show it to the rest of the jury while Elizabeth handed me the haversack.

'Do you have a haversack, Daniel?'

'No.'

'Yet only this morning I found this haversack, which contains a powder horn and bullets. It was in your bedroom.'

Daniel did not respond. His face was set in a scowl, the lips forming a tight arch.

'It looks exactly like the one I saw Mr Tree carrying last Friday evening. It was as he set off into the woods to meet, as he thought, Mr Bowden. Do you know why he thought Mr Bowden would be waiting for him?'

Daniel's face was still stony.

'A message was brought by a boy who pretended it was from Mr Bowden. That boy was you, wasn't it?'

Again he refused to reply.

'What is your family name? Is it Bennett?'

'No.'

'Then what is it? Who is your father?'

'If you want to know, it's Brabner. My dad's Ted Brabner.'

'Ted Brabner. The same who was forced out of his farm when his own father died, because the Squire threatened to exact a new higher rate of the tax called heriot? The same who is said to have burned the house in anger and despair before he left?'

Daniel, who had until now been so stolid, banged his hands on the chair's arms and sprang up, shouting. 'He never burned our house! It were Squire's doin' or his men. An' my Dad. My Ma. Our Dorothy. Dead an' gone, an' our Philip and Charlie gone away. Only me left. An' our house gone an' all. It's wicked. Wicked!'

His passion subsided as quickly as it had risen and he again stood still, looking at me through eyelids formed into slits.

'So what did you do, Daniel?' I said, trying a softer tone. 'I ask because it may be that you were the last person to see Wilkin Tree alive. And that is important because the reason why we are all here is to find out what happened when he died.'

Daniel made a fist of one hand and pressed it to his mouth. I persisted.

'Did you go up with Limer that night, Daniel, up to the woods to find Mr Tree? What did you mean your dog to do? I have seen your power over him and have no doubt he could kill a man, if you ordered him to. But perhaps your idea was only to frighten Mr Tree? So, which is it, Daniel?'

Daniel stood looking at me with his knuckles sullen in his mouth, saying nothing.

At one time there were professional torturers, whose duty was to go around putting suspects to the question and extorting their answers. The coroners of today have no such luxury to call on and, short of screwing Daniel's thumbs, or stretching him on the rack by exquisite degrees, there was nothing I could do to break his steadfast and defiant silence. Yet, although it can provide no detail, silence is a kind of statement in itself and I allowed the jury to draw their conclusions from Daniel Brabner's. When they had done so, the inquest verdict on the death of Wilkin Tree that Foreman Brook put up to me now gave a different slant on the facts.

> . . . that the said Wilkin Tree did accidentally die by a broken neck sustained after falling into a gully in the Ingolside Wood while fleeing in the dark of the woods at night from a dog belonging to Daniel Brabner, with the name of Limer being a very large Mastiff which he thought to be a wolf.

I asked if they had all agreed and Brook said they had.

'Then you may sign it, Mr Brook and, when you have done so, these proceedings will be at an end and the late Mr Tree can be buried and lie in peace.'

# THIRTY-THREE

As Elizabeth and I left the Dissenters' Hall carrying away the papers and paraphernalia of the inquest, we heard voices calling our names. The Rector and his lady were perambulating towards us.

'Cragg, and Mrs Cragg!' said Mr Cumberledge. 'How do you both do? A horrid few days, has it not been?'

'Yes, the death of Mr Wilkin Tree following so close after that of his associate Mr Lavenham has indeed been shocking.'

'Death? Mr Tree? Lavenham? I didn't know those fellows. No, no! I refer to those drunken Ales, and the bestial boxing performance, and then, oh then! The dreadful occurrence at the Market Cross.'

'Dreadful, *dreadful* occurrence,' echoed Mrs Cumberledge. 'And so wicked it was quite unsuitable even to be condemned in the Rector's Whitsunday sermon.'

'It was,' her husband agreed. 'Did you hear my remarks at all?'

'Oh yes,' said Elizabeth. 'You spoke with great force, Mr Cumberledge.'

'Then you must have noticed, I am more than happy to pit myself against the devil of drink, and even of the sport of prize-fighting and of any gambling that attends it. But such indecency as Thomas Moorhouse displayed in putting his wife up for— Oh! I cannot say the word. His action was, well, I must use the word unconscionable.'

'Unconscionable, unconscionable,' agreed Mrs Cumberledge.

A silence fell. The Rector laced his hands together over his belly and twiddled his thumbs. Mrs Cumberledge looked at him worshipfully.

'I suppose you shall now be returning whence you came,' said the Rector at last.

'We shall leave tomorrow.'

'And we shall be thankful.'

He sighed.

'It has indeed been a most terrible few days.'

'I hope you do not blame us for them, Rector.'

'Not entirely. But the sooner all of you outsiders leave this parish, the happier we shall be, shall we not, my dear?'

'We shall be,' said Mrs Cumberledge with emphasis. 'We shall indeed be.'

After dinner with Mr Holloway and Amelia Hart, which we had a little later than usual, Elizabeth went out with Amelia to visit Mrs Booth, and to bid her goodbye. I knew I ought not leave Ingolside without having a final conversation with Arthur Lumsden, so I walked in the other direction to the Manor House.

The Squire was sitting alone in his comfortable oak-paneled parlour reading legal papers. He took off his spectacles as I was shown in.

'Thank you for your conclusion on poor Tree's death. Scared by the wolf. Very satisfactory.'

'We have just finished the inquest,' I said. 'The verdict is a little different from my report because new information came to my attention only as we began.'

'New information?'

'We found that a young member of the population had developed a grudge against Wilkin Tree. He used his dog to frighten him. Otherwise the verdict was very much as Dr Fidelis and I described. It was dark. Wilkin Tree ran from the dog, fell into the gully and died. The important difference is that there is no wolf.'

'No wolf? Of course there is a wolf. There must be a wolf.'

'It was this boy's mastiff, not a wolf.'

'And has the boy – I assume you mean the idiot Daniel, who is the only villager that I am aware has a mastiff – has he confessed?'

'No. He refuses to speak. But the evidence is impossible to ignore. He had the gun carried by Tree hidden in his room.'

'Oh, dear, no. Is that all you have? He could have simply found it lying around. There's no doubt about the wolf, though. None whatever. I cannot manage without the wolf.'

'May I ask why the wolf is so important?'

Lumsden closed his eyes for a moment, breathing out.

'I need the wolf to prey on my sheep. Or at the very least I want the real threat of a wolf. I want people to think there is a flesh-and-blood predator in the woods. The most damaging thing I am faced with as an improving squire is this superstition about the wicked witch haunting these parts in everlasting struggle with a spirit wolf. These peasants who think there is such a witch and a bogey wolf are imprisoned in the past, clinging to their out-of-date beliefs. A real wolf, not a bogey wolf, is the ticket. It will make them all see the need to put up physical barriers, for protection. In other words – do you see? – they will understand the imperative to enclose, and they will no longer be afraid to fell trees.'

'If I may point out, it is your determination to fell trees and enclose the common that has caused all the ill feeling here. It is not the superstition of the cottagers that turns them against you, it's their losing their homes and livelihoods. Daniel Brabner, the idiot as you call him, has lost his family because of it, and he is not such an idiot that he can't understand that.'

'I will not debate with you, Cragg. I am on the side of history, that is all I know. They, the cottagers and small farmers, are the pitiful losers in this war. Enclosure of common land is a rising tide and cannot be stopped. You may remember what happened to King Canute. He drowned.'

He rose from his wing chair and extended his hand.

'I bid you farewell, Cragg, and I wish you and Mrs Cragg a comfortable journey back to Preston.'

Out in the hall I found Fidelis loitering.

'I heard your voice through the parlour door. Better to wait for you than burst in, I thought.'

'You are back on duty at Sarah Lumsden's sick bed, Luke?'

'I thought I was, but circumstances have changed. It makes me think I have been entirely wasting my time ministering to her. My medicines, treatments, diets – all have been utterly useless.'

If I had had my hat on, I would have respectfully removed it.

'My condolences, Luke. She made a good fight of it, I think, but surely the morbidity was stronger than she was, in the end.'

'What do you mean, in the end? What on earth are you talking about?'

'I take it from what you said Mrs Lumsden has at last succumbed.'

Fidelis looked at me then started to laugh, shaking his head.

'Oh no! On the contrary, Titus. On the contrary. I am quite confounded and cannot explain it. She has apparently regained her strength. She eats triple helpings. She sings in front of the mirror while the maid brushes her hair. She speaks of re-marrying, of going out riding, of re-planting the rose garden. She says she will hold a ball here at the Manor House for all of the county and then travel to Bath, not to take the water but for the society and entertainments.'

'I noticed she was energized rather by the Ales, but there was no indication that she was cured.'

'I really think she is, now. Of course, I have seen cases where a tumour shrinks and disappears, or a consumption ceases to consume. Patients get well without notice almost as often as they unexpectedly die. But they never do so from the state she was in. I am tempted to call it a miracle.'

'No, Luke, no. The miracle is your experience and skill. You must take the credit.'

'I am not deceived, Titus. In this I did no better than a hobble-dehoy. I despaired of the patient almost from the moment I saw her. Yes, I tried to do a cure, but I was not confident anything would work. In the end I was giving her nostrums with the simple hope of making her as comfortable as possible. And now this! Well, if diseases were well-behaved there would be no need for doctors, only apothecaries.'

'I must see the results of this miracle. I shall go up and call on her.'

Sarah Lumsden was even more cheerful than when I had seen her on the day of the Ales. Now fully dressed, and with her bath chair nowhere to be seen, she stood looking out of the window at Ingolmere, as it stretched away northwards towards the violet-grey northern mountains beyond.

'I have looked out at this country and loved it all my life, Mr Cragg,' she said as soon as I came in. 'I despaired of ever walking or driving in it again. But now, as you see, I am as well as a young girl. I shall walk out again. I might go fishing. I used to do that with old Jim Bowden, when he was our gamekeeper forty years ago. Old Jim had been at the Battle of Marston Moor. His father was in Ireland with the Earl of Essex. They are long-lived memories, Mr Cragg, and I hold them dear.'

I stood beside her and tried to see the lake as she might be seeing it. It was not just a work of nature, at times picturesque, at times sublime. It was a kind of enormous pool in which history resided. Men had worked its waters for a thousand years, or more. Creatures had lived in it, and flown over it, for far longer. After just a short journey I would be back in humdrum Preston, with its dirty rain and never-ending business, remembering Ingolmere as a strange and distant province in which life had for the most part, and in spite of Arthur Lumsden, changed little in centuries. Here farming was still done in open fields, and spirit wolves and shape-shifting witches were still capable of making a nuisance of themselves.

But for how long? As I have just mentioned, that country is just a day's ride away from Preston's Market Place. The tide of improvement, as Lumsden had called it, was coming in dangerously fast. There was melancholy in that.

'I have come to say goodbye, Mrs Lumsden,' I said. 'I will leave with Mrs Cragg tomorrow in the early morning.'

'Mr Cumberledge has told me. I join with him in rejoicing. It is an end to a time of distress and I for one am looking forward to more tranquil times ahead.'

I left her with a note of caution. I could not help myself.

'I fear, if I may tell you, Madam, that times will not continue tranquil here for long, if your son does not desist in his project to modernize.'

She sighed.

'I know you are right, Mr Cragg. But God and Mr Cumberledge are with me and with their help my son may yet be persuaded.'

It was only when I had reached the bottom of the stair and gone out of the Manor House that it occurred to me: she had not once mispronounced my name.

After an early breakfast with Mr Holloway and Amelia, Elizabeth and I were mounted and ready to ride at seven the next morning. Luke came to say goodbye and with him Mrs Booth.

'Are you not yet ready to return to Preston, Luke?' I said. 'Your work with Mrs Lumsden is over, is it not?'

Luke exchanged glances with his hostess.

'Oh, I will stay on a few more days, Titus. Just a few. In the meantime, God speed you.'

He turned again to Mrs Booth, who lowered her eyelids for fractionally longer than a blink. It was, as Elizabeth later said, a signal not of modesty but of pleasure.

The crossing of Morecambe Bay can be a nerve-wrenching ride for anyone that hasn't done it before. Although the glistening sand stretches away so far that the sea's edge looks miles distant, we had been warned as we urged our horses on to the wet surface of the bay that when the tide turns it does so in near a single bound. Many who set off too late, or travel too slow, are caught by it and drown as surely, according to Arthur Lumsden, as King Canute.

On the other hand we had calculated correctly and so reached the little fishing village of Morecambe without accident. From there we soon came to Lancaster where Elizabeth's mount was left at the livery stable. A ticket for the southbound coach was bought for her, and it left for Preston in the early afternoon, with me riding behind.

Our turbulent visit to Ingolside was over, but there were sequels that I must record before putting down my pen.

# THIRTY-FOUR

I t was many weeks later, with Martinmas coming and Elizabeth's birthday in mind, that I entered Sweeting's bookshop to buy her a present. I thought she would like a copy for herself of John Gay's *Fables*, the book she had borrowed at Ingolside from Amelia Hart, and been so beguiled by. Mr Sweeting gave me snuff as usual and, when I had taken it, asked what I was looking for.

'Do you have Gay's *Fables*?'

He retreated into his back room and came back with two volumes, laying them on the counter.

'Here they are, in two volumes, the first and the second series. The latter is published after the unfortunate death of the author.'

'Do you have only these, Sweeting? It is the third series I require.'

Sweeting frowned.

'The *third* series? Are you quite sure?'

'Yes. Mrs Cragg was reading it at the house of her relatives some weeks ago.'

'Well, I for one have never heard of a third series of Gay's *Fables*. There have been only two. These two.'

I picked up one and then the other of the volumes on the counter, and consulted their tables of contents. Neither book had among its poems either 'The Slug and the Grasshopper' or 'The Philosophers and the Ass'. I tried to recall what else Elizabeth had read. Then I remembered 'Peterkin and the Bear' but it, too, was not among the fables of either the first or the second series. I put the books down.

'The third has a quite different choice of fables in it compared to these, Sweeting.'

'Can you tell me anything more about this book? Its date of publication, perhaps.'

'I don't know the date, but that it was the third series was clearly printed on the title page of the book, beneath the title and before the author's name.'

Sweeting scratched his head. As the premier bookseller in Preston he hated to be wrong on any literary question.

'And are the verses up to the usual standard?' he said.

'I think so. And very much to the point in some cases. There was one strange thing about the book, though. A careless typographical error. By some mischance the author's name was misprinted as John Guy.'

Sweeting took a pinch of snuff, inhaled and said, with some relief, 'Ah! Is that so? Then it is not a mischance, Mr Cragg. I remember now, there have been rumours of this edition and I must tell you that the verses in it are not by the author of *The Beggar's Opera*.'

'What do you mean? Are they forgeries?'

'Certainly they are. The whole book is a deliberate fraud.'

'I see. So the author's name was not misprinted. It is that of a certain person coincidentally named John Guy.'

'It is no coincidence. The name was adopted with the idea that purchasers would never notice the substitution of "Guy" for "Gay". This poet, if you can call him that, would be some hack producer of feeble and inferior imitations of the celebrated John Gay who, being dead, does not complain.'

'As I say, I thought Mr Guy's verses were rather good. Will you obtain the volume for me?'

Sweeting was incredulous. 'You want a copy of *Fables* by John Guy?'

'Yes. That is the book that Mrs Cragg so enjoyed.'

'I am surprised, Mr Cragg, not to say shocked. You have long been one of my best customers, but surely you would not admit such a book into your library.'

'Yes, as a matter of fact I would, because as I say Mrs Cragg—'

'No, Sir. With regret, no!'

Sweeting held up his hand in a gesture of stern refusal.

'I am unable to assist you. Or to be more precise, I refuse to. We sell respectable literature in this shop and never handle the indecent scribblings of Grub Street pirates.'

I left the shop disappointed. I would have to think of another birthday gift for Elizabeth. Walking back, I heard raised voices in the centre of Market Place and I went across to have a look. Several men were engaged in unwinding a long length of what

looked like a ship's hawser from a large drum, and taking meas-
urements. They were arguing with one or two passers-by, one
of whom was Luke Fidelis. Since the great unforeseen upheaval
of his life during the summer – I mean of course his marriage
to Helen Booth – I had been seeing less of him. Fidelis still
lived at Scrafton's Roost but, as he now had a wife, and was
working harder than ever to expand his medical practice, he was
seen less often among the denizens of our favourite coffee house,
the Turk's Head.

'It is simple mathematics,' I heard Fidelis say as I drew nearer
to the argument. 'If you want the circle to have a radius of ten
feet, you can easily calculate the length of rope required using
pi. The formula is—'

'Bugger your mathematics, Doctor,' said the man in charge of
laying out the ring. 'This is a hell of a lot wider than any pie.
Trial and error will do it. Come on, lads! Unroll the rope and
hand me that ten-foot rod.'

'What is going on, Luke?' I said to my friend. 'What are they
doing?'

'They are ignoring reason, Titus. They are blockheads.'

'But what's that rope for?'

'To define a boxing ring of – in the unlikely event that they
get it right – twenty feet in diameter. It's for the fight. Have you
not read about it?'

He pointed to the board alongside the Moot Hall, on which
advertisements for various events were posted. On it was a newly
printed notice, which I had not seen. I went over to read it.

TO BE FOUGHT ON MICHAELMAS EVE
IN THE MARKET PLACE
A GREAT TRIAL OF PUGILATION BETWEEN
'PRESTON'S OWN'
JACK STONE
&
CHARLIE JOHNSON
OF COVENT GARDEN IN LONDON
FOR A PURSE OF
150 GUINEAS

'Charlie Johnson, here in Preston!' I said, returning to Fidelis. 'Have you seen him? And what about Quexton?'

'I have seen them both. They are staying with Helen and me. It is better for Johnson's preparation than to stay in an inn. It is away from the public gaze.'

'So Quexton still trains him?'

'Yes, despite his change of circumstance.'

'Oh? What change is that?'

'It's the same one as my own, Titus. You see—'

He was interrupted by a hail from the side of Market Place.

'Doctor! Mr Cragg!'

Cornelius Quexton strode up to us, full of geniality and vigour. He shook my hand.

'Very good to see you, Cragg. And look here, I have brought my missus, that I married after her unexpected widowhood not six weeks ago.'

He turned and extended his arm proudly towards the woman following him. I suppose my face registered considerable surprise, for both Quexton and she laughed in delight. His new wife was Françoise Siran du Bressac.

When she heard that Quexton had come to town, and heard also (with amazement) the name of his recently acquired wife, Elizabeth proposed that we have a Michaelmas feast at our house as a reunion of those who were last together in Ingolside. The Fidelises and the Quextons were invited and so were Charlie Johnson and Robert Furzey.

Boiled mutton was served as, inevitably, the talked turned to the events at Whitsuntide. It was I who opened the subject.

'This mutton will be less expensive if Arthur Lumsden at Ingolside has his way. He told me that, once he had cleared the open fields and the forests for pasture, he will sell sheep meat in such quantity and so cheap that it will become the staple of the people. There will be no call for bully beef or sausage meat any longer.'

'He may never do so,' said Elizabeth. 'Cousin Amelia has written to me that, since we were there, Mr Lumsden's enthusiasm for taking the commons into his own hands has cooled.'

'I have heard the same,' said Helen. 'His mother is in such

good fettle that he cannot go forward with the project. She thwarts him at every turn.'

I looked at Quexton. He was eating steadily, while exchanging occasional glances with his wife. I wondered he was not more visibly affected by the news.

'You must be happy, Cornelius,' I said. 'All your endeavours at Ingolside are bearing fruit.'

'Oh, yes,' he said lightly. 'But Ingolside is only one small place. The common land is being stolen all over England.'

'But speaking of Ingolside,' said Fidelis, 'it is frustrating that we never reached the absolute bottom of what happened to the two agents Lumsden brought from London, Lavenham and Tree.'

'We all agree that John Lavenham died from smoke in the fire,' said Quexton.

'And Wilkin Tree fell into a gully and broke his neck,' I said. 'That is the inquest verdict, and it still stands.'

'You cannot fully persuade me,' said Fidelis, 'that two men came to Ingolside to work towards much hated enclosures, and both had separate fatal accidents. No reasonable person would think their deaths unrelated.'

'The Squire might,' I said. 'He was very anxious that both deaths be treated as random events.'

'There is a deal more to explain than that,' said Furzey, who had up to this point been drinking silently.

His voice had that pugnacious edge to it that I noted with a degree of alarm. He drained his glass of wine and held it out for a refill, then said, 'There was things going on behind the scenes in that place and you, Sir—'

He pointed an accusing finger at Cornelius Quexton.

'You were behind most of them, if I am not very much mistaken.'

He smiled, but it was the smile of a prosecutor rather than a friend.

'Now look here, Furzey,' I said. 'Mr Quexton is our guest.'

'A guest who has got away with much, and has much to answer for,' growled Furzey.

'Mr Furzey,' said Quexton's wife. 'Do you remember that I had come to the north because I wanted to know the truth about what happened to John Lavenham?'

Furzey drained his glass again.

'Your lover, who you loved so much that, since he died, you hitched up with the fellow who disgracefully abused the other one's body. The scoundrel who—'

'Robert Furzey!' said Elizabeth sharply. 'You bring shame on my hospitality, Sir.'

Mrs Quexton repeatedly struck the side of her glass with a spoon.

'Let me be heard, please,' she said. 'Mr Furzey has made suggestions that should have an answer. I wish that we give him one by telling the truth.'

She looked around the table, from face to face. No one said a word.

'Yes, John Lavenham was my lover,' she went on. 'And helper in my business, but he was not a good man, under that friendly manner. He was, as you know, a forger of documents and he drank excessively. I am sure that when the fire broke out in the Three Horns he was already in an ale coma and could not help himself. The smoke suffocated him dead and it was his own fault. Charlie, you know this. You saw him.'

Johnson nodded his huge head.

'Aye, Mrs Q. It was me carried him out.'

'You told Mr Cragg you did not know whether you did or not,' said Furzey. 'You lied.'

Johnson shook his head slowly.

'Where I was brung up, you don't say yea or nay unless you know why you're being asked the question.'

There was no more than a brief silence before Mrs Quexton said, 'I insist to go on. Will you let me?'

We settled down once more to listen.

'John,' she said, 'was not a good man in many other ways as well, which I need not tell you here. But when it was found he was dead, dear Mr Quexton thought of a way he could become good. I mean be of some good.'

Again she exchanged affectionate glances with Lavenham's successor, her new beloved.

'What good?' said I.

'The good of frightening Mr Arthur Lumsden to make him change his course. It is why John's dead body was shot and then put down against the Market Cross, to make the Squire think he had been assassinated. To make him stop the enclosures. So what

I say is, what Mr Quexton did was not the deed of a scoundrel, but of a good man.'

'Mr Cragg will not find this surprising,' said Elizabeth. 'He and I had already thought something like it might be true. Remember the philosophers' donkey, Titus?'

Mrs Quexton stood up and whispered to Elizabeth to show her the necessary house. Elizabeth took her out through the scullery and into the garden while the death of Lavenham continued to occupy the rest of us.

'I suppose you shot the body also, Quexton?' said Fidelis.

'And did you also write the note that was pinned to it?' I put in.

'The note was written by the same hand as wrote all the anonymous notes,' said Quexton.

'Whose?' I asked. 'Was it Thomas Moorhouse?'

'Perhaps I had better continue the story which my wife began,' he said, 'because Mrs Quexton knows it only at second-hand. I say first that you are very wide of the mark in your questions, for there were many of us in it. Yes, it was my idea to use Lavenham's corpse to deceive the Squire, though I knew it could not be done on the same night as the fire.'

'You told me you were not at Ingolside at that time,' I said.

'I was not there when the fire started, but I came back the same night and saw what was happening. The scene was very confused. Attempts were being made to extinguish the fire. Those who had been brought out were attended to on the ground in Street, and one by one were taken away to their homes. Finally only Lavenham was left, and he was found to be dead. Oswald Gillow, who was very outspoken against Lumsden, agreed to my suggestion that we say nothing in public, and hide the body in his hops store while we considered a plan. We met the next day at Gillow's home.'

'This is as good as the Gunpowder Conspiracy,' growled Furzey. 'So tell us who was in it.'

'As well as myself and Charlie here, there were Mr and Mrs Gillow, Mrs Bennett and her nephew Daniel Brabner. They all had a connection with the Brabner family that had some time before been made homeless, lost one of their children and been chased out of Ingolside. Also there was Curly Berry, and a few others.'

'Berry?' I said.

'It was he who wanted to make out Lavenham had been shot. I tried to dissuade him. I said it was not a good notion, but he wouldn't listen. He went away for his pistol and on his return pointed it at the dead man's breast without warning and fired. Although no else approved what he'd done, we decided to go ahead with the plan in spite of it.'

'And the anonymous note?'

'The work of Daniel Brabner, and his idea. I had got to know him well as we were almost neighbours. He wrote all the notes.'

'Why did he send one to me?' I asked.

'He was angry that you reached a verdict of accidental death. He burned with hatred for Lumsden and wanted to frighten him with the fear of murder. He is not such a goose cap as most believe, though his spelling is atrocious.'

'And on the night of the riot, when Lavenham's body was discovered,' said Fidelis. 'How did you work it, placing the body?'

'We carried it in the midst of the crowd, with difficulty but we managed it, down Street towards Manor House. We stopped for some speeches at the Market Cross and it was then that we left Lavenham sitting, with Daniel's note pinned on him. I had no more to do with him after.'

'Do you mean that the whole enterprise was an open secret? That everyone in the village was in on it?'

'Just those objecting to Squire's project, but that's not a few.'

'Then what about Tree? What did you have to do with him?'

'Oh, very little. But if I may say a few words about that. I am not ashamed of the work I did at Ingolside – the speeches and the meetings – but I do regret that we set loose the fear of death there. I am sorry in particular for encouraging Daniel's idea of sending Tree mad from fear and guilt.'

'Did he talk to you about it?'

'Yes. He had heard of such things happening. He thought it would complete his revenge for his family. And he reckoned he had the means in the form of his dog, Limer. It miscarried, however, when Wilkin Tree fell into that gully.'

'So you are telling me there was no intention to kill Tree.'

'None whatever. It was only to frighten him. But it was a reckless plan and I regret that I did not talk him out of it.'

He bowed his head as if seeking absolution, and I sensed that all of us present silently granted it. All except Furzey. He answered Quexton with a single contemptuous snort.

'I must tell you, my love, what Mrs Quexton told me when I showed her the way to the necessary house.'

It was much later. Our guests had gone and Elizabeth and I were lying in bed. The smell of our snuffed candles permeated the darkness.

'I asked her about Alice Moorhouse, who she bought from her husband in that extraordinary way. I said I could hardly bear to think of Alice's life now, but she took my hand and patted it and said the outcome is not what I might suppose. Alice has been left in charge of the business in Covent Garden. It seems she is an able and trusted administrator. In the words of Françoise, she has blossomed.'

'She is not a strumpet?'

'That, we do not know. We can only guess at the kind of business it is, as Françoise does not specify.'

'Basket-making is unlikely, though. Numbers of gentlemen do not call at night to buy baskets.'

We lay for a time in silence, each thinking over the evening's conversation.

'It is all quite a story, Titus,' Elizabeth said at last. 'A novelist could make much of those ingredients: the superstitions of the people, the wolf legend, the resentment against the Squire and his evictions, the people of a small village and their attachment to old ways.'

'With the world of the city or town coming in to disturb them.'

'And all ending, like any good comedy play, with marriages.'

'Or should that be like a poem by John Gay? Called, let's say, "The Outsiders and the Ingolsiders", and capped off with a moral.'

'What moral, do you think?'

'Beware of the wolf. And the whole might be entitled *The Murders of Ingolside.*'

'But there is no wolf, Titus. And there were, after all, no murders.'

'Are you sure of that, my love? Are you entirely sure there was no wolf?'

# EPILOGUE

**Three Fables**
by
**John Guy**
*Author of The B\*gger's Opera*

## The Slug and the Grasshopper

A slug call'd out to a grasshopper, 'Ho!
Where do you, friend, so hurriedly go?
Jumping and whirring with horrid dispatch,
Not stopping except on occasion to scratch
Your legs one on t'other and making a noise
For no earthly reason, except it annoys.'
The grasshopper smil'd at the slug's tart enquiry.
'I've nowhere to go, I've a quite empty diary.
No creditor's bringing a Chancery suit of me,
No Parish Constable's hot in pursuit of me.
To jump and rub legs is my simple delight.
Far better, my friend, than your crawling plight.'
'My plight,' said the slug, 'as you're choosing to call it
Is no wise a plight, and this isn't a crawl. It
Lets me proceed round this garden quite easy.
To go any quicker would make me feel queasy.
Rather I keep philosophical measure
And *festina lente*'s the adage I treasure.'
So which is more worthy? The sagacious slug,
Whose body resembles a glutinous plug?
Or the slender bundle of green twigs, which leaps
From garden to garden and never sleeps?
I'll say this: while grasshopper's giddily happy,
And slug's frowsy life's not infrequently crappy,
The hopper hops on and is lost in the west,
But the slug's silver trail leads him home to his rest.

## The Greek Philosophers and the Ass

Three Grecian wise men travel together
Giving their lectures in all sorts of weather.
Unlike the Magi they have no rich baggage
The load of one donkey is all of their luggage.
The donkey however is scrannel and old.
The load makes her stagger, she coughs in the cold.
They feed her on nothing but leavings and crumbs,
And flog her so hard that at last she succumbs.
The philosophers three are angry. They say,
'Jenny our donkey has failed us this day.
We've no means of carrying, no beast to ride,
Just bowels and bones in the bag of her hide.
Such is the ingratitude of our Jenny.'
Their wailing is loud in the hearing of many
Till a tanner from Crete delivers good news:
'Your Jenny, though dead, can still be of use.
I'll tan and curry the skin of her back
And cure it and stretch it as if on the rack
And we'll make a kettledrum out of that skin
To drum up more custom, bring many folk in
To hear your wise discourse.' This pleases the sages.
Their audience hasn't been many for ages.
And so it is done by the cunning old Cretan
And Jenny's again being reg'larly beaten.

## Peterkin and the Bear

There's nowhere on earth more awful than
The crags and snows above Lake Van.
The valley people speak of the fell
And frightful creatures that in them dwell:
The Oozium Bird, the Manticore,
The Cockatrice and Ophiotaur,
The four-legg'd bird, the fish-tail'd goat,
The Dragon whose teeth will rip out your throat.
There's just one familiar presence up there:

That's Bruin the mischievous shaggy-haired bear
Who guddles for trout and scampers up trees
To pilfer the honey away from the bees.
A boy called Peterkin lov'd to imagine
Bruin the bear, his rogu'ry and cadging,
And asked could he climb up and play with him. 'No,'
His mother said, 'I forbid you to go.
The Werewolf will get you (from him there's no running)
And have you for dinner. When hungry, he's cunning.
E'en if you escape him you'll soon run the risk
Of the poisonous stare of the Basilisk
Or else the Chimera's fiery breath.
You cannot imagine a more painful death.'
But Peterkin vowed, too headstrong to listen,
To climb up that mountain without permission.
So early one morn as his family slept
Out of his window young Peterkin crept.
He hurried uphill and looked all about
For the Bear in his den. He was feeling no doubt
He could dodge the Minotaur, hide from the Drake
And creep past the Wyvern-haunted lake.
When he spotted his playfellow, he seemed quite tame
So he ran to him laughing to start up the game.
The Bear, looking cuddlesome, held out his paws
And set upon Peter with murderous claws.

When they found what was left on the side of the hill,
Savaged and bloody and lifelessly still,
All agreed that the Dragon brought Peter to ruin
And no one suspected the murd'rer in Bruin.